On the 28th June 1914 there occurred the beginnin changing historic event. The young Archduke acknowledged heir to the powerful Austrian-Hungarian Empire, was assassinated in Sarajevo, Bosnia, a province in far off Serbia, a country most British people had never even heard of.

The belligerent Austria-Hungarian Empire demanded vengeance for the Archduke's assassination and threatened dire consequences against little Bosnia if she did not comply. On the 23rd July 1914, and ignoring the strongest warnings from Russia, to which Serbia was allied, the Austria-Hungarian Empire issued the Serbian government with an ultimatum, the terms of which that country deemed impossible to meet.

Serbia desperately tried to diffuse the critical situation, agreeing to most of the Austrian-Hungarian demands, but with one main exception. Serbia rejected the requirement for Austria-Hungary to be allowed to be represented in the judicial procedure in the trial of the assassin. This was interpreted by the Austrian-Hungarian Empire to be a direct refusal to accede to their demands and in their view could not be tolerated.

Great Britain tried its very best to act as a moderator and asked for a meeting of the Great Powers to discuss the rapidly deteriorating situation, but this was ignored. On the 31st July 1914, Austria-Hungary's strongest ally, Germany, demanded that Russia stop mobilising her manpower, but Russia refused to do so, preparing to go to the aid of her ally, Serbia, should Austria-Hungary attack. Russia assured Germany that she was only mobilising her manpower to protect herself against the Austrian-Hungarian Empire, and not that of Germany. On July 31st, 1914, ignoring this response, Germany declared war on Russia.

On August 2nd, 1914, Germany threw all pretence aside and invaded Luxembourg, and at the same time activated secret war plans by declaring war on France. The following day, on August 3rd, 1914, Belgium refused to allow Germany free passage through its country to France, and so, on the 4th August 1914, Germany declared war on Belgium.

Britain was allied to Belgium through a long-standing treaty. When Germany declared war on Belgium, European life was about to be drastically changed. Great Britain fulfilled her obligations and affirmed its war on Germany. Treaties entered into by other countries were hastily activated, and World War One began; slowly at first, and then it rapidly developed into outright slaughter and mayhem. History confirms that the "Rape of Belgium" was really that.

In the sleepy county of Somerset, England, where nothing exciting at all seemed to be taking place, particularly in the City of Bath, all that was about to dramatically change.

This is the tale of the North Somerset Yeomanry (Territorials) whose headquarters was based in Bath, Somerset. It follows the unit from its mobilisation right through to its first fully fledged battle against the Prussian Guards, at Ypres, Belgium.

Monday, 3rd August 1914.

The landlord of the Full Moon public house, Alf Cleall, stretched himself across a huge wooden barrel. It lay between several others that were strategically arranged behind the long oaken bar. He paused for a moment to carefully stand up, feeling a little twinge of pain in his lower lumbar region as he did so. Taking a small step backwards he surveyed the fastidiously hand-written copperplate notice displayed in front of it. He inwardly smiled at the precise handiwork of his beloved wife. This barrel boasted the legend, "Dry Zummerzet Farmhouse Cider."

A slight frown momentarily flickered across his rugged features as he again bent forward and carefully lifted the cask from the rear with his huge left hand. Skilfully he slipped a vee shaped wooden wedge beneath it and gently raised the back of the barrel by another inch or so. He wiggled the cork bung in the top of it, ensuring that the last few pints of its contents would flow out unhindered by the vacuum that would have occurred had he not done so.

He knew exactly what he was doing, but this time he willed his ministrations to produce the desired effect, for his friends were discretely eyeing his every move. Any mistake he made now that resulted in a pint of cloudy cider would surely mean an evening of ribaldry at his expense. Nonchalantly he forced himself to glance down at the old-fashioned double handed earthenware cider mug that he had picked up and was now holding in his hand.

He turned the barrel's wooden tap and a golden liquid gushed out, flowing smoothly into the pot he was holding. Carefully he filled it to its brim, allowing its pleasant apple smell to waft upwards towards his grateful nostrils. He smiled in self-appreciation, for none of the cider lees (the remnants of apples and perhaps odd bits of barley straw), were evident in the brew. Confidently he slammed the now full mug upon the polished wooden bar in front of him, spilling a bare tablespoonful.

He ran his finger over the place where the cider had overflowed and licked it, testing its fulsome flavour. "There it is, Charlie, and it is a nice drop of the real stuff too, if you don't mind me saying so!"

Charlie Gibbs counted out 2 pence on to the bar. The coins were made up of a penny piece, 1 halfpenny and 2 farthings. "Starting to get a bit pricey for a quart of cider aren't you pal?" he complained, but in a good-natured way.

His best mate, Alf, the owner of the public house in which they were standing, gave him a rueful smile and explained in his heavy Somerset accent; "It isn't my fault, me bird! Them their buggers that carts it over here from Taunton have raised the price by quite something! They reckon it's because the bloody war that everyone says is coming!"

"What bloody war? We aren't in the fight yet, are we?" grumbled Charlie.

On that beautifully warm bank holiday evening of the 3rd August 1914 it was indeed true that England was not at war with Germany - or at least, not yet. "Can't be far off though, can it?" he said, in an excitable voice. He retrieved the Bath Chronicle out of his deep jacket pocket and stabbed his stubby finger at the front page. "It says here that the bloody Huns have declared war on France - and that the plucky little Belgians have turned down the bugger's demand to pass through their country unhindered."

Alf Cleall nodded. "If the Belgians do that, then I reckon that those Huns will invade them anyway."

"Do you reckon we'll be called up Alf?"

The genial landlord glanced down the bar to locate his dumpy and homely wife, Winifred, making sure that she was busily serving another customer and was not looking at him. He beckoned Charlie towards him and whispered conspiratorially into his ear. "I'll tell you something, my pigeon, I am ready to go. Aren't you? I've got everything packed. All I have to do is jump into my uniform and pop off down to headquarters. I suggest you do the same," he offered.

Charlie nodded. He greatly respected Alf, for he was an old soldier and some forty years of age, but one who had experienced battle in the Boer War. Despite a disparity in ranks between them, Charlie being a serjeant and Alf a corporal in the North Somerset Yeomanry Territorials, they were both firm and loyal friends, playing rugby together in the local team, the Bath Rugby Football "A" team.

Their regiment had been disbanded on return from the South African campaign but was again reformed in 1908 as another territorial unit to defend the homeland. Both had elected to stay within its ranks.

Charlie thoughtfully stroked his chin and stated firmly, "I think you are right, you know. Them there bloody Hun's be spoiling for a fight and I don't think bugger all is going to stop them."

He raised his stoneware quart pot and offered it towards Alf. The men solemnly chinked their cider pots together in a companionable way and silently drank each other's health. In a practised manner, Charlie swiftly drained the contents of his pot before giving a satisfied "Ahhh!" He glanced thoughtfully about him before reflecting aloud, "I think I shall be going home now to pack my things. I reckon that it won't do me any harm to be ready, for we don't know what the morrow will bring."

"Aye," nodded Alf. "You are damn well right in that, Charlie." His friend nodded in farewell and gave Winifred a friendly wave as he strolled away from the bar, adjusting his flat cap in a rakish angle as he did so. Alf's wife gave a suspicious frown, and carefully wiping her hands upon her apron approached him with a wary look in her eyes, drawing herself up to her full 4 feet 2 inches in height as she did so.

Winifred nodded towards Alf's departing friend and said in a suspicious tone, "Charlie's gone home early then?"

Alf looked at Winnie and smiled. God, how he loved that woman, even after all these years. Winifred looked at Alf and saw that look in his eyes, that old glint of fire. She put her hand to her mouth and said, "Alfie my love! I'm scared! What is going to happen?"

Her husband gently placed his arm comfortingly around her waist and whispered encouragingly, "There, there, Winnie. Don't you fret about it, my beauty. I think I need to be ready for my country's call." He looked around the bar and counted about thirty people. "Can you manage by yourself for a bit?"

"Why?"

"I just want to go upstairs and get some paperwork straight, that's all."

Winifred's eyes moistened, but she steadfastly held her husband's icy blue eyes. She steeled herself, barely concealing the lump in her throat. "You go ahead, my love. I shall be alright." Secretly she tried to smother the thought that she might have to cope by herself sooner, rather than later.

Tuesday, 4th August 1914.

The cuddlesome blonde woman lay completely naked in her bed and glanced lovingly down at the man that lay snoring loudly beside her, but she didn't mind that at all. Gently she pulled back the white linen sheet to look hungrily at his muscled body. Alice smiled at the strong manly features that were those of her lover. The sandy hair, the downy and broad chest and, well, the 'man smell' she loved so much about him. He stirred slightly, and she smiled knowingly to herself. Looking towards the window she saw that the dawn was quickly approaching, and as if to support her view, a Blackbird began to whistle its morning choral. It was time to wake him up. She gently placed her hand upon his manhood and playfully shook it.

"Albert, darling," she cooed. "It's time for you to get up, my dearest."

The stocky dark-haired man beside her stirred and he yawned, stretching his thick arms up and above his head. His eyes opened, and he grinned at her, an impish smile playing across his handsome face. "We've got time yet, my dear," he reasoned.

She giggled as he rolled over on top of her and rubbed his face in her ample breasts, grabbing an erect and pink nipple in each hand as he did so. She moaned in pure joy as they made robust and unashamed love. There was no tenderness is this love making, just an urgent rutting of a young man of 20 summers to a woman of 30. In a minute or so it was all over. With a satisfied grunt, Albert rolled off her and flopped on to his broad back, grinning hugely. "Morning, my love," he said.

She giggled girlishly again as Albert jumped out of bed and quickly dressed. Setting his flat cap straight on his head he leaned over and kissed her, giving her left nipple a little loving tweak as he did so. She reached for him, but he danced away, giggling as he did so. He gave her a little wave as he ran out of the bedroom and went lightly down the stairs.

She lay quietly there for a moment before giving a huge sigh. A little tear trickled out of her eye as she gently stroked it away. Alice threw back the bed clothes and jumped out. She swiftly made up the large bed, making sure that she had puffed up the eiderdown pillows so that no head prints would show. Quietly she opened the window a little to air it. Then she put on a thick and creamy nightgown and checking the room thoroughly to make sure that no clues were left behind, she opened the bedroom door and left. She walked across the tiny landing and into the matrimonial bedroom and looked bleakly at the cold and empty feather-down bedstead. Placing her hand beneath the thick sheet she quickly located the stone hot water bottle that she had placed there the night before and removed it. The bottle was barely warm now, but it would do to help the deception. Having removed it and placed it on the floor next to the bed, she lifted the sheet and slipped beneath it.

An hour later she heard the metallic clunk of the latch turning downstairs. This was followed by the soft click of the closing of the front door. She heard him get into the tin bath full of cold water that she had left prepared last night. It wouldn't be long now. Fifteen minutes later the bedroom door silently opened, the merest creak betraying the event. Alice feigned a deep sleep. Ernest gently pulled back the bedclothes and checking that he had got all the coal dust off him from the night shift at Radstock Colliery, he slipped quietly in beside her, trying his best not to disturb her. He sniffed the air as he recognised a familiar smell, but he could not place it.

His wife felt his cool hand touch her thigh and she gave an involuntary shudder. She closed her eyes as Ernest whispered her name. After all, they had been married for some ten years or so. Alice grimaced, knowing that her husband could not see her face. She had been sleeping with his best friend for over six months, but she knew that someday he would surely find it out for she knew that she could not keep it a secret for much longer.

Lieutenant Colonel Geoffrey Carr Glynn, D.S.O., made his way down the stairs on that bright summer's day at 8 a.m. in the morning and muttered softly to himself, feeling every one of his 51 years of age.

With a start he recalled that only the previous day he had had ridden to the Bank Holiday hounds with his family, and as usual he had been the genial host, buying copious amounts of alcohol for the whole Blackmore Vale Hunt. It was expected of him.

He had enjoyed a very lively social event which saw his stirrup cup refilled several times before riding away in pursuit of their elusive quarry, Reynard the fox. A very successful day's hunting had then been followed by an enjoyable evening dinner at his house where the subject of Germany and the likelihood of war had been the main subject of discussion. He bitterly regretted taking that last 3 large glasses of brandy, for his head was now pounding and he was taking some time in getting his thoughts together. His only consolation was that he knew that his other male guests would be feeling the same way as he.

The colonel was slightly irritated at having been called upon so early in the morning, for he was officially on leave. His manservant had awoken him with the news that a military despatch rider had arrived with an urgent message for him, and he insisted that he had to deliver it personally to the colonel.

The Commanding Officer of the North Somerset Yeomanry, a Territorial Army unit, stopped as he descended the circular stairs. He placed a small cheroot, his first of the day, firmly into his thin mouth. Striking a Lucifer match, he lit it. He shook the match to put it out, a trail of black smoke evident as he did so and drew a deep inhalation of tobacco smoke down into his lungs. The colonel coughed wretchedly for a while, the smoke coming back out of his mouth in little white spurts as he did so. He wiped the back of his hand across his mouth and frowned at the little spot of blood that manifested itself upon it. He wiped it off in his dressing gown, instantly dismissing it as a minor irritation.

Geoffrey Glynn stood motionless for a moment as he regained his gentleman's composure, for it would not do for anyone to see him being breathless. They might mistake it for a lack of fitness. He glanced around furtively, making sure no-one was watching him. When he was ready, he gave his magnificent moustache a twirl at the end with his fingers, and with another slight cough carried on down the stairs of his large country house. His manservant, Adams, had silently appeared at the drawing room and was already holding the door open for him. As the colonel passed him by the servant readily bowed his head in acknowledgement of his master. The matchstick was handed to him to dispose of.

The colonel entered the room, fastening the cord around his dressing gown more securely. A despatch rider with the rank of serjeant stood before him, still smartly dressed even though his khaki uniform was covered in dust from his mad-cap ride. His army pattern regulation motor cyclist goggles were perched precariously on top of his cap.

The serjeant saluted stiffly. "Good morning, sir," he said crisply. "I am ordered to deliver this personally into your hands, sir, and no-one else!" The colonel took the proffered piece of yellow paper, an official War Office telegram, from the outstretched hand of the serjeant. He noticed that the serjeant's hand that held the message had a little tremor. "Excitement?" speculated the colonel to himself. The Senior Non-Commissioned Officer then offered the colonel another piece of paper with a space for his signature on it. "Would you please sign it to acknowledge receipt, sir," he requested. The colonel took the piece of paper and placing it on a little writing desk in the drawing room, calmly took a fountain pen from the desk. Removing its top, he signed his elegant signature in the relevant box and returned the form to the outstretched hand of the despatch rider.

"Thank you, serjeant," he said. "Would you care for a cup of tea before you go?"

The serjeant grinned broadly, for he had driven from the headquarters of the 1st South West Mounted Brigade in Salisbury to Shepton Mallet along dusty roads with no chance for a break, such was the urgency of the mission he had been ordered to complete. "Thank you very much sir," he said. "A quick cup of tea would do nicely."

The colonel nodded at Adams who then indicated the door to the serjeant with an outstretched hand. "If you would care to follow me," he obliged. The serjeant saluted the colonel and followed the manservant out and down the stairs to the servant's quarters.

Glynn sat down at his writing desk and carefully slit open the telegraph message with a thin ivory paper knife that he had made for him in South Africa, a memento of the days he had served there in the Boer War. The colonel read it and then put it down on the table. He frowned before picking it up again and looked at it. He had been half expecting it.

He rummaged around the top draw of his table and selected a large cigar from those in a box that he kept there. He sat back in his chair and smiled hugely. It was no surprise really. The Germans had been given an ultimatum by Britain only yesterday to respect Belgium's neutrality or else take the consequences, and the Germans had promptly invaded that poor little country.

The colonel looked at the telegram from the Brigade Headquarters again. It ordered "The North Somerset Yeomanry is to fully mobilise on a war footing forthwith. This headquarters is to be notified immediately when your headquarters is functioning."

The colonel sighed when he realised that the word "functioning" had been carefully chosen, as opposed to the word "operational." This gave him some indication of the urgency of the task. He tugged the bell cord that lay on his left-hand side in a brisk manner and grunted in satisfaction as he heard the strident bell call ringing noisily in the servant's ready room in the room below.

There was almost an instantaneous knock on the door, and his manservant appeared before him, almost as if he had been expecting the summons. "You rang, sir," he said.

"Ah, Adams," he replied, nodding at him and speaking in a calm and matter-of-fact voice. "Get my uniform ready would you and get into yours too! Send word to all of my men on the farm who are in the Yeomanry to report to the Drill Hall in Bath immediately, fully prepared to ride!"

Adams blinked in astonishment. He took a deep breath and said, "Immediately, sir?"

He said tersely, "Must I repeat myself? Immediately I said, and immediately I meant!"

"At once, sir," the startled man responded.

As his valet turned to leave the colonel called after him, and almost as an afterthought. "And Adams; get the groom to saddle up our horses by 10 a.m. Full military equipment," he ordered.

His personal valet nodded again, for he was an intelligent man and could guess as to what the telegram contained.

The colonel leaned forward and picked up the telephone. The operator answered at the Exchange of the telephone in a bored voice, for it had been a long night. "Number please?"

"Mells number 2" he said gruffly.

The phone rang at the other end for at least four times before it was answered, and a calm voice responded, "Mells Park!"

"Captain Bates, please."

The man's voice at the other end said defensively, "I'm afraid that Captain Bates is indisposed now, sir. Whom shall I say has called?"

"It's Lieutenant Colonel Glynn calling." A note of annoyance quickly became apparent to the servant as the colonel spoke in a clipped and authoritative manner. "I don't care how indisposed he is. He is to call me immediately. It is a matter of great national importance. Do you understand?"

There was a moment's hesitation at the end of the telephone. "I understand, sir," he said.

"Good!" The colonel slammed the speaker back on to the telephone receiver with some annoyance, sharply ending the conversation.

He sat drumming his fingers on the writing table, thinking things through. He had to mobilise his battalion and mobilise it now! The first man he needed was his Adjutant, Captain Bates, and he was in the process of contacting him. Bates was the only regular officer in the Yeomanry. He really belonged to the 7th (Queen's Own) Hussars, and as such he could be totally relied upon.

Then he would need to get hold of his quartermaster, Lieutenant Holwell, for the brunt of the mobilisation and equipping of the Yeomanry to a war footing would fall upon him. He hoped his quartermaster was up to it, for he was not a gentleman officer but a "ranker"', one who had worked himself up through the other ranks structure to become an officer. He wasn't really a gentleman and, in his view, could not be taken seriously as a real officer.

He looked at his desk and with a smile on his face picked up a letter he had received the day before. Yesterday he had strongly considered suicide. The communication was from his bank. They had outlined that his debts were so many that they had no other option but to make out a bankruptcy case against him, unless, of course, he immediately paid off his overdraft of £15,000.

With a twitch he brought himself back to face the real issue. He frowned a little to himself, trying to work out how long it would take before he could establish his Yeomanry to be accepted as a true fighting unit, for they were essentially a territorial unit and had never been to war; well, not at least since the South African campaign.

Serving in that war as a captain in the Rhodesia Regiment, Glynn had won his Distinguished Service Order "In recognition of services during the operations in South Africa" was how the London Gazette's reported it. In his and the unit's favour, it could be argued that he was a colonel who had seen some active service and successfully led his men. Luckily for him he had some seasoned and veteran soldiers still left from that campaign that had served in his squadrons. Immediately he thought of Corporal Cleall, a good and steady man if ever there was one. He, also, had been a veteran of that hard-fought campaign and they had served together under active service conditions.

Although he thought of his North Somerset Yeomanry as a fighting unit, the truth was that Yeomanry units of the new Territorial Forces constituted in 1908 were not expected to fight outside of the United Kingdom; they were formed purely for the Home Defence of Britain. Although his predecessor had been asked if he would volunteer the Yeomanry for service abroad if the need arose, he had replied with an emphatic "No!"

The telephone rang loudly, disturbing his logical thoughts. He picked it up immediately, almost snatching it off its cradle. "Glynn!" he said precisely.

The voice at the other end seemed a little surprised and replied in a calm and resonant tone, "Morning sir, Stanley Bates. I believe you wish to speak with me urgently?"

The colonel nodded to himself, a smile on his lips, for not only was Stanley his Adjutant, but he was also a personal friend. "Ah, Stanley," he said. "Sorry to disturb you my boy, but the balloon has just gone up. We are to mobilise forthwith."

There was a hint of excitement from the other end of the telephone. "Oh, I say," drawled a cultured reply, a hint of breathlessness being evident as the captain realised the importance of the words. "Do you think we'll have a chance of action sir?"

The colonel's bright blue eyes sparkled for a moment, and then he replied. "They will send the regular battalions first, I suspect, and then perhaps they will let us have a go."

"Do you really think so, sir?"

"Never mind that for the moment, as time is pressing. This is what I want to happen, Stanley. Have you a pen and paper ready?"

"Just a moment, sir," he responded. The colonel waited, his fingers once again drumming impatiently on the wooden desk on which he now rested his elbow. He heard a rustling of paper over the crackling telephone. There was an unexpected "click" on the phone and the colonel was sure that the exchange operator was eavesdropping.

The Adjutant picked up the receiver once more. "I'm ready, sir."

"Good! I want you to contact all our headquarters staff, the second in command first. They are to be told that we are mobilising and that they are to report to the Bath headquarters immediately. Got that?"

"Yes sir."

"Excellent. After that contact the quartermaster. He is to report to me personally and immediately on arrival at headquarters with a complete state of equipment for each man, and certainly with a list of our deficiencies."

"Right ho, sir."

"Stanley, the state of equipment reported to me is to be that of the full War Equipment."

The voice came back, a bit more subdued this time. "I understand completely, colonel."

"Good. Then you are to contact each of the Squadron Commanders to order them to report to their headquarters immediately and mobilise their troops. From now on, they are to have their squadron headquarters telephones continually manned. Is that understood?"

"Yes sir. The telephones are to be continually manned."

"Once the Squadron Commanders are in situation, they are to report over the telephone personally to you with a Squadron State Report. Is that comprehended?"

"Of course, sir!"

The colonel smiled, for he had complete and utter faith in his young Adjutant. "Good! But there is one more thing, Stanley, my boy."

"And what's that sir?"

"This really is war, you know."

"I know, sir."

"Good." The colonel's voice took on a softer tone as he said, "Take some little time in saying goodbye to your new fiancée, for it may be a long while before you get the chance to see her again."

"Thank you, sir. What are your movements going to be for the rest of the day?"

The colonel's voice immediately assumed a business-like tone, for he had not anticipated that question from his Adjutant. He smiled ironically to himself, for he should have. "Good man, Stanley," he said. "Trust you to think of that." The colonel paused for a moment before saying; "I will have my telephone here manned by one of the servants for the remainder of the morning." The colonel looked at the clock in the drawing room. "It is now a quarter-past nine, Stanley. I intend to be in the saddle with my orderly, Adams, by 10 a.m. We will ride to the headquarters to be there by ten-thirty. All of my headquarters officers are to personally report to me upon arrival there." As an after-thought he added: "Please ensure that the gate-keeper is made aware of my proposed arrival time."

"Very good, sir," replied the Adjutant.

"Goodbye, Stanley." He replaced the earpiece on to the handset.

He smiled as he walked across to the made-up fireplace. It had not yet been lit. At the bottom of the fire grid there was some paper, and on top of that some thin kindling wood. Upon that rested lumps of the best Mendip coal. Looking around to check that there was no-one else about, he threw the letter from the bank upon it. Grinning, he took a match and struck it, applying it first to the offending letter. It burst into flames. He chuckled aloud, for the announcement of war had given him just the respite he needed. No bank would dare to make him bankrupt in the countries hour of need!

12

The colonel looked up from the fireplace as the door to the drawing room unexpectedly clicked open. His wife, Marjorie, stood there before him in her pretty pink silk dressing gown, her hand at her mouth. "Geoffrey!" she cried. "Is it really happening? Are we at war?"

The colonel nodded. His wife ran over to him, smothering her face in his shoulder. Her shoulders shook as she sobbed, "Are you going away to the war?"

The colonel kissed the top of her head affectionately. "There, there, old thing. Don't you worry about anything, my dear! Yes, we are going to war, but not straight away, and the likelihood of us having to serve abroad is remote. Besides, I must get the Yeomanry ready yet!" he exclaimed, "and that may take some time!"

He looked up at him through eyes that were brim-full of tears. "Darling," she said softly. "I'm so afraid for us, for the country. What is going to happen?"

The colonel laughed as he gently pushed his wife away from him. "Why, we are going to give the Hun a damn good thrashing, my love, that's what! Don't you worry my dearest; it'll all be all over by Christmas."

She pulled a handkerchief out of her dressing room sleeve and dabbed her eyes and, taking a deep breath asked in a suddenly determined voice, "What am I to do?"

The colonel grinned at her. "That's the spirit, old girl! While I am getting dressed into my uniform it would be most helpful if you gathered my personal stuff together and put it in my valise. For I, and the servants and all the employees of the farm who are in the Yeomanry, will have to go to Bath immediately."

She looked at him, bravely fighting back her tears. "Will you be coming home tonight?"

The colonel shook his head. He took his wife into his arms once more and kissed her tenderly of her forehead. "I doubt it, my dear," he said. "God only knows when I'll be back again."

His wife pushed herself out of his arms and ran away up the stairs, calling for her maid as she did so. The quiet house was beginning to become a bustling hive of activity.

The newly installed telephone unexpectedly jangled in the Full Moon Hotel. Winifred jumped, momentarily startled by the noise. She put down her cloth and stopped polishing the bar. Carefully she took the hearing piece off the telephone. Putting on what she thought sounded like an extremely posh voice she spoke slowly into the mouthpiece. "This is the Full Moon Hotel. Mrs Cleall speaking. How may I be of service to you?"

An authoritative but friendly voice on the other end of the line said: "Good morning Mrs Cleall. It's Captain Lubbock here, the officer commanding "A" squadron. May I speak to your husband please; most urgently?"

The little woman's eyes took on a look of fear and she gulped down a breath of fresh air. Steeling herself to make her voice sound normal, she replied sweetly, "Of course, sir. Could you 'ang on for a minute or so?" She hadn't realised that her voice had slipped back into her soft Somerset accent.

"Of course I can, my dear."

Mrs Cleall placed the earpiece of the telephone on the top of the counter behind the bar. She opened the door that led directly from the door upstairs to the office. "Alf!" she shouted loudly. "It's Captain Lubbock on the telephone for you."

Alf popped his head around the door of the office. "I'm on my way!" he shouted as he came hurrying out of his office door. With a pounding of feet Alf rushed down the stairs. He picked up the earpiece in one hand and the telephone in the other. "Corporal Cleall, sir," he stated firmly. Unbeknown to him he was standing rigidly to attention.

"Ah! Corporal Cleall! We are to mobilise immediately. Is there any chance of you getting down to the headquarters as soon as possible? The colonel will be arriving by 10.30 a.m. and I shall be leaving home myself shortly. I should be at the H.Q. by 11 a.m."

"I'm on my way, sir."

"Good man!" The telephone clicked at the other end, indicating that the conversation was plainly over.

Alf replaced the receiver on the telephone and placed the whole apparatus carefully down on the counter behind the bar. Winifred stood there, motionless, looking at him. She held her hand held across her mouth. She said fearfully, "Alfie?"

He strode across to her in a few brief steps and wrapped her in his arms, his wife clinging to him. They kissed. Alf brushed the hair away from Winifred's eyes and said, "It's time, my dove. We knew it was coming now, didn't we?"

Winifred sniffled. "I know, I know," she cried gently. "But I was hoping it would be a little longer yet." Alf kissed her on the top of her head and then hurried back up the stairs. Within five minutes he was on his way back down, fully dressed in his uniform and carrying his already pre-packed equipment.

He placed his kitbag on the bar room floor and reached out to hold his wife in his arms again for a brief and precious moment. He looked her sternly in the eyes and said in an authorative tone, "Tell my brother Wilfred to come in daily now. I've left him written instructions in an envelope that he will find on my desk. You know, banking details, accounts and things. He'll have to take over running the pub with you while I am away." Winifred nodded her head. "The accounts are fully up to date and we have no outstanding bills. I have already placed the next order and that should be here on Friday."

His wife gave a little sniffle. "There, there, Winnie old thing. I'll have none of that now. I don't know when I'll be back, but you can always pop over to see me at the headquarters, you know," he admonished, gently. Winifred nodded glumly. He lifted her chin up with his fingers and said, "Come on, Winnie. Give me a smile. I can't go to the war with you looking like that!" His wife forced a smile upon her face as Corporal Alf Cleall of the North Somerset Yeomanry kissed her once again. Letting Winnie go, he picked up his kit bag. Effortlessly he threw it across his shoulders and marched purposefully out of the hotel's main door.

Winifred ran to the door and kept it open, watching her soldier husband disappear down the street to travel the small distance to the "A" Squadron headquarters. Unbeknown to her, and at the same time, the same scene was being re-enacted all over the country.

At the end of the street Alf turned and waved furiously to his watching wife. She waved back, and she saw a huge smile on his face. As Alf turned to go, a couple of bystanders slapped him on the back and gave him a cheer. As he disappeared around the corner Winifred closed the main door. Almost collapsing into a chair at a nearby table, she sobbed uncontrollably.

The colonel and his servant, Adams, cantered into the Upper Bristol Road in Bath, heading for Ivy Lodge, the drill hall that housed the headquarters of the North Somerset Yeomanry and "A" Squadron. Glynn's black horse, Elizabeth, held her head high and stepped in a lively manner along the street, with Trooper Adams following a respectful length or so behind. The horse could sense the excitement in the air and she carried herself proudly.

Adam's wore the typical trooper's uniform of khaki with a leather bandolier of five pouches that ran from the top of his left shoulder and down to his right waist. A peaked cap was firmly placed upon his head, its strap underneath his chin to stop it from falling off.

As they trotted through the City of Bath people stopped and cheered, waving enthusiastically at them. Uniformed soldiers of other Battalions and troops were hastily making their way to wherever they had to go, the colonel receiving so many salutes that eventually he resorted to nodding an acknowledgement at each soldier who did so.

They arrived at the drill hall, a 2-storey high structure that looked somewhat Gothic in appearance. The whole place was set behind a high brick wall and it was tall enough to stop anybody from looking over it. The flat drill halls were on either side of the building, no doubt added as an afterthought once the original had been built. The whole thing had a sloped and slated roof, and the windows set into it reminded one more of medieval castle arrow slits. Exactly in the middle of building was the imposing archway with its massive gateway into which was set a large iron gate.

The colonel was pleased to see that an armed sentry already stood on guard there, bayonet fixed. The sentry, immediately recognising the colonel, gave a "Present

Arms" to him. Glynn grimly saluted back. His face broke into a smile as Corporal Cleall, the old veteran soldier from the Boer War Days, came out of the little guardhouse to swing open the gate for him. He rode inside along with Adams and both men dismounted. The colonel handed the reins of Elizabeth to his manservant, and he led the 2 horses away to the stables at the rear of the headquarters.

Corporal Cleall saluted smartly. "Good morning sir," he greeted.

"Good morning to you, Corporal Cleall. What's happening so far?"

The corporal gave his concise report to his colonel. "Myself and 5 troopers are here, sir. No officers or S.N.C.Os present at yet, but Captain Lubbock should be here by eleven a.m. I have set a guard on the main gate, sir, if you approve."

The colonel nodded his head. "Yes, corporal; I do approve. I approve it very much. Is there anything else?"

"I have a man sitting next to the telephone sir, taking messages down. There are a couple there that need urgent answering from the Brigade H.Q., and a few men ringing in to say they will be getting here a bit later than expected. I have the man writing everything down in a log, so you can see what is going on."

"Damn good show, Corporal Cleall; its initiatives like yours that will win us this war!"

"Orders sir?" he asked.

"Get all the officers to report to me personally as soon as they arrive, corporal, if you please. The first N.C.O. that comes in is to relieve you. You are then to take on the responsibilities of the serjeant major until he arrives. After that you are to report to me personally to be at my disposal."

"Yes sir!" Corporal Cleall saluted and the colonel used the end of his horsewhip to touch the tip of his peaked cap, acknowledging it. The sound of some more troopers arriving on horses, men from his farm so it seemed, announced that the Yeomanry was beginning to form and that the heart of the regiment was, at last, slowly beginning to beat.

The colonel entered the building that housed his and the squadron's headquarters. At the top of the stairs he saw a trooper in the adjutant's office, busily writing down a telephone message with one hand while the other held the telephone piece to his ear. The man stopped for a moment, uncertain as what to do.

"Keep writing, Davis!" instructed the colonel.

Colonel Glynn walked over to where the trooper stood, now busily transcribing a message. It was Lieutenant Gibbs of "B" Squadron reporting that he was now at his headquarters in Weston-super-Mare and he was mobilising his men, of which fourteen of them had so far had reported in. The colonel smiled in satisfaction. Gibbs was a good man and he could be relied upon to do the right things. The colonel's eyes wandered down the page where three other messages had been recorded, thankfully because Cleall had the common sense and forethought to ensure that someone did so. He thought to himself that it was about time that Cleall received his third stripe, and when the opportunity arose he would make every effort to ensure that he did.

The first message the corporal had talked about came from the headquarters of the Brigade, ordering the unit to mobilise. The colonel gave a rueful smile and thought, "That's a bit late!" The second message called for an urgent ammunition return. "Well," thought the colonel, "that would have to wait until the quartermaster arrived." The third was the most important. At the very first opportunity a real-time manpower report was to be sent. The colonel grunted in dissatisfaction, knowing the answer to that already. The North Somerset Yeomanry was already greatly undermanned, but he had a terrible suspicion that the real meaning of this enquiry that would probably take some of his best men to make up the deficiencies in manpower in other regular cavalry units.

He heard footsteps running up the stairway and saw his Adjutant standing before him. "Ah! Stanley. Glad to see you my boy," he said. "Get someone to put the kettle on for us and come on into my office. Let's see how your mobilisation plan stands up to the actual events as they unfold."

Captain Bates grinned. "Yes, sir," he grinned.

It was 3 p.m. in the afternoon and the North Somerset Yeomanry rapidly began to take shape. Staff officers from Brigade had already arrived in Bath and were beginning to find and allocate billets for the men. The idea was that quite soon all of the Regiment would be housed together in Bath and near to the headquarters. The adjutant had given permission for Corporal Cleall to billet himself in his own hotel. Cleall already had a telephone installed there and was literally only five minutes away.

The colonel was taking his first Orders Group, or "O" Group as it was known in the army. He was patiently listening to each officer's report where he outlined in detail his squadron deficiencies. The colonel noted that the quartermaster seemed to have aged considerably as he hurriedly jotted down notes in a large notepad. It would be his job to make good those shortages.

After the last man had spoken, the colonel glanced down at his calculations. "Well gentlemen," he said. "It seems to me that we have some considerable shortcomings to overcome, but overcome them we will. I will tolerate nothing less than a 100% effort from every officer and each man. Currently, as I understand it, we are four officers short, and we need another 102 men to bring us up to our authorised war strength of 500. We are also supposed to be a cavalry unit, gentlemen, and what worries me is that we are also 200 horses short, more or less, of what we should have."

The telephone rang, and the Adjutant hurriedly snatched up the phone, turning his back on the colonel and gathered officers and speaking quietly into the telephone. He nodded his head and smiled. Putting the telephone down, he grinned hugely at the colonel.

"Well Captain Bates, it seems as if you may have some good news for us, at last!"

"Yes sir. That was the recruiting officer in charge of the offices in Bath. It seems as if those men on the Army Reserve are clamouring to join the colours since war has been declared. We can expect our first mobilised Reserve men to join us almost immediately!"

The colonel smiled, happy that things were beginning to take shape at last. He pointed towards one of his junior lieutenants. "Lieutenant Longrigg; you are to be responsible for the physical training of those men. Contact the Bath Recruiting Officer immediately. Tell him that I will not accept any man who cannot sit and ride a horse or cannot take a four-foot jump over a fence with his horse. Captain English!"

"Yes sir?"

"You will be our training officer for these new recruits. Submit a training programme to me within the next 2 days, concentrating on the horsemanship side of things. Talking of which," he said meaningfully, "I assume that you have some horses coming to the regiment, Lieutenant Holwell."

The clearly nervous officer cleared his throat before he replied. "I have spoken to the Quartermaster's Corps, sir, and they assure me that we will be receiving a full complement of horses and accoutrements during the week, as well as the remainder of our weapons."

The colonel looked at his quartermaster coldly, for in truth he did not like him, for he was no gentleman. He was also quite poor and could not afford to maintain himself in the mess in the custom that other officers could and did. The colonel found it hard, try as he might, to hide his disdain for this little man.

Putting that aside for a moment the colonel became quite brusque as he ordered, "Just do it, quartermaster. I will accept no less. In one week you shall have to get those horses, or, by God sir, you will have to find yourself another regiment."

A couple of the other officers exchanged secret smiles, for they too thought of the poor quartermaster as a bureaucratic oaf, and indeed had often ridiculed him in the mess. The ridicule did not last for long, however, as the quartermaster never felt up to arguing with his "betters", even though he carried greater seniority as an officer than some of the junior officers that made fun of him. That always infuriated the adjutant, a regular officer himself, who once snapped at the poor quartermaster, "For God's sake man, can't you stand up for yourself? You served 15 years in the ranks before your promotion. Surely you remember how to deal with men such as those who make so much fun of you?" But it had been to no avail, and the adjutant threw his hands up in despair and left the poor man to fend for himself.

The colonel looked around him and gave each officer a personal look in the eye. Apart from his quartermaster, he was relatively content that each one of them would do his duty. Some of the younger officers were quite raw, of course, and had yet to be blooded in war.

The colonel opened the top drawer of his green leather topped desk and took out an ornately carved cigarette box. He took out a cigarette and sniffed it. "Gentlemen, you may smoke," he said, and offered the box around.

When the officers who wished to smoke were doing so, the colonel inhaled a deep breath and blew out a cloud of white smoke intentionally towards the quartermaster. The poor little fellow was an avid non-smoker, and he immediately started to cough. A few of the officers nudged each other and quietly laughed.

The colonel waited for the tittering to stop before he continued. "As you know, gentlemen, this regiment was formed to operate within England only, and then only in a self-defence role. In 1908, territorial regiments were given the opportunity to serve abroad in England's service, should the occasion arise. I regret to say that this regiment was one of the 80% who elected to stay in service but within England's bounds."

"Bad form," someone said quietly.

The colonel looked up sharply and said nothing, but the look on his face plainly told that he did not like to be interrupted when speaking. "Yes," replied the colonel. "As one of you quite rightly commentated, "bad form". It was bad form for the regiment and bad form for us. Would you not agree gentlemen?"

"Hear, hear," offered the adjutant, and nods from most of the officer's present displayed that the sentiment expressed was wholly felt.

The colonel grinned. "What would be your feelings, gentlemen, if I offered the North Somerset Yeomanry for service in France on active duty?"

Captain Lubbock, the most senior of the territorial officers' present, bar the colonel, quickly spoke. "I believe, sir, that you will find every one of us in favour of that!"

A chorus of "Hear, hear!" echoed around the table and the colonel put his hands up for silence. "Very well gentlemen, I hear what you say." The colonel paused for a moment before asking, "And what about the men? How do you think they would feel?"

Captain Bates was quick to intercede. "Without doubt, colonel, they would support us. Ask any man you like, and I think that I could almost guarantee that they would be only too willing and anxious to serve their country anywhere in the world!"

Captain Spencer grinned and said in a sly sort of way, "Why don't we put it to the test colonel?"

"Eh?"

"May I have your permission to try something, sir?"

The colonel grunted his assent. The captain stood up and opened the office door and called, "Corporal Cleall! Adams!" The 2 men in the outer office jumped up from the wooden chairs on which they had been sitting and quickly stood at attention. Spencer nodded in acknowledgement to them and ordered, "Report to the colonel, please."

They both exchanged surprised glances. "Very good, sir!" Cleall at once responded. He nodded at Adams. "By the left, quick march!" The men marched into the office. Corporal Cleall gave the command to halt and both men snapped up smart salutes. "Reporting to the colonel as ordered, sir!" said Corporal Cleall stiffly. He and Adams were both standing rigidly at attention.

The colonel smiled. "Stand at ease and stand easy men," he said. "There is a question I would like to put to you."

The 2 men looked at each other, a fact that was not missed by Captain Lubbock. "Relax, Cleall," he said encouragingly. "You have done no wrong, but we do seek your opinion on a certain matter."

The colonel looked towards Spencer and addressed him by his first name. "Well, Huntley, seeing as it was your suggestion, I think I will let you do the asking."

"Thank you, colonel." Captain Spencer placed himself next to the men. "Well, Corporal Cleall. What are the men of the regiment saying?"

"Saying sir?"

"Yes, about the mobilisation."

Cleall and Adams grinned at each other. "Why sir, we hope that we can have a chance to teach them Huns a lesson, don't we Adams?"

Adams nodded in assent and said with feeling, "Too bloody true, colonel!" Then, suddenly remembering his place, said, "I am sorry for swearing, sir, but we are just spoiling for a fight with them!"

The colonel smiled. "Are you telling me that the men of the regiment are willing to go to France or Belgium to meet with the enemy?"

"Just give us the chance, sir, that's all we are asking for!" pleaded Cleall.

"Alright Huntley, I think I am getting the message!" The colonel smiled and nodded towards the captain.

Spencer said to the men. "Alright, chaps. Thank you. You can go now." Both men sprang back to the position of attention and saluted. Turning about, they marched out of the room.

After the men had left and Lieutenant Longrigg had closed the door behind them, the colonel spoke with self-assurance. "Right then, gentlemen. Here is your task. Set about the training with a will. When I am confident that we are at the right point I will offer the Regiment to Brigade for Foreign Service. I can do no more than that."

"When will that be, sir?" asked Bates.

The officers craned their heads forward, eagerly awaiting the colonel's reply. Having made his mind up he said, "Within 5 days, gentlemen. 5 days!"

Captain Bates was busily dealing with an unusually full tray of correspondence and other duties that adjutants always found themselves with. He smiled ruefully and thought of the easy time that he had previously found in this territorial regiment, where the demands made upon him were relatively few compared to that of a regular unit. Disciplinary problems hardly ever occurred because the men only appeared for 2 hours or so a week at training. They were also dispersed around the county of Somerset in one of the many drill halls that catered for them.

A sharp knock sounded on the door. "Come in," he said curtly. The door opened, and four young officers entered, all strangers to him.

They saluted the adjutant. The tallest of the four, a gangly looking youngster with a spotted face said, "Second Lieutenants Davey, Fry, Mitchell and Wills, sir." Davey thrust forward his hand containing their orders. "The War Office has directed us to join your regiment, sir."

"Good lord!" exclaimed the Adjutant. "This is news to me, gentlemen. Please, take a seat." The Adjutant quickly scanned the orders of the new officers and gave a broad grin. "Well gentlemen, you are certainly most welcome to your regiment." The adjutant stood up and walked around his desk, proffering his outstretched hand towards them. "Captain Stanley Bates," he said, introducing himself. He added unnecessarily, "I am the adjutant here."

The gangly youth shook the adjutant's hand first. "John Davey, sir. Glad to be here."

The next officer said, "Leonard Fry, sir. Good to be a part of this regiment." His hair was slightly ginger in tone and was matched with a thick moustache. The adjutant suspected that he was trying to make himself look far older then he really was, and he was tempted to ask him "how old are you?" but thought better of it.

The third officer had fair hair and strikingly blue eyes. He introduced himself in a polished and cultured voice. "Alexander Mitchell, sir. I look forward to my time in the regiment." The adjutant smiled and nodded.

The fourth officer was a little hesitant, but quite clearly the youngest of the bunch. His pale face was covered in bum fluff and the adjutant made a mental note to get him shaving properly at once. "Alec Wills, sir. From Bristol"

"Wills? The name sounds familiar."

"My father is William Wills, sir. Perhaps you have heard of him? He owns the cigarette company in Bristol."

"Ah!" responded the adjutant. Mr W.H. Wills was well known around the Bristol area. "That might be handy. The colonel does love a fine cigar."

The young lieutenant grinned, his confidence growing. "I'm sure I'll be able to manage something for the Mess, sir," he said.

The adjutant nodded in appreciation. Looking at the orders once more his voice took on a business-like tone and he said, "Just wait here for a moment, gentlemen. I

am sure that the colonel would wish to welcome you personally into the regiment."
He walked across to a wooden communicating hatch that was set in the wall and
knocking on it he pulled it briskly open and put his head though the hatch. "Are you
free, sir?" he asked.

The colonel looked up from something he was reading. "Is there a problem,
Stanley?" he frowned.

The adjutant beamed. "On the contrary, sir. Four brand new second lieutenants
and just out of the box have just reported themselves to me and are now standing in
my office."

"Capital!" cried the colonel. "That's the best bit of news I've had all day. Wheel
'em in, adjutant!" he said exultantly; "wheel 'em in!"

The adjutant slid the hatch door closed. "Colonel Glynn D.S.O. will see you now,
gentlemen," he said. "Please go next door and report yourself to him. Once you have
done that, come back to me and I'll allocate you your billets and assign you a batman."

The four officers saluted the adjutant. "Very good, sir," said Davey.

After the young officers had left the adjutant hurriedly took up the piece of paper
on which he was handwriting the Regimental Orders for the next day. Below the space
where he had written, "Alarm for HQ and A Squadron at Norfolk Crescent" he added;
"Assigned to A Squadron: Second Lieutenants A.B. Mitchell, Lieutenant A.D. Wills.
Assigned to B Squadron: Second Lieutenants J.S. Davey and Lt L.H. Fry. With a
satisfied sigh, he shouted to the Company Clerk to come and get the orders for typing
up.

The bar of the Half Moon Hotel was full of men drinking, and in some instances so
were the wives and girlfriends of those present. The inn had an excitable atmosphere
about it, and to speak and be heard a man had to raise his voice, which added to the
general hubbub of the place.

Alf Cleall noted with surprise that over half of the customers in the bar were
already in uniform, including four sailors whom he had never seen before. His ears
were attuned to the cash register which seemed to be ceaselessly ringing.

Alf's younger brother, his usually silent partner in the hotel business, was behind
the big bar, looking somewhat harassed. Wilf was more at home running the other
business that he shared with his brother, the snooker hall. Cleall heard him curse as
he dropped an earthen mug that shattered on the stone floor. Alf automatically rose
out of his chair to go and lend his brother a hand. "Don't you dare, Alf Cleall!" his
wife called out in a firm rebuff. "He's got to learn how to do these things without you.
You carry on with your drinking, my love, and enjoy yourself."

Wilf looked sheepishly from over the bar. "She is right, of course, Alf. I've got to
learn how to do things now; what with you probably going away and all."

Charlie Gibbs laughed and, placing his hand lightly upon his friend's shoulder, pushed him gently back down into his wooden chair. "Sit down, you silly old sod, and have a draught of your own cider!" he admonished light heartedly. "And that is an order!" Alf looked a little uncertain, but he reluctantly did as he was told. Winifred handed Wilf a hand brush and coal shovel to brush up the broken shards of pottery.

The friends began to quietly discuss the events of the day that had taken place in the North Somerset Yeomanry. The news that the colonel had asked Cleall if the regiment was willing to serve abroad had spread like wildfire, so now everyone seemed to know about it and had made an assumption that at some point the unit would be going to either France or Belgium. They had also heard that the colonel hadn't quite made up his mind yet, and it was up to the men to prove that they were ready and fit enough to fight, if need be.

This was what the men had trained for and looked forward to. Only as recently as a couple of months ago and on their annual exercise on Salisbury Plain, the Yeomanry had acquitted itself well, particularly in the mass brigade cavalry charge against entrenched troops with Maxim machine guns. "Of course," Alf had thought, "the machine guns were not firing real bullets."

He wondered again how charging cavalry would fare against modern Vickers machine guns, (which hardly ever went out of action due to a mechanical defect), compared to the British Army's current weapon of choice, the Maxim machine guns. He had seen the Vickers machine gun being demonstrated only last year on Salisbury Plain, and the havoc that the team of eight men with only one Vickers gun wrought against its targets beggared belief and stayed firmly fixed within his memory, for the water-cooled weapon never jammed once. Rumour had it that the ancient Maxim machine gun that was on the Yeomanry's strength would be replaced in due course by the Vickers.

He speculated with Charlie if there would truly be a role for the cavalry again in modern warfare against such a formidable weapon as the new Vickers machine gun. What was certain was that a Machine Gun Section, armed with Maxim machine guns, was even at this moment being formed in the Yeomanry and under the command of the respected Lieutenant Tyssen.

A small man in smart civilian clothing walked into the hotel and patiently took his turn in the queue at the bar. At last Winifred got to serve him. "What be you drinking then, my lover?"

The man looked around uncertainly before speaking hesitatingly in a noticeable and heavily accented broken English. "Please, vrouw. I sink ze beer vould be nice, Ja?"

The place went as quiet as a mouse. Somebody exclaimed, "Bloody hell! The bugger be a German spy!"

The stranger looked concerned. "No! No!" he hurriedly corrected, "I am Netherlander! Dutch!" He almost shouted the last bit.

One of the sailors, who had a little too much rum in him, suddenly lurched towards the man. He grabbed him by his coat collar and snarled, "Bloody German!"

Alf leapt swiftly to his feet with Charlie immediately behind him. He quickly forced himself between the 2 men, making the sailor let go of the scared little man. His eyes pleaded with Alf. "I am Dutch, please!"

Alf looked at him, trying to remember the little bit of Afrikaners that he had picked up when he was soldiering in South Africa. He had been taught a few words of the language by one of the captured Boer soldiers. Afrikaners was basically Dutch but with some variations. He screwed up his eyes as he tried to think of a suitable phrase that he could use. Suddenly he remembered the basic one. "Wie bent U? Wat doet u heir?" (Who are you? What are you doing here?).

The man's face broke into a huge grin as he grasped Alf's shoulders, a look of sheer relief in his eyes. "U spreekt Nederland's!" (You speak Dutch!) he cried.

Sadly, Alf shook his head. "Nee, heel weinig (No, very little), he replied.

The Dutchman looked around him, slightly afraid of what the people in the bar were going to do to him. "God zij dank! Ze zeg ik als Nederlandse!" (Thank God! Tell them I am Dutch!).

Alf grinned. "It's alright boys," he said. "He really is a Dutchman, although he can't speak much English, it seems!"

The sailor looked a bit sheepish and held out his hand for the Dutchman to shake, which he quickly did. Alf spoke slowly and deliberately to the man. "Wat is uw naam?" (What is your name?).

The Dutchman grinned broadly. "Mijn naam is Peter," (My name is Peter).

Alf put out his hand and shook that of the Dutchman's. "Boys," he said, "meet Dutch Peter, from Holland."

The bar immediately resumed its cheerful chatter and the incident was over. The Dutchman quickly thought better of being out alone in a strange city and one who spoke with such a strong accent.

He swiftly downed his drink and turn to leave. "Deze mijn vriend," (Thank you my friend), he acknowledged gratefully, and quickly left the premises.

Charlie grinned at Alf. "You crafty old fox! I didn't know you spoke Dutch, Alf?"

Alf laughed. "Just a smattering I picked up during my time in South Africa. Never thought it would come in handy here, though." The men laughed and carried on drinking and talking in the way that only men who immensely enjoyed each other's company could.

Wednesday, 5th August 1914.

Ernest Summers was enjoying the last moments of what, in those days, would just about pass as making love to his wife. He thought ruefully that it wasn't really like that anymore. She just lay there like a log and he felt that he was merely going through the actions, despite his best intentions to re-awaken the desires of the young maiden he had once wed. As if to prove his unspoken point she said in a grumpy voice, "Hurry up, Ernie, and finish will you. I gotta get up in a minute to make your lunch." Any remaining love died in that moment. He grunted and withdrew himself.

Immediately Alice hopped out of bed, and with her back to him slipped off her nightdress and in a single fluid movement was suddenly dressed in her simple worsted smock. Silently she walked out of the room, her mind on other things. Drowsily he heard her moving around downstairs as she expertly made up the fire in the small pot-bellied stove, and in a moment or so he heard the bang of the large iron frying pan as it was slapped down onto its flat top.

He lay with his hands behind his head, staring moodily up at the ceiling. He closed his eyes, but he could not put the damning picture out of his mind. Only yesterday he had finished work at the local colliery, for later on this afternoon he had to report himself to the North Somerset Yeomanry, ready to go to war.

He had noticed how Alice had gotten so very morose lately, but when young Albert, one of his skittles team, came around to collect him to go to the pub on a Saturday night, she would brighten up considerably and it seemed to him, carefully prepare herself. He had thought that she had been treating Albie as a son, but now he was not so sure.

His last night at work in the colliery had been on Monday, for he had received his mobilisation orders and had quit his job after his shift and on the Tuesday morning. He had not told his wife this news. He had to know if anything was going on before he went away. He spent the Tuesday morning in bed, as was his practice, rising for his lunch at 1 p.m. precisely.

That evening, at 9 p.m. he had pretended to go off to his evening shift of work as normal, from 10 p.m. until 7 a.m, but instead he settled himself down with a flagon of cider in the little copse opposite his cottage to keep watch on the house. Nothing happened for a long time and for a moment he thought that all his suspicions were just that, unfounded suspicions. He had even thought about going back to his house.

The summer darkness had quickly gathered, and the day rapidly gave way to night. He saw his wife through the front bedroom window, a shimmering shadow behind the flimsy curtains. She lit a candle and was gone. Then to his complete surprise he saw another candlelight suddenly appear in the window of the spare bedroom. Ernie moved closer to the edge of the copse to obtain a better view.

At 10 p.m. he had heard hobnailed boots crunching along the slate garden path and going towards his front door. He opened it and he saw the man against the lamp light. It was his comrade, Albert! Confidently his best friend opened the front door, and he heard him running up the stairs. Suddenly there was loud laughing. Grimly Ernie walked towards the house on the well-cut grass alongside the garden path, for he did not want to be heard. He quietly opened the front door, and, habitually removing his boots first, crept silently up the stairs. The door to the spare bedroom was closed.

He hovered next to it, listening, his balled fist pushed firmly in his mouth to stop him from crying out aloud. From behind the door he heard his wife moaning in sheer carnal desire, something she never did for him. He heard her cry out in absolute pleasure, "Oh Albert! More! More! More!" A look of pure hatred came over his face as he went to put his hand on the latch. Then he stopped. He knew that if he entered the bedroom now there would be 2 dead bodies to explain.

Sullenly he made his way back downstairs and out of the house. He walked to the end of the garden and by the iron water pump put his boots back on. His face had a grim resolve set up on it.

On Wednesday afternoon, he and Albie would both be reporting to the North Somerset Yeomanry. It was rumoured that they were going to war. He looked towards the spare bedroom of his house and spat out in a low and hate filled voice, "You won't be coming back, you bastard!"

Thursday, 6th August 1914.

Much to the relief of the harassed quartermaster, one of the several special supply trains that pulled into Bath station that day had arrived with the regiment's supply of missing horses, their regulated half docked tails and clearly numbered brands marking them down as army steeds. He had some misgivings about them, for the North Somerset Yeomanry considered itself to be an elite Light Calvary unit and did not accept any mounts below the statutory 15 hands in height. Without doubt a few of the horses barely managed 14 hands high and should have been rated as ponies and therefore not cavalry mounts at all. Some of the animals were clearly the farm horses that they had until very recently been. He was sure that one of them allocated to him was almost blind in one eye.

He had complained bitterly to the Brigade Major, "These aren't horses, they are ponies!"

The Brigade Major fixed him with a stony stare. "All of the *proper* horses have gone to the *proper* cavalry regiments."

"But, sir!" he protested.

The Brigade Major held his hand up, palm first towards the Quartermaster, his meaning quite clear. He said tiredly, "Your regiment is a territorial unit." He held the Quartermaster with his pale grey eyes once more as he twiddled with his white moustache. "*If* your regiment," he said, enunciating the "if", "ever does get sent to the Front, which is highly unlikely, then surely you will receive the correct horses." The Brigade Major waited before he added, "Consider yourself damn lucky to get what you have got."

"The C.O. won't like being given ponies," pointed out the quartermaster by way of a mitigating explanation.

He received another icy stare from the Brigade Major's grey eyes. "Your Commanding Officer's brigadier is aware of the situation. Tell him to complain to him!" That was clearly the end of the matter.

Another train arrived shortly after the first, simply brimming full of ammunition and the items of saddlery that had been so absent and virtually unobtainable in the past when the unit was carrying out its peace time role. Even another train brought the remaining missing items, including the shortfall of rifles and the 4 wheeled Maxim machine guns that the regiment had always experienced as a territorial unit.

Lieutenant Tyssen was the Officer in Command of the Machine Gun Section and he was busily training up the sixteen men selected from the squadrons to form this machine gun troop. He was eagerly loading his new "toys", as he called them, into one of the quartermaster's wagons and was handling his recent acquisitions as if they were newly laid eggs. The quartermaster, ever eager to avoid the wrath of the colonel, allocated the horse with the almost blind eye to the machine gun troop, and Lieutenant

Tyssen was quite happy to sign for it. The regiment was now equipped to its war time standard, and training really began in earnest.

The quartermaster frowned at the invoice for the horses feed. Each horse should have had allocated to it 12 pounds of oats and 14 lbs of hay a day. Quite clearly when he totalled up the figures, he could immediately see that they had only received about 70% of a week's rations for the animals. He thought glumly that the colonel would not be very happy at this news and would surely lay the blame for the deficiency on his shoulders. He had been assured by the Brigade Major that the shortfall would be made up "within the next 2 or 3 days."

The good news was that there would now be enough of the standard Lee Enfield Number 1 Mark II rifles to equip each trooper. These would be carried slung across their shoulders whenever they rode. Each weapon would hold ten rounds when loaded, with the man either charging the magazine one at a time or by 2 chargers which held 5 rounds each.

When getting ready for action the troopers would simply slip these rifles off their backs and firmly ram the butts of the rifles into a small bucket shaped leather cup holder that hung from the right-hand side of the saddle and behind the man. The trooper would then ride forward with the left hand on the reins and the other holding his weapon. By this method, he could quite confidently gallop forward. If all else failed, the trooper could fall back on the heavy cavalry sabre that he carried on the left-hand side of the saddle.

Lieutenant Longrigg had finally devised a workable training programme, and after a few major amendments to it by Captain English, it was finally forwarded to the colonel for his approval. Much to his surprise and delight the training programme was accepted as it was shown, with the colonel hardly making any changes to it at all. All in all, things appeared to be going rather splendidly. The only fly in the ointment was getting the new recruits to ride their horses.

Because most of the new recruits came from the town of Bath itself, and despite them being army reservists, quite a few of them had never ridden a horse as they had been in infantry regiments beforehand. Some had even been previously in the Royal Navy! Constant practice in riding began to pay dividends, but 2 of the men just could not stay on their horses when they took the statutory jump that the colonel had forced upon them to qualify as Troopers in the North Somerset Yeomanry.

Captain English and Lieutenant Longrigg were looking on in exasperation as the same troopers repeatedly fell off their horses taking the "Colonel's Jump" as the fence was now called. "Bloody hell! Those men are useless, Longrigg. Get them to take the jump again."

"Yes sir!" Lieutenant Longrigg walked over to where the troopers stood sheepishly holding their recaptured horses, for they were well trained mounts. As soon as their reins fell loosely to the ground they stopped and calmly started to graze, awaiting their riders to remount them once more.

Corporal Cleall marched up to the captain and saluted. "Still having trouble with those men, sir?" he asked, nodding towards them.

Captain English agreed. "Yes, I'm afraid I am, corporal. Those men will never make Troopers if they can't sit a horse while taking a jump."

Cleall asked, "Would you like me to talk to them sir and give them some advice?"

The captain nodded. "It wouldn't do any harm, corporal. Toddle over and see what you can do will you, please. Tell Mr Longrigg that I have sent you."

Captain English watched Corporal Cleall go over to the three men. Lieutenant Longrigg was clearly in the throes of giving the 2 errant troopers the sharp edge of his tongue. He watched with interest as Cleall reported himself to Longrigg, saluting as he did so, and then pointed back at him. Longrigg returned to his captain.

The new recruits were standing stiffly at attention while Corporal Cleall was talking to them, but they were too far away for either officer to hear what was being said. The men suddenly mounted, and riding at the "Colonel's Jump" both cleared it with ease, and this time both managing to stay solidly in their saddles. Cleall indicated that they should jump the fence one more time, which both men did. They then rode off to rejoin the rest of the squadron.

Captain English was shaking his head from side to side in disbelief as the corporal approached him. "My God, Cleall! What did you say to them that made them take the jump like that?"

Corporal Cleall grinned. "Nothing much, sir. I know those men, Simmons and Haskell, quite well. They can tend to be a little bit lazy. I just reminded them that the colonel would not allow anyone into the regiment who couldn't stay on his horse when taking that jump."

Longrigg frowned. "I told them both that, several times."

Cleall grinned cheekily. "Ah, sirs! I also told them that the Somerset Light Infantry were urgently seeking men to go to France with their reinforcements next week. I told them riding to war was far better than walking to war. I also told them that if they failed to clear the jump this time, then they would be transferred to the infantry tomorrow. It seems to have worked." Cleall saluted and walked away.

Longrigg gave a quiet chuckle. "I'd hate to upset that particular corporal," he opined.

"Best not, then," grinned Captain English. Both men laughed, for they had been friends for a long time.

Friday, 7th August 1914.

The adjutant was sitting behind his desk when there came a polite knock on the door. "Come in", he called. A captain in the uniform of a North Somerset Yeomanry officer entered his office.

The adjutant raised his eyebrows in surprise. "Hello," he said, rising from his chair and walking around his desk to greet the newcomer. "I am the adjutant, Stanley Bates." The 2 men shook hands.

"Hugh Brooking, old man. I have been recalled to duty and appointed again to my old regiment in the role of a temporary captain."

Stanley smiled. "So you have served with us before then?"

The officer, who was about 44 years of age, gave a boyish grin. "Yes. I served in South Africa and......."

He had hardly finished his sentence when the hatchway was suddenly drawn aside and a delighted Colonel Glynn called out loudly: "Hughie! You old scoundrel. I'd recognise that voice anywhere!"

Captain Brooking smiled broadly. "Hello sir! We meet again!"

The colonel grinned hugely. "Come on through and let's have a chin wag. God! It's beginning to feel like old times already!"

2 new officer arrivals joined the regiment that day. The first, temporary Captain Hugh Cyril Arthur Brooking, was immediately assigned to "B" Squadron to be its second in command. The second arrival was Surgeon Captain Charles Wright Edwards, an important addition to the regiment and a local general practitioner whose home was in nearby Wincanton, Somerset. His remit was to be the unit's medical officer. He was now in urgent consultation with the colonel.

"I have been ordered to carry out a medical inspection of every man in the Yeomanry, sir. They all are to be seen by me and must undergo a full examination, including a dental one. Each man must be fully fit and up to the war time standard."

The colonel frowned. "All of the men underwent a medical before they joined us," he said.

The doctor nodded. "Of course, sir, and the War Office accepts that. However, the standard required for a territorial soldier has not been set as high as that for regular troops. In addition, there are a lot of men in the regiment that have not had a medical since they joined it in 1908"

The colonel nodded in agreement. "I have to concede you that fact, doctor," he agreed.

The doctor smiled. "Not only that, sir. I believe that you are contemplating offering your regiment for active service?"

The colonel's eyes twinkled. "You are most certainly correct doctor."

"If the men in your regiment are all given an up to date medical and passed fit for active service, sir, would that not aid your case?"

The colonel grinned. "My, my, doctor. You are a crafty one!" The colonel thumped the table with his hand. "But damme' if you aren't right! A fully fit regiment up to active service standard certainly would be a trump card I could play!"

The doctor nodded. "Thank you, sir. Then I take it that I have your full support?"

The colonel stood up and walked across to the hatch in the wall. Pulling it back he saw his adjutant on the telephone. The adjutant turned and saw the colonel looking at him and recognised the uncompromising look upon his face, so he rapidly finished his conversation with whoever whom he was speaking to and rose to his feet. "Colonel?"

"Priority number one for you, Stanley. Make sure our doctor here, Captain Edwards, gets everything he needs." The adjutant nodded. "He is going to give every man in the regiment a thorough medical inspection and then report back the results to me. This is to be done as soon as possible. Is that clear?"

"Perfectly, sir."

"Good!" The colonel closed the hatch and sat down again at his desk. "Well doctor, is that good enough for you?"

"Wonderful, sir. There are a lot of men I have to see."

The colonel stood up and started to unbutton his tunic. "No time like the present, doctor. As the colonel of the regiment I insist to be the first man to be examined."

"I'll just go and fetch my bag and stethoscope, sir," he replied.

The adjutant looked at the new set of orders in his hand that had just arrived from the Brigade and were marked "Immediate." "Things are definitely beginning to move," he thought to himself. These orders set out that there were serious concerns from the Brigade that spies were actively operating in the area, and a mysterious fire at a stores depot within the brigade's area of responsibility had been thought to have been the work of fifth columnists. The saboteurs were out!

The most obvious target in the North Yeomanry's area of responsibility was the Great Western Railway Station in Bath itself. There were plenty of people about during the day to ensure that fifth columnists could not do their work, but at night it was a totally different story. The station was an open one and therefore vulnerable to attack and sabotage.

The regiment was ordered to provide a guard of 1 non-commissioned officer and 3 ranks daily, from 9 p.m. at night to 6 a.m. each morning. They were to report to the Station Master each time upon their arrival and departure.

The adjutant rose from behind his desk and walked across the tired old blue coloured Axminster carpet that covered the floor. He opened the door and looked along the landing and towards the notice board where the regimental orders were displayed daily. Second Lieutenant Mitchell was studying the board, his notebook and pencil in hand.

"Ah! Mitchell!" called the adjutant.

The young second lieutenant spun around, taken by surprise. "Sir?"

"Come here. I have a task for you."

The adjutant left the door open and returned to the seat behind the light-coloured desk covered by a green beige covering. On his left was his "In-tray" and fairly brimming with work to do. On his right his black tin "Out-tray" which contained only one file. He really was a busy man.

Mitchell knocked on the door and came in. "Sir?"

The adjutant indicated a chair and said, "Take a seat, lieutenant." The nervous young man sat down, not quite knowing what to expect. The adjutant glanced at him and sensed his nervousness. "I have a task for you, quite a straightforward one really. As from 9 p.m. tonight and until 6 a.m. each morning, we are to mount a guard at the Great Western Railway Station." Mitchell nodded. The adjutant suppressed a grin and prompted gently, "You might want to take some notes, Mitchell?"

Mitchell blushed. "Sorry sir," he said and took out his notebook and pencil and quickly caught up with proceedings.

The adjutant nodded and gave a rueful smile. "Don't worry about it. We all have to start properly at some time."

Again, Mitchell blushed, but not too deeply this time. "Thank you, sir."

"Your guard will consist of 1 non-commissioned officer and 3 other ranks each night and all from "A" Squadron. They are to report to the Station Master on arrival and on departure. Now, what you are required to do, Mitchell, is to pop along to the railway station and find the Station Master. Take a note of his areas of concern about the security of the place at night and find out where the men are to be. Make sure that they have access to a telephone. When you have done that, I want you to get back here and create a set of orders for the guard, the standard sort of thing. I also want you to create the duty roster from your squadron for the next week, keeping it a week in advance all the time. When you have done that, I want you to bring all the orders to me for my approval. Have you got that?"

Second Lieutenant Mitchell was a happy man. After arriving so soon in the regiment he did not expect to be given any responsibility such as this for a while. He was anxious and willing to prove himself. "Consider it done, sir," he beamed.

The adjutant's demeanour became that of a serious one as he said stiffly, and putting the young subaltern back in his place, "I will consider it done when I have approved the orders and the duty list!"

The sharp tone of the adjutant's voice quickly took the smile away from the young officer's face. "I'll go there immediately, sir," he said. The adjutant nodded, indicating that the meeting was over.

As an afterthought, the adjutant called after the departing young officer. "Make sure that you brief your squadron commander first on the orders I have just given you."

Mitchell blushed. For without that gentle reminder he would have rushed straight off to the station.

After the second lieutenant had departed, the adjutant clasped his hands behind his head to give thought to the real and immediate problem that he had – Newton Bridge. The regiment had also been ordered to place an immediate guard on it to stop it being sabotaged. The old bridge with its curiously pointed parapet and 2 large circular holes in each end of it was the main artery of transport into Bath over the River Avon. It was now in constant use by the Army Service Corps transport vehicles as they trundled their way throughout the south west delivering whatever war-time cargo they held. He had to act swiftly. He again got up from behind his desk and opened the door to the corridor, sighing as he did so. It had worked for him the last time, he thought, so why not try it again.

Looking out he saw a small group of seven men gathered around the notice board, reading the latest set of regimental orders. He smiled as he recognised Corporal Cleall. "Just the man!" he thought. "Corporal Cleall!" he called.

Alf Cleall turned at the shout and saw the adjutant. "Sir?"

"Report to me, Corporal Cleall, if you please." To the rest of the men standing there he ordered, "You men! Remain where you are until Corporal Cleall comes back for you."

Corporal Cleall reported himself to the adjutant who by now was once again sitting behind his desk. "Corporal Cleall, take those 6 men out there and ride over to Newton Bridge. Do you know it?"

Alf Cleall had lived his whole life in Bath and he knew the bridge well. "Aye, sir. That I do!"

The adjutant nodded. "Good, good. Take the men, each fully armed and carrying 10 live rounds, and establish yourself on Newton Bridge. Your task is to stop any potential enemy saboteur from carrying out any mischief there. I am now going to give you a direct order, Corporal Cleall, which you must confirm that you understand to me. If you give an order to someone to stop and they do not, then under the articles of war you have the right to shoot them, after giving them due warning. Do you understand that?"

The old soldier did. "Aye, sir. If them buggers don't do as we say, then we can shoot 'em but tell 'em first so they have a chance to surrender. Is that right?"

"That's right, Corporal Cleall. We are at war, so war time regulations are now in force. Before you go there, and I want you there as quickly as possible, find the "A" Squadron commander and send him to me."

"How long do you want us to be there for, sir?"

"Until you are relieved by a standing guard from "A" Squadron, which is why I want you to send me the squadron commander."

"Very good, sir. I'll be established up there within the hour." Corporal Cleall saluted and marched out of the office.

The adjutant watched him leave his office and thought that if ever he trusted one of his non-commissioned officers, it was Corporal Cleall. The colonel had already spoken to him about his rank and had instructed him to promote Cleall to a serjeant as soon as a senior non-commissioned officer vacancy occurred in the regiment. As it was, regrettably, it would probably be some time before a vacancy would occur. Peacetime promotion was notoriously slow, but in war things could rapidly change.

Saturday, 8th August 1914.

The colonel was very pleased with his regiment. The mobilisation mechanism had really kicked in by now and the Yeomanry was almost complete. "B" and "C" Squadrons had left their drill halls in Weston-super-Mare and Shepton Mallet and were both now located in Bath. It was time for the remaining squadron to join them.

The hatch door was open, so the colonel called out to his adjutant. "Stanley! Can you come in here for a moment please? We have a little work before us today."

The door to the colonel's office opened after a respectful knock and the adjutant entered, holding a wooden flatboard in his hand. On the board a strong metal clip held a sheaf of clean A4 sized paper upon it. The colonel held out his hand and indicated a chair for him to sit in, which the adjutant did, pencil poised and ready to write.

"I want you to check with the billeting officer from Brigade where the men from "D" Squadron are going to be placed when they arrive here. Please instruct the officer commanding to evacuate Bristol tomorrow and report his squadron here by 4 o'clock. The men of "D" Squadron are to be distributed evenly between "A", "B" and "C" to give them roughly the same strength. After 4 p.m. tomorrow the North Somerset Yeomanry will consist only of these 3 squadrons, together with the headquarters, all based here, in Bath."

"The same with the officer's, sir?"

The colonel nodded. "Yes, please. Make it so."

"Is there anything else, colonel?"

The colonel grinned and pushed across a handwritten signal. "I want you to get this off to Brigade by despatch rider immediately, please."

The adjutant picked up the message and read it. His face broke into a broad grin as he read what the colonel had written: *"I have the honour to report that the Regiment under my command have requested me to offer their services for active service abroad and are ready."*

He nodded and said, "When do you want me to make this public?"

"Put it in tomorrow's Regimental Daily Orders, if you please. By the time they are published, I am rather hoping that the Brigade will have responded to me."

"I understand, sir."

The colonel nodded. "Thank you, Stanley." The adjutant got up from his chair and walked swiftly from the room. When he got out into the corridor the colonel heard him calling for the despatch rider. The motor cyclist attached to the regiment from Brigade would take no time at all in getting into Bristol and delivering the message addressed personally to the brigadier from the Commanding Officer, North Somerset Yeomanry.

Alf was grumbling to himself because he was no longer living in the Half Moon Hotel but had been re-billeted along with a few others in the Weekes Men's Club. That was not a bad thing as he was quartered in the large room at the back of the club with another twenty or so men from "A" Squadron.

A few of the older men who had been with the regiment for a long time were also there and the men considered it a prime billet. The old soldier did not object to sleeping on a wooden canvas bunk bed with its feather pillow and army issue blankets; he could even get a drink in the bar because they had all been made honorary members of the club. What he felt aggrieved about was that that he couldn't go home after 9 p.m. because all the Yeomanry were barred from the public houses after that time, and they all had to be back in their billets by 10 p.m.

What annoyed him most was the fact that his pub was less than 500 yards from the men's club. He had asked for permission to be able to stay in his own home, but the adjutant had reluctantly refused. His argument was that if he allowed one person to do so then many others would expect the same privilege.

Alf also felt a little bit left out of it as his best friend, Charlie Gibbs, because he was a serjeant, was now billeted with the remaining sergeants of the regiment. He felt strangely at a loss because of this as they were true comrades. Admittedly he had stepped in to help behind the bar of the club when the regular man failed to turn up and that had placated him somewhat. Apparently, the bar steward he had gone off without a word and joined the Somerset Light Infantry.

Weekes Men's Club was also beginning to feel the effects of the war, in common with many other places. The membership of the club had virtually halved overnight, as members who were in the reserves had been called up and other younger men had gone straight to the local recruiting office in Bath to enlist.

It still left Alf in the queer position of having to leave the bar area of the club, in common with the remainder of the North Somerset Yeomanry men who were billeted there, to get to the large hall which had been taken over as their sleeping quarters. He, as the senior corporal, had been delegated the task by his new Squadron Serjeant Major (the original one had failed his recent medical badly and had already been discharged from the North Somerset Yeomanry) of ensuring that everyone was back in the club and in the club room where they slept by 10 p.m. Anyone who was not would be in trouble. To cap it all, the duty officer of the squadron would come around anytime between 10 p.m. and 11 p.m. to ensure that everyman was accounted for. Alf looked anxiously at his pocket watch. Trooper Alex Davis would have to get a move on if he were to get back in time.

Sunday, 9th August 1914.

The Church Parade was held on the green outside of Norfolk Crescent at 10 a.m. that morning. The whole regiment, less their horses, had paraded in their 3 squadrons, the men of "D" Squadron having not yet arrived. The North Somerset Yeomanry did not yet have their own padre, although the colonel was aware that the Reverend Gibbs, a Chaplain of the Forces, was due to join them on the morrow, with the rank of Captain. He had tried to get him to join yesterday so that he could be present on the Church Parade. It would have been a good way for him to meet the men. It was not to be, however, for the Brigade Major had insisted that the new padre reported to him at 10 a.m. on this day for Brigade business. He would be required until the supper time and so he would not be available to take the Church Parade. The colonel understood this.

This was the first time the regiment had paraded in such large numbers in public, other than their annual training, and the 350 or so of the men gathered in the one place almost filled the open space to its capacity. Because they were a local regiment, the wives and children of the men had also gathered there to join in the service. It was the colonel's view that the regiment was a family, and that wives and children were always welcome. He looked across to the dais that had been placed there and smiled fondly towards his wife. She gave a little wave to him. Quickly the colonel turned his mind to other regimental matters.

The Bishop of Bath and Wells, Bishop George Kennion, was taking the service today. He was an old friend of the colonel's and often had stayed at his house. For a bishop, he had a noticeable craving for a fine brandy and cigars. Often, they would stay up into the early hours of the morning after a dinner party and discuss Australia. Bishop Kennion had, before returning to England, been the Bishop of Adelaide. He had loved the country and had been instrumental in the building of a lot more churches in South Australia. He had also increased the number of clergy in that State from 50 to 75, not a mean feat.

The regiment's band was in attendance and at 10 a.m. precisely the adjutant called the parade to attention and the band struck up 'God Save the King.' After this the parade was stood at ease and the Bishop of Bath and Wells began the proceedings. The first hymn, and one specifically chosen by the Bishop, was 'Onward Christian Soldiers' and the men sang this with much gusto. After that the Bishop delivered a short sermon about how it was right for soldiers to defend their country against the Germans and made a sober reference to the fact that perhaps some of the men standing here now would not return. The colonel felt a little uncomfortable about this, but it was the Bishop who was delivering the sermon and he probably felt he had a moral duty to get the men prepared to meet their maker. When this had finished, the last hymn, "Abide with Me", was sung. The colonel felt that he had never heard such feeling in the song than as he did then.

After the service was over the colonel stood on the dais alone whilst the adjutant and squadron commanders gathered the men around him. With so many of the soldier's families in attendance he thought it was an opportune time to speak to them. When all was ready the adjutant called the men to attention and reported the regiment to the colonel.

"Thank you, adjutant," he said. "Stand the men at ease please."

"Very good, sir! R.S.M.!"

"Sah!"

"Stand the regiment at ease please."

R.S.M. Shakespeare threw out his barrel sized chest and bellowed: "Regiment! Stand at - ease!" The men did as they were ordered, and the colonel waited for a moment for absolute silence. "Men," he shouted, for the large assembly needed to hear a loud voice. "I have instructed the adjutant to add something to our Regimental Daily Orders today. The adjutant will now read it out to you."

The adjutant stepped up to the dais and held out a copy of the day's Regimental Daily Orders, which had yet to be published. He read, "The Commanding Officer has sent a telegram: "I have the honour to report that the Regiment under my command have requested me to offer their services for active service abroad and are ready."

A buzz of excitement spread like wildfire around the crescent. "Silence!" shouted the R.S.M.

The colonel stepped forward again. "I sent this message yesterday to our Brigade. I have not yet received an official answer, although a little bird tells me that probably our offer will be accepted." Again, a little buzz of excitement ran through the soldiers and the colonel held his hand up for silence. "As soon as I receive the official answer I will post it on Regimental Orders. All I can say is that I have the utmost faith in you. I know that, whatever happens, you will never let me, or the regiment, down. God bless you all in the days to come." The colonel turned to leave the dais.

From somewhere within the soldiers ranks a voice shouted eagerly, "Three cheers for the colonel! Hip! Hip! Hip!" and a resounding chorus of "Hooray!" echoed around Norfolk Crescent, the cheering resonating off the old building which only increased the intensity of the noise. Somewhere a child began to cry loudly. The soldiers were still cheering when the colonel escorted his lady away.

The Reverend A.S. Gibbs sat respectfully with his new colonel. He felt at ease, for although he carried the paid rank of a captain, whenever he spoke to someone he unofficially took on the rank of that person he was speaking to. The colonel looked at him and said in a gruff voice, "And what had the brigade to say to you that was so very important that it kept you away from your very first church parade with the regiment, padre?" The colonel had made his point.

He felt very guilty about this and spread his hands open wide in a conciliatory gesture. "It's not something that I would want to raise colonel, but it is vitally important one." The minister paused before he continued. "The Brigade has made it known to us of the absolute importance they place upon the subject." The padre's face frowned as he screwed up his eyes and he gently rocked back and forth a little, searching for the words that he would need to emphasise the matter. He decided that the best approach would be to speak directly about it. "It could have an exceedingly demoralising affect upon the regiment if handled wrongly, colonel!"

The commanding officer of the North Somerset Yeomanry raised one of his eyebrows. He became alert when the rector acknowledged the fact the he really was the colonel in charge of the regiment. He nonchalantly shuffled some papers and gave the impression of carelessly placing them in his out tray. He waited a short while before he finally encouraged, "Really?"

The Chaplain of the Forces gave a cough of embarrassment. He sighed as he said firmly, his mind made up, "It is a rather delicate subject, but one that has to be broached and dealt with."

The colonel waved his hand in a condescending manner. "Feel free to tell me directly, padre."

The Reverend Gibbs looked closely at his notes before he spoke, taking a moment or so to gather together his thoughts. "I trust that what I am about to say will be kept in utter confidence, sir?"

The colonel was irritated a little by the thought that the padre had the temerity to question this aspect about him, but he recognised that the padre did not know him – yet. He said, with a note of sternness in his voice, "Of course - and it always will be!"

The padre's face became a bright red as he recognised the serious error that he had just made. He took out a white handkerchief and blew into it, taking time to recover himself. Eventually he said, "The Brigade has informed me that there is a good chance that the regiment could be sent to the front, so all of the officers are to receive special instructions from me."

"Special instructions?" said the colonel, a frown across his brow, but a little elated by the unexpected information that that the Reverend Gibbs had inadvertently revealed to him.

The minister nodded sadly, "I am afraid, colonel, that my duty has been clearly spelt out to me. I am to immediately instruct your officers in letter writing."

"Letter writing! Damned if I can see the sense in that padre. They are all literate men and can easily pen a letter."

"I don't doubt that for a moment colonel, but I am sorry to say that these will be special letters, and ones that will need to be written with care." The military chaplain paused for a moment and cleared his throat before he said emphatically, "I am to instruct the officers in how to write to the next-of-kin of the men under their command who will fall in battle."

The colonel suddenly understood. He sat quietly for a moment, drumming his fingertips upon the top of the wooden desk, a habit he had recently fallen into when weighing up the pros and cons of something. The sound made an unintentional rhythmic pattern before he quickly stopped. "I see. Well, I can see the sense of it. It has to be done, I suppose."

"I would like to see all of the officers in the officers' mess at some time, colonel. I will only need them for an hour at the most."

The colonel nodded in agreement. "I'll get the adjutant to make it so."

"Thank you. It must be done discretely though. It wouldn't do to publish anything on regimental orders, and the Brigade Major has forbidden that anyway."

"Very well. How about after dinner in the mess tomorrow night? I will, of course, be in attendance myself."

"Thank you, colonel."

There came a crisp rap upon the colonel's door, and the adjutant entered. "I am sorry to disturb you, sir, but I thought that you should see this at once." The adjutant passed the message to the colonel, a huge smile upon his face.

The colonel grinned as he read the military telegraph. He looked towards his newly appointed padre and said, "This makes our conversation more important!" He passed the message across to the padre. It read, *From Brigadier General Commanding 1st South West Mounted Division. "Your fine offer received and much appreciated. BRIGADIER."*

"I have taken the liberty of putting it on the regimental orders, to be published later, sir," said the adjutant, a note of quiet satisfaction evident in his voice.

The colonel nodded wisely. "Good, good," he said. He waited a moment before he directed, "Now then, Stanley, Captain Gibbs has something to say to you, and I want it to be put into action immediately."

The adjutant looked expectantly towards the padre, who immediately began to tell him about the letter writing exercise that had to take place.

Four new recruits stood at attention before the adjutant. They had just joined the regiment after being sent to them by the recruiting officer of Bath. The adjutant's clerk, Trooper Harding, held a list in front of him. "Here are the new men's regimental numbers, sir," he said, for army units in those days had their own numbering systems. The adjutant smiled, for his clerk was an efficient man.

"All four of you are drafted to "A" squadron. Here are your regimental numbers. Remember them!"

"Henry Reed, 593," said the clerk.

"Sir," replied Reed.

The adjutant fixed him with a stern gaze. "How old are you, Reed?"

The lad blushed. He hesitated and said, "Eighteen, sir!"

"The truth now, boy! Come on, out with it! You don't look eighteen to me!" The lad cast his eyes downwards. The adjutant added, "I can soon send a man around to your mothers to find out, so you had better tell me the truth!"

The lad looked up. "W-ell, I am almost eighteen, sir."

"When is your birthday?"

"It is the 4th of December, sir. I shall be 18 years old then."

The adjutant sighed. The lad was old enough to join the regiment but not old enough to go to France just yet. He had several men like that now, and they were going to have to go into a reserve squadron.

"Does that mean you don't want me, sir?" he said timidly.

The adjutant was quick to respond. "Oh, we want you alright lad, but you'll have to wait until you are 18 should we go to France. Next man."

Harding nodded. "Arthur Hopkins, 594."

"Sir!"

"George Nicholls, 592."

"Sir!"

"Leonard Smythe, 591."

"Welcome to the regiment, men. Trooper Harding here will take charge of you now and allocate you your billets. Once you have done that, Harding, take them around to the training officer."

"Very good, sir." Harding called the men to attention, and after saluting, he about turned the men and marched them away.

"Good man, Harding," the adjutant thought.

Wednesday, 12th August 1914.

The adjutant grinned triumphantly. At last he had got all the billeting of the men and officers finally worked out. It had taken a little time to get it right, but now at least he knew where every man was. He got up and knocked on the hatch separating his offices from the colonel's. "Yes, Stanley," invited the colonel.

The adjutant slid back the hatch. "Morning sir," he greeted.

"Good morning."

"I would like your permission to publish the whereabouts of the men's billets on our regimental orders today, sir, if possible."

The colonel nodded. "Of course, of course. Where are they all?"

Captain Bates smiled. "I have billeted "A" Squadron and the headquarters in the following places, sir. In Weston Schools we have 140 men from "A" Squadron and part of our H.Q. I have 25 men placed in the Weekes Men's Club and another 35 headquarters staff at number 1, Clifton Terrace. For "B" Squadron, there are 30 men at Christchurch School, 80 at numbers 3 and 4 Clifton Terrace and 26 in number at 6 Clifton Terrace. There are 115 men from "C" Squadron at St. Thomas's School and the remaining 21 are in billeted in 8, Clifton Terrace. A total of 472 other ranks."

"A grand job, Stanley. I am so pleased that you have achieved getting the men in billets and all in the same area. It makes life that much simpler. And the officers?"

"All of the officers are now accommodated in Litton Lodge, sir."

"Horses?"

"All at Oram Arbour, sir."

The colonel nodded his understanding. "An excellent piece of work, Stanley," he praised. "I would wish to visit each location at some time, starting with the horses."

"Very good, sir, I'll make the arrangements at once." The adjutant beamed and closed the hatch.

After dinner that night the adjutant cleared the officer's mess completely. Even the bar steward had been stood down, for the adjutant did not want the "letter writing exercise" to become common knowledge. When he had done this and made sure that all the officers were in attendance, he went to the Commanding Officer's Office to fetch the colonel.

The officers went quiet as the colonel entered the mess, with the adjutant coming behind him carry a sheaf of clean paper and some pencils.

"Alright, gentlemen. Please be seated," said the colonel. The officers sat down while he remained standing. "You will recall from orders that our offer to go to France has been accepted from the brigadier." The colonel's eyes wandered around the room, noting the murmur of appreciation and expectation that was abuzz. He said, coolly, "Well, if we do go to France gentlemen there is one thing that we can expect to happen.

In any fight there will be casualties." He waited a moment for the fact to slowly register, and then nodded towards the padre. "Padre, take over please."

The Chaplain of the Forces got to his feet and the adjutant began to hand out pieces of papers and pencils to each officer present. He waited a moment and then said, "Well, gentlemen, the colonel is very correct in what he says. Each unit that goes to war can expect to lose as many as six men, and the next of kin of those men will have to be informed. That means that you, as the officer commanding your men, will have to write directly to them with the sad news of the loss of their loved one."

The minister took a sip of water. Lieutenant Longrigg said, "Oh come now padre. To lose six men is somewhat careless is it not?" There was a titter of amusement.

The colonel held his hand up for silence. "Very amusing, Mr. Longrigg," he said, "but that is the brigade forecast of casualties per unit – at least six."

The minister spoke again, "Well then, Mr. Longrigg, let's start with you. Who is your best man, do you think?"

The officer grinned broadly and said without any hesitation, "Without a doubt I think that Corporal Cleall is one of the very finest man we have."

The colonel and adjutant both nodded agreement.

"Well then," responded the cleric. "Image that Corporal Cleall has been killed and it is your responsibility to write to his family to break the bad news to them. Just how do you start your letter?"

"Dear Mrs Cleall, I suppose."

"That is just a good a place as any to start. But what do you write after that? Do you simply say: Dear Mrs. Cleall, your husband is dead?"

Lieutenant Longrigg stroked his chin. "H-m-m, I see your point," he accepted.

The padre looked at a list in front of him. "The Brigade is quite keen that any casualties be notified immediately to their next of kin by a hand-written letter of an officer. Think about your men as individuals, men who would not be going home. How about, "My dear Mrs. Cleall, it is with the heaviest of hearts that I have to write to tell you of the loss of your gallant husband. How does that sound?"

He smiled. "I like that, but God forbid that I will ever have to say that."

"You may have to, Mr. Longrigg." The colonel thought for a moment and explained, "I don't really like to tell you this, and what I am about to say does not go outside this room. Is that clear, gentlemen?"

The expressions of the officer's present took on a sober vista. The colonel cleared his throat and continued. "When I was in South Africa I lost one of my young officers through a Boer howitzer shell." The colonel closed his eyes as he recalled the event. "The shell caught him full in the stomach and blew his guts out, and when I got to him he was trying to push his intestines back in and crying out for his mother."

The officers' present exchanged glances, feeling the colonel's horror at the situation. The colonel suddenly slammed his fist on the table in front of him, causing those present to give a nervous start. "How do you explain that to a mother!" he said, feeling the old anger and remorse that he should have done more for the boy.

The Chaplain of the Forces stood up and looked meaningfully at all those present. "We can ease this moment, gentlemen. Brigade have suggested that you write something like, "Your son died gallantly. He was leading his men at the time and was caught in the explosion of a shell. I am sure he felt no pain and died an instantaneous death."

The colonel saw that the officers' present were now taking the exercise seriously and that they had begun to take notes. He thought ruefully to himself, "Only six casualties? Brigade must be off their heads, why, I lost fourteen men in one day alone when I was in the Transvaal."

"One more thing," the padre added. "Please do not get into the habit of using the same statement twice. Loved ones will want to know exactly what happened to their son, brother, husband, father etc. You must tell the truth about the death each time, for the man's comrades will surely write home about their friend's death at some point or another. So be honest in what you write, but write with feeling. Think about how you would like to be told about the death of your loved one."

The colonel added, "Get your letters started gentlemen, and show them to the padre on completion. That is all."

Thursday, 13th August 1914.

The colonel was holding his daily "O" group at 8.30 a.m. All the officers were gathered there, except for Lieutenant Longrigg, who was the duty officer. The adjutant would brief him later. Once everyone had settled down he colonel broke the news to them.

"Well gentlemen," he began. "Everything is now moving at a very fast pace indeed. We are to move as a regiment *en bloc* with the brigade to Windsor, Berkshire. We will stay for about a week or so before we go to Forest Row, which will be our main camp. There we will begin training with the brigade." He looked towards the machine guns officer, Lieutenant Tyssen, and said, "On completion of this briefing the machine gun section is to leave immediately for Winchester. Brigade are sending over 3 lorries and an omnibus to transport you at 11 p.m." The Machine Gun Officer's eyes widened in surprise, but he was up to it. "The lorries are being provided and driven by the Army Service Corps. There will be a serjeant with them who knows directly where you have to go, so liaise with him on his arrival."

"Thank you, colonel," he said.

The colonel nodded and continued, "Adjutant, if you please."

"Captain Lubbock," he said, addressing the officer directly. "It's very short notice, as we know, but you are to take the headquarters element and the unallocated horses to Winchester by train, departing tomorrow night from the Great Western Rail Station at Westmoreland at 6.50 p.m. I have the manifest ready and will pass it to you on completion of the "O" Group. Suffice to say that there will be 156 officers and men from the regiment, plus 175 horses. You will need to be at the station by 5 p.m."

Captain Lubbock gulped. He really had been thrown in at the deep end and there was nothing that he could do about it. He said in an ironic tone, "Thank you so much, adjutant." There was a ripple of laughter.

"Happy to oblige," grinned the adjutant. He then unveiled a blackboard that until that moment had been covered with an army issue blanket. On it was a large-scale map that displayed the west-country. "For the squadrons, we will move from Bath, here," he said, as the adjutant tapped the city of Bath on the map with his swagger stick, "to Winchester, there." Again, the adjutant tapped the map to show where it was. "We will be moving into previously pitched tented accommodation, although of course the officers will be billeted in a local hotel."

He looked directly at the poor quartermaster who quickly averted his gaze from the colonels, but the colonel would not let that be. "Lieutenant Holwell," he snapped.

The quartermaster instantly leapt to his feet. "See the adjutant after this briefing. You are to move to Pirbright tomorrow, taking a wagon and 2 horses with you. The adjutant has allocated 1 serjeant and 14 men, plus Corporal Corben from your staff, to accompany you. You ride out by 11 a.m. tomorrow. Your Regimental Quartermaster Serjeant, with the remainder of the staff, are to stay here to close the headquarters and field camp before joining us at our new location in Winchester. Is that understood?"

"Yes sir," he replied promptly.

The colonel smiled at the rest of his officers. "Now then, gentlemen, I have, I hope, some good news for you. We have been ordered to leave on Monday morning, so I have decided that this Saturday night will be a lady's night in the mess. You are all required to be there, including the duty officer. You are to attend in normal uniform gentlemen, as I am sure most of your mess dress uniform has already been packed in anticipation of a move. You are to be here by 7 p.m. prompt for a 7.30 p.m. start." He noticed that some of the officers' looked towards each other, some frowning. "Don't you worry about the logistics of it gentlemen. I do appreciate the damnably short notice for the whole event, which is why I am not insisting on mess dress." He waited for a moment before adding, with a broad grin, "Why, even my wife does not know about it yet!" The officers laughed gaily.

The colonel's eyes twinkled as he played with the tip of his moustache. "I am keen for this to happen because this may be the last time we get a chance to have our ladies together as a group, gentlemen, before we go away! One more thing, which I am sure you will find agreeable. On completion of this "O" group, apart from the duty officer, I want all of you married men who have their wives living nearby to go home and get your 'little woman' sorted out. I do not expect to see you until Saturday night's dinner." The married officers who could bring their wives to the dinner smiled at each other, grateful for the chance to go home, albeit for such a relatively short time.

"One more thing for you, gentlemen. Things are beginning to move now at an unstoppable pace. We welcome Lieutenant Liebert to the regiment and he has been appointed as the officer commanding "C" Squadron." The new officer stood up and nodded his formal greeting to the mess members present. "Tomorrow, another new officer, Lieutenant Horner, will also join us. I am sure that the adjutant can tell you more about that particular officer," he said, turning his head to look at him.

The adjutant stepped forward so that all the officers could see him. "Thank you, colonel. The new officer assigned to us is named Lieutenant Edward Horner, and he will be assigned to Lieutenant Liebert's "C" squadron." Captain Bates grinned as he continued. "I know Lieutenant Horner very well, gentlemen, for he also hails from Mells. He received his education at Eton and Balliol College, Oxford. He is also a lawyer, so no doubt he can give you some free advice if needed!" The officers grinned. "One more thing about him, gentlemen, is that he has an unusual family history. Please don't ask him about it – and he is not to know this, - the colonel intends to get him to tell us that history over dinner on Saturday. I promise you, gentlemen that you will be extremely interested in what he has to say."

Friday, 14th August 1914.

The quartermaster made a final check of his wagon and the big shire horses that would draw it. From Bath to Pirbright was a long way, about 100 miles. That journey would take about 4 days to cover, but it had to be done. He had asked for rail transportation but had been bluntly told by the Brigade Major to carry out the task assigned to him by his commanding officer.

Feeling somewhat chastised by the events, the quartermaster set about making sure that everything was ready for the journey. Lieutenant Holwell was really looking forward to the chance to command 15 men, including a serjeant, as he would actually be in charge with no-one over him for the first time. For a second time he re-checked that the tents were on top of the load, for after reaching his 25 miles target a day he would have to set up camp in a place of his choosing.

Serjeant Bristow and his men were waiting patiently whilst he made a final check of the wagon. On completion, the quartermaster reported to the adjutant at 10.45 a.m. that he was ready to leave.

The adjutant liked Holwell, despite his failings, and did his best to assure him. "Enjoy the trip," he said, "for I think now that we are going to the war you will be given more opportunities to display your leadership skills." He held out his hand and shook the quartermasters. "Ring me each day to keep me informed of your progress, Arthur."

"Yes sir." Lieutenant Holwell left the office with a spring in his step.

The serjeant was holding the reins of his horse for him, and he nodded towards his corporal. "Ready to go, Corporal Corben?"

"Yes sir."

He took the reins of his horse and mounted it. "Well, Serjeant Bristow, we have a long ride ahead of us. I want to make Chippenham, which is about 13 miles away, in about 3 hours. Once there we will stop for an hour to rest the horses before we move on again. I intend to make our first camp somewhere near Avebury."

"Yes sir. We await your orders, sir."

Lieutenant Holwell nodded, and took out his khaki coloured map holder. He had already marked out the route on it and showed it to the serjeant again. "We move off now and follow the main road to Chippenham. Everything ready?" he checked.

Serjeant Bristow nodded. "All ready sir," he confirmed.

Lieutenant Holwell turned on his horse and said, "Alright Corporal Corben. Roll the wagon and follow me." The quartermaster set off at a walking pace and his corporal slapped the reins on the back of the 2 horses. They needed no urging and the laden cart moved slowly forward. The second part of the regiment's move was now underway.

Later that afternoon Captain Lubbock paraded the elements of the headquarters squadron and the "odds and sods" of the regiment that would accompany him on the train journey. In addition a serjeant and 4 members of the Army Ordnance Corps had been seconded to him and would take a permanent place within the regiment. The third part of the regiment's move then took place.

Saturday, 15th August 1914.

"Well, Stanley, how did the last nights move go?" enquired the colonel, sipping his hot cup of tea from behind his desk.

The adjutant gave a little grimace and responded, "Not quite as we planned sir, but eventually the move happened."

The colonel took another sip from his cup and returned it to its saucer. "Oh really?" he said. "You had better tell me everything then. Take a pew."

The tired adjutant sat down and took a sip of the tea that had already been poured for him by the colonel's batman, Adams. He pulled back the top sheet of the paper that lay on his wooden millboard and studied it briefly. "The quartermaster and the Machine Gun Section have gone and there was no trouble with them. Lieutenant Holwell and his group have successfully completed their first part of their road journey and stayed overnight at Avebury. By now they should have left there and are headed towards Newbury."

Captain Bates paused and took another sip from his cup. "As you know, the men under Captain Lubbock paraded at 4 p.m. prior to their move and arrived at the station at 5 p.m. That part went exactly as planned, and despite the short notice. Captain Lubbock's planning went extremely well and I commend him for it." The colonel nodded his approval and made a note on a pad in front of him. "Due to circumstances beyond his control it then started to go somewhat wrong, but Captain Lubbock, again, responded magnificently."

The colonel started to drum his fingers on the table. "Go on," he invited.

"The trains were running late, and the large crowds that had assembled to watch the departure impeded the movement of the men and horses somewhat. The police had to be informed so that they could exercise some sort of crowd control. The original schedule had them departing at 6.50 p.m., but this was delayed by several hours. They did not leave until about 10.30 p.m., amid the great cheering of the citizenry who had gathered there to watch their departure."

"What caused the delay?"

"The horses."

"The horses?"

"Yes, the men were on a steep learning curve themselves and had not loaded horses into goods wagons before. These 175 horses are also relatively untrained army mounts, the only thing about them that made them military mounts was their docked tails. Getting them into the wagons took some doing, I can assure you. The easiest way I can describe it was that most of them were very excitable!"

"A bit like my Yeomanry then," grinned the colonel.

The adjutant laughed at the comparison. "I'm afraid so, colonel," he conceded.

"Are they there yet?"

"Yes sir. I had a phone call from the guardroom at Windsor informing me that they had arrived about 15 minutes ago."

The colonel nodded. "Good, good," he said.

"I left a message for Captain Lubbock to ring me direct at midday, sir. Should I pass him on to you colonel, or would you wish me to deal with it?"

"I would like to speak to him directly, Stanley. When I have finished you can deal with any other matters with him."

"Yes sir."

"Now then, how is the planning going for the squadrons move?"

The adjutant replied, "It just so happens that I have it all written down for you."

His eyes twinkled as he answered, "I thought that you might have!"

All the officers' mess silver had been carefully laid out, each piece in its allocated place, and much to the extreme annoyance of the Mess Corporal. After carefully storing it away for transportation, he had been told to unpack it all from the large case that the North Somerset Yeomanry was going to take with them to their new home. The unexpected mess ladies evening had taken everyone by surprise, but the staff were up to the task and had set a wonderful table.

The officers and their ladies were met by the colonel and his wife as they entered the dining room and introductions were made and old acquaintances struck up. In the background musicians from the Yeomanry's own band, conducted by the rotund little bandmaster, were unobtrusively performing some music from one of Beethoven's string quartets. The officers entered in order of their seniority to be formally greeted by the colonel and then helped themselves and their guests to a pre-poured glass of sherry that stood on silver trays on the large oak sideboard.

After that each officer and his guest were escorted to his assigned place at the massive mahogany table that was to seat them by one of the mess orderlies. The table was covered by a brilliant white damask tablecloth that had a wide scarlet strip of red beige running down the centre line. Several silver trophies decorated the table, one so large that it had taken 2 men to lift it safely onto the table. Evenly spaced out along the scarlet runner were four big silver candelabras, each holding eight large candles. They gave extra heat to what was already a warm evening. On the walls of the dining room several gas lights threw out a spluttering white light, sometimes accompanied by a hissing sound as the gentle breeze from one of the open windows caught the flame. One of the gas mantles suddenly flared up and burnt itself out, the ashes fluttering harmlessly to the floor. A mess orderly quickly replaced it with a new one and within minutes it was burning brightly again.

All in all, some eighteen officers and eleven ladies were seated around the table. Lieutenant Horner, the newest officer to join the regiment, was the last man to enter the dining room. As custom dictated he was placed at the end of the table and furthest away from the colonel and his lady and giving the responsibility of "guarding" the full port decanter.

When everyone was seated, the colonel took the arm of his wife and led her to the head of the table. The sitting officers and their ladies then stood up as the mess corporal seated the colonel's wife. Then the colonel himself took his place. "Thank you, ladies and gentlemen," he said. "Ladies, please be seated. The colonel waited until they were all sat down before sitting down himself. The standing officers then followed suit.

There were ten mess orderlies placed strategically about the table, each with a bottle of red wine in his hand. The Mess Corporal looked after the colonel and his wife personally, pouring the colonel's crystal goblet full of blood red liquid before filling his lady's glass with the same. Once that had been done, the mess orderlies quickly advanced upon the table and filled the glasses of the remaining officers and their guests. The ladies wine glasses were about half the size of the men's in deference to their genteel upbringing.

The colonel watched and waited until all the glasses of the regiment's officers and their ladies had been fully charged with the robust wine. He inclined his head to the Mess Corporal who then stood back behind the colonel's chair. This was the signal for the string quartet to stop playing. The bandmaster held his baton up high above his head and waited.

He paused before he stood up and raised his glass, the remainder of the mess doing the same. "Ladies and gentlemen – the King!" The band immediately broke into the first verse of "God Save the King." When the last note had sounded, and following the colonel's example, they each took a sip out of their glass. The colonel then sat down, and the rest of the mess followed suit.

The meal was of the usual mess fare, carrot soup with croutons followed by roast beef and all the trimmings. In deference to the warm weather they had been experiencing, the colonel had allowed dishes of ice cream to be served. After that, they finished their meal with the usual cheese tray and biscuits. Talk was random around the table, neighbour talking to neighbour, exchanging small talk and general chit-chat. But of course, the main topic of conversation was about the war and the regiment's move.

The Mess Corporal silently placed himself by the colonel and placed a gavel and block on the table. These were a regimental heirloom, having been presented to the North Somerset Yeomanry by Lord Roberts, who, at the end of the Boer War, had donated it to the regiment in grateful thanks for their loyalty as his personal bodyguard.

He then hovered around cautiously, ensuring that everyone had a charged glass. When he was satisfied he whispered into the colonel's ear. "All glasses charged, sir."

The colonel nodded in approval. He picked up the gavel and banged the block loudly twice. Conversation immediately ceased as all eyes looked towards him.

"Ladies and gentlemen, I have the honour to thank you tonight for attending this ladies night in the Mess. I am saddened to say that this may be the last one for some time." He looked his wife in her eyes and patted her gloved hand. "War is a terrible thing, and we are about to embark upon it. It brings untold dangers and unknown terrors. But it also brings new friends and comrades."

He paused for a moment. "I would like to officially welcome to the North Somerset Yeomanry our latest addition to the mess, Lieutenant Edward Horner, the son of Sir John and Lady Horner of Mells. Not unknown to our adjutant, I might add."

"Ah, sir!" interjected the adjutant, a wicked smile on his face and right on cue. "Lieutenant Horner has an interesting family background, if he would care to relate it."

The colonel grinned. "Well, Lieutenant Horner."

Lieutenant Horner was used to mixing with high society and with senior officer's, and he held no fear in his ability to socialise. He smiled and nodded towards the colonel. "Thank you, sir, but I am sure that my family background will be of no particular interest to anyone gathered here."

The colonel's wife, Winifred, her curiosity aroused, thought otherwise. "Oh, come now, Lieutenant Horner, can't you see how intrigued we ladies are? What is this mystery? Does it involve murder and mayhem, or perhaps something even spicier?" Everyone laughed, including the colonel.

Jessica Bowen, the fiancée of the adjutant smiled wickedly. She came from the village of Mells and knew Horner socially. Laughingly she said to the colonel's lady, "Oh come now, Winifred, we wouldn't want to embarrass our newest lieutenant now, would we." The ladies around the table giggled in unison.

"Do tell," pleaded the colonel's wife.

"Yes, do tell," resounded a delighted chorus of voices, for their imagination had been titillated by the supposed mystery.

Lieutenant Horner took a sip of wine and looked towards the colonel. "May I have your permission, sir?"

The colonel smiled. "Please, Edward. Do enlighten us or my wife will never stop nagging me about it."

"Geoffrey!" his wife cried in mock horror. "How could you tease me so?"

There was a general ripple of good natured laughter around the table. Lieutenant Horner wiped his napkin over his lips and stood up. There was a slight babble of conversation and the colonel banged his gavel once on the table and the talking immediately subsided.

Horner was a tall man, somewhere around 6 feet 2 inches in height and 32 years of age. His slim figure was topped by a mop of unruly black hair which had a parting in the middle. Despite his careful attention to it, the hair still looked like a black woolly cap. His uniform had quickly been made for him by a local tailor and it fitted him perfectly.

The latest addition to the North Somerset Yeomanry began to speak in a mysterious tone and recited an old English nursery rhyme. "Little Jack Horner sat in the corner, eating his Christmas pie; he put in his thumb and pulled out a plum, and said "What a good boy am I!"

When he had finished he stopped talking and took another sip of wine before replacing the glass on the table. Tapping the side of his nose he said; "Ah, 'tis an old nursery rhyme as you well know, and I am sure all of you have heard of it at some time or another. But as you rightly suspect, the rhyme has something to do with my family?"

The colonel's wife clapped her hands together and squealed in delight. "Edward! Is Jack Horner one of your ancestors?"

The confident young lieutenant elegantly bowed from his waist towards Winifred Glynn. He smiled a dazzling white smile that caused the hearts of a few of the ladies present to flutter. He said, "Yes, madam, you are absolutely correct." He had them now, so he remained silent, a mischievous grin playing upon his face.

Jessica Bowen looked towards the colonel's wife. "Oh, look who has now joined our company, Winifred. He is going to be such a terrible tease to us ladies!"

Captain Edwards wife, Isobel, could contain herself no longer. "Oh, come along Edward, please. You know how we women love a good gossip!"

The colonel laughed loudly. "Damned if he hasn't got my curiosity stirred now. Come along Edward, out with it!"

Lieutenant Horner inclined his head. "It all involves a bit of history, sir, and it goes something like this. Between the years of 1536 and 1540, after breaking away from the Catholic Church, King Henry the VIIIth was busily dissolving all the monasteries in England. The real reason for this was so that the King and his minister, Thomas Cromwell, could steal all the wealth the church had. By 1539, Glastonbury Abbey was the only religious house left in Somerset that had not been seized, but it was only a matter of time before it was. Glastonbury Abbey also happened to be probably the richest abbey in England.

The then Bishop of Glastonbury, Bishop Whiting, came up with the idea of bribing the King to leave his religious affairs alone. He decided to gift the title of twelve wealthy manors in Somerset to the King, hoping that this act would placate him; but alas he entrusted his steward, who was not an entirely honourable man, with the mission. The deeds were secreted inside a pie to hide them from any would be robbers and, in his steward's care, sent to London. The steward realised that this attempted bribery would be of no use. After all, why should the king accept the deeds to twelve manors when he could have them all? So, the steward stole the deeds to the manor of Mells, which was said to be the richest plum of the bunch."

"Oh my!" exclaimed Jessica. "So how is it that Horner..........?"

"Ah!" interjected the lieutenant. "Let me tell you what happened then." He took another sip of his wine and looked at the glass meaningfully before he replaced it on the table. One of the mess stewards moved over to it and quietly and discreetly refilled the glass. "The steward was quite right. It did not matter a bit. The Bishop was tried for treason for being a member of the Roman Catholic Church and was hung, drawn and quartered on Glastonbury Tor."

Mrs Edwards gave a little gasp of horror, her hand flying to her mouth. Captain Edwards grinned and comfortingly took her hand and gave it a gentle pat. "There, there, my dear. That's how it was in those days."

Horner laughed. "I forgot to say that Bishop Whiting's steward was also on the jury that convicted him of treason. And that steward, ladies and gentlemen, was my ancestor Sir John (or Jack as he was known) Horner!"

Everyone laughed and clapped their hands at the story. "Is it really true Edward?" asked a delighted Mrs Edwards. "All that skulduggery got you Mells Manor?"

"Well, that's the story, Mrs Edwards," he smiled back. "But really, as far as I know Sir John bought the deeds to the manor legally off Cromwell."

"Well really!" cried Jessica indignantly. "You almost had me believing you!"

Edward laughed. "Well," he said, shrugging his shoulders, "that's what we were told. But if that is not the truth, then what is the nursery rhyme all about?"

Everyone clapped their hands. The colonel shook his head in mirth and chuckled aloud. "If nothing else, Edward, it makes a damnable good story!" Everyone laughed.

Colonel Glynn bided his time, savouring the pleasantness of the evening. He had one more duty to attend to with the lady's present. He nodded to the Mess Corporal who once more took up his position behind the colonel's chair. As before, this was the signal for the band to stop playing. He banged the gavel and rose to his feet, picking up his wine glass as he did so. "Gentlemen," he enthused. "I give you a toast. A toast to the flowers of England gathered around this table. I toast "the ladies of the regiment!" There was a scraping of chairs as the officer's rose to their feet and responded. Once they had done this, and taking the tip from the colonel, they remained standing. The band played the first few bars of "Their will always be an England" and stopped.

"Gentlemen,' he said. 'That concludes our ladies' night." He turned to his wife and said, "Winifred, my dear, would you take the ladies out please. Unfortunately, I have business that I need to urgently attend to with my officers."

Winifred blushed. "Of course, my dearest." She stood up and said, "Come, ladies of the regiment. It is time to leave the men to their awful war."

Mess orderlies moved hurriedly to pull back the chairs so that the ladies could stand unhindered. The colonel's wife held her eyes open in surprise as the colonel and the officers suddenly left the table and headed towards the door. As they reached the door area, mess orderlies handed each officer his sword. Raising their swords tip to tip they formed in a line opposite each other and produced an aisle through which the ladies had to pass. The bandmaster started to play the popular dance tune, "Gary Owen" as the ladies walked towards it.

The Mess Corporal opened the door to the lounge of the officer's mess, and as the ladies passed through the smiling men, the men began to tap the tips of their heavy cavalry sabres together in applause. Some of the ladies' eyes went moist and the odd handkerchief appeared, suddenly dabbing at their eyes as they left the dining room.

The colonel and the officers returned to their seats, replacing their swords in the scabbards before doing so. Whilst the officers had been applauding the ladies the mess staff had swiftly put out decanters of port onto the tables and had quickly cleared them of everything else. The colonel said to the Mess Corporal, "That will be all, corporal. Leave us alone now." The Mess Corporal nodded and withdrew with all of his staff. Looking towards the orchestra he said, "Thank you, bandmaster. You and your quartet may now withdraw, if you please." As the bandmaster and his band withdrew, the sitting officers applauded them.

After the room had been cleared of everyone but the officers, the colonel poured himself a glass of port, indicating to the officers that they should do so as well. "You may smoke, gentlemen," he said. On the table the silver cigarette boxes were opened, but to their surprise they did not contain cigarettes, but small cigars. The colonel laughed. "No telling when we will get the chance again for a good cigar, gentlemen, so I thought that it would be a good idea to take the opportunity to do so now." From the delighted grins of the officers he knew that he had made the right choice. Glynn looked at one of his young officers. "Thank you, Mr Wills," he said. Lieutenant Wills blushed in appreciation.

The colonel waited until everyone had a cigar lighted and their glasses filled with port. He then rose to his feet and held his glass out in front of him. "Gentlemen," he said firmly. "The toast is to the regiment and to the honour and glory it will earn in France."

The officer's responded with "the regiment." Some of them chinked their glasses together before drinking, and following the colonel's lead, emptied them. Sitting down again, the colonel refilled his glass. He waited for a moment for the officers to do so.

He smiled and said, "I can see from some of your faces you noticed what I said about the regiment during the toast, "and to the honour and glory it will earn in France." No, gentlemen, it was not a slip of the tongue." All went suddenly quiet within the mess and the officers' listened in high expectation. The colonel held the moment in his mind before he said, "Brigade notified me this morning that the regiment will undergo no more than ten weeks training in Sussex. Once that has been completed, they are going to send us to France as part of the Third Cavalry Division."

"Oh, I say!" said Captain Edwards, echoing the thoughts of those around him. The officer's cheered and slapped each other's backs, anticipating the chance for real action as last.

Alf Cleall and Charlie Gibbs had been joined by a friend of theirs who was a serjeant in "A" Squadron, George Britton, for a drink in the Weekes Men's Club. The place was full and there were no empty seats anywhere, apart from one at their table that Alf was keeping free. Behind the bar the till rang a small bell each time as money was rung in. Alf noticed in professional irritation that one of the large kegs of beer had already run out, and there was no replacement for it. The carter who usually brought over his ale from Oakhill Brewery had lost his horses to the army and had nothing to replace them. They had been commandeered to pull artillery pieces and at that very moment they were all on their way to France. Already the war was beginning to be felt by those at home.

It was no accident that Alf and his 2 friends were there. He had organised it. Harry George was acting as the Mess Corporal that night and the young twenty-one-year-old lance corporal was a member of his squadron. He also worked at the Billiard Hall that his brother Wilf normally ran on their behalf.

Alf knew that sometimes the best intelligence came from the officers' mess functions. Relaxing in their mess and after a few drinks the wily landlord had long since learned that sometimes the information picked up at these types of social gatherings was worth its weight in gold. That was one of the reasons he always volunteered some of the brighter men of his squadrons to be waiters or cooks at these events. As far as he was aware of, no officer knew of his method of gathering this type of intelligence. Captain Lubbock had looked at him curiously once when he had delivered to "A" Squadron some important news. Alf had shown no surprise in the news imparted, but from that little incident he had learned to act in a startled manner when future news came to him by way of the official line.

Harry burst through the front door, puffing a little as he had been running. Alf glanced up from his beer and saw him, for they did not sell cider in the Men's Club. He waved and said, "Over here, Harry." Charlie Gibbs got to his feet and went over to the bar to get Harry a pint.

Alf pushed back the empty chair he had been saving for the Mess Corporal and he gratefully sat down in it. Charlie returned with the pint of beer and plonked it down on the wooden table. "Have a drink, Harry."

"Cheers!" he said and gulped down a refreshing draught of warm beer.

Alf waited for Harry to catch his breath and he said, "Well?"

Harry looked around him and leaned forward, beckoning his companions towards him. He said in a low voice, "The colonel was told this morning that the regiment is going into action. We are to be part of the Third Cavalry Division in France!"

"Bloody hell!" exclaimed George.

"Bloody hell!" repeated Charlie.

"Beggar me, we be for it now, for sure my lads," responded Alf.

Harry George took another swig of his beer. "That's not all," he said. The ears of the three friends pricked up as Harry gave them his final bit of information. "Our training before we are sent to France will take no longer than ten weeks."

Alf frowned as he made the calculation in his head. "That means we'll probably be over there during the first week of November. Christ! That aren't much time to whip the regiment into shape!"

Charlie Gibbs picked up his beer glass and raised it high. "To us, me likely lads. It's up to us beggars here to make sure that the regiment is ready!"

The four men chinked their mugs together. "To us!" they responded.

Sunday, 16th August 1914.

The day was one of rest for the Yeomanry. They were still finishing off preparing the move on the morrow, but in truth they were ready to go now. The men attended Church Parade where the regiment's chaplain led them in prayers. At the colonel's behest it was a short event, lasting no more than 20 minutes before the solemn men were dismissed to return to their billets.

The last Yeomanry to be completely ready were the officers' mess servants. They had to clear up and pack up the mess silver and other accoutrements after the social gathering that had taken place the night before. The adjutant, who was also President of the Mess Committee, was most pleased when Lance Corporal George reported to him that all was safely stored and packed away by 2 p.m. that afternoon.

Although the men's club was just that, and women were not normally allowed to enter it socially. The Club Committee, as a gesture of good will, had decided that they would allow the wives and girlfriends of those soldiers billeted there to enter the club premises from 8 p.m. to 9 p.m. Those soldiers would have at least the benefit of seeing their wives for a little while before the adventure that lay before them unfolded.

Winifred Cleall had taken time off from her public house duties to spend her last hour with Alf before he went away. The couple just sat at the table, making small talk and holding hands. Winnie was a bit tearful but Alf made her put a brave face on it. Gesturing around him he said, "We aren't the only ones who are going to be parted for a while, my dear. We all are."

"I know Alf, but it is hard." Tears welled up in her eyes but did not flow.

At last 9 p.m. came and the soldiers dutifully escorted their ladies to the doors and many a fond and sad farewell was made. They were the lucky ones in the regiment. Many of the other troopers had no chance to see their loved ones before they departed the City of Bath.

Most of the married officers had their wives staying locally and had the pleasure of having their evening meal, with the permission of the colonel, at home with their family. Not so for the men. They had to remain in their billets.

Monday, 17th August 1914.

At 6.30 a.m. that morning the regiment were all on parade and ready to make the move from Bath to Winchester, a good distance away. This would be the first time that the regiment would passage as a complete unit in squadron order, for although they had carried out training camps prior to the war, they had, in truth, only been at half strength.

"What do you think, adjutant?" asked the colonel.

Bates responded immediately. "We've about 60 miles to cover to the camp in Winchester, sir," he opined. "In a fully trained cavalry unit I could expect to average at least 7 miles per hour, making it about an eight and a half hours ride."

The colonel nodded. "But?"

"I don't think that the horses, or come to that, some of the newer men, are quite up to it yet."

Again, the colonel nodded. "That's my opinion also. I think that we'll spread the journey out over 2 days. We will use the whole repositioning of the regiment as an exercise to give the horses, a lot of them new to the regiment and previously civilian animals, an actual hard work out in carrying their troopers."

"I think that it would be much better, sir. We'll have some trouble on the way with some of the farm horses that are just not used to going long distances yet. Besides, Brigade has allowed us 2 days in their planning to get to Winchester. We just as well make use of the experience."

Captain Brooking and the squadron officers approached them on their horses. They reined in and saluted the colonel, Captain Brooking saying, "Good morning, colonel. It's a fine day for a ride."

The colonel looked about him. It was already beginning to be a warm day and only a few fluffy white clouds were scattered against the blue of the sky. Somewhere a blackbird shrilled a sharp warning. It would be hot later. Off to his right the regimental band of the 4th Battalion Somerset Light Infantry (Territorials) were practising quietly on their instruments, ready to form up and lead the North Somerset Yeomanry through Bath on the first part of their journey. "Right ho, Brooking. This is what we are going to do," said the colonel decisively. "The band of the Somersets will lead us off and we will proceed at a walking pace through the city. I have had some discussion with the adjutant already and I can confirm to you that what we talked about yesterday will happen today."

"Very good sir," replied Captain Brooking.

The adjutant confirmed the colonel's orders. "Once the band has left us after we have reached the other side of Bath, we are to adopt a running walk pace."

"Ah! The good old fox-trot!" beamed Brooking.

The adjutant nodded. "We keep going until we reach our first objective and then we shall call a halt for an hour. During this time the men will have to closely inspect their horses and equipment to ensure that they are not in need of anything. Saddle girths are to be loosened and stirrups up when the horses are watered. The serjeant farrier's wagon left an hour and a half ago and should be nearing our first stopping point soon."

"How far are you hoping to make, sir?" asked the Lieutenant Liebert.

"At a running walk I would expect to make between 6 and 8 miles an hour, with a fully trained regiment. We shall not stop until we get to Bradford-on-Avon. That is where the first watering spot and the farrier will be located."

The band struck up a jaunty tune and marched out of the encampment and on to the main Bath road. The colonel rode proudly at the head of his Yeomanry with his regimental staff, followed by "A", "B" and "C" squadrons. Despite it being so early in the morning, many a citizen of Bath had turned out to watch the men depart. Weeping wives and girlfriends were much in evidence, waving farewell to their men-folk. They had no idea when they would meet, if ever, again.

The only irritation to the colonel was that 2 of his men from "A" Squadron, Troopers Simmons and Haskell, had absented themselves and would not be riding with the regiment. The colonel made a vow to himself that when they were apprehended, and they would be, he would make sure that it went hard for them. Already the police had been informed of their non-appearance and they were sending some constables around to arrest them, if they were at home.

As the regiment passed the Roman Baths the local gentry and the Mayor were gathered together, the more important of them standing on a little raised dais surrounded by flowers. As the colonel passed by, he saluted. The gentlemen doffed their hats and bowed in respect. The noise around them was deafening as the local population cheered and shouted encouragement, roaring in approval. Occasionally, one of the not so well-trained horses would rebel against the sound and its rider was hard pressed to keep the animal under control.

After twenty minutes or so the regiment had passed out of the city of Bath proper and on to its very outskirts. The band moved aside and kept playing as the regiment rode by. The colonel nodded to his adjutant. Turning about in his saddle Captain Bates called out his orders: "The regiment will advance in a running-walk. Advance!"

The colonel broke into the traditional fast walking pace for a horse known as the fox-trot gait and took his horse, Elizabeth, up to about an even 7 miles per hour. Down along the line of the regiment he could hear the order being repeated and gradually the whole organisation picked up speed.

The colonel smiled in satisfaction as he noted that the Brigade had sent out its military policemen on motor-cycles, as he had asked for, and they were keeping the way clear for them. It would be hard to stop such a moving mass of men and horses such as this.

Just ahead of him a noisy traction engine heading towards the regiment had been halted by the military police and told to wait whilst the regiment passed by. It hissed and blew clouds of steam and smoke out of its tall chimney. The colonel grinned ruefully to himself. This would be the first test of real horsemanship for many of his men. He expected some sort of incident involving one of the steeds as even Elizabeth shied a little as she pranced past the noisy and smoky machine. He glanced back anxiously over his shoulder but to his pleasant surprise the mounts of the regiment seemed to be taking the event in their stride. The adjutant gave the colonel a wave, acknowledging the fact that he, too, had been a little worried about the possible consequences.

It took just over an hour to reach the small but pretty village of Bradord-on-Avon. The farrier was already there with his mobile furnace blazing fiercely as the regiment arrived. Soon the anvils began to ring with the sound of horseshoes being fitted to those that had worked their way loose or had simply fallen off on the way.

Lieutenant Davey approached his commanding officer with some trepidation. "I'm afraid one of the horses of my troop has just collapsed and died, sir," he apologised.

The colonel raised his eyebrows. "Damn it!" he exploded. "A Board of Inquiry already and we have only been going for just over an hour." Whenever a cavalry unit lost an animal it was mandatory that a Board of Inquiry be convened as soon as possible. They were valuable items of equipment. "Any ideas at this stage, John?" he asked quietly.

The young officer nodded. "Yes sir. It's one of the fourteen hand high ponies that we were forced to take. The vet had serious doubts about this one before we started. It seemed to get winded quite easily during training. He said that the animal's heart just gave out."

Captain Bates added briskly, "We told brigade that we should have had no animals under 15 hands high. They said that it was a risk they were prepared to take, due to the shortage of war horses."

The colonel made his decision. "Sell the dead horse to the local butcher, Stanley. The money can go into the regimental funds."

The adjutant saluted. "Yes sir." He walked away to quickly carry out his task.

A riderless horse suddenly bolted past, its saddle hanging carelessly around its left side as opposed to sitting squarely on its back. Wide eyed and nostril's flaring, the frightened animal galloped down towards the river with several men hotly chasing in pursuit. The colonel looked on in interest as the frightened steed flashed by him and noticed that the Saddler Serjeant Baynton had already jumped on the back of a horse he had just finished fixing a loose fitment on. Like a flash, he was after the animal.

The horse, finding its way blocked by troopers who had quickly spotted the incident and barred its way, ran into the River Avon and suddenly it was up to its neck in water and was forced to swim. The river at this part was quite deep. It neighed as it tried to turn around, but the saddle seemed to be acting like a rudder and sent it upstream instead of back to the bank. The Saddler Serjeant, and old and experienced hand, rode up the bank a little way and fearlessly plunged his animal into the water, ahead of the panicking horse.

The colonel looked on approvingly as the man angled his horse towards the other animal and without stopping leant over and grabbed it's trailing reins. Nudging his swimming steed in the ribs the serjeant guided it back towards the riverbank and within a minute or so was splashing through the shallows and up the bank.

He passed the colonel who said approvingly, "Well done, Serjeant Baynton; very well done indeed."

Captain English suddenly appeared with 2 soldiers. One of them looked crestfallen as he took the reins of his animal from the serjeant. The other soldier pushed the saddle upright and tightened the girth.

Colonel Glynn pointed at the animal. "What happened?" he asked.

Captain English blushed as he furiously stabbed a finger towards one of the soldiers. "Trooper Fitch did not secure his mount properly with his peg and heel rope, sir, and somehow the horse broke loose and bolted."

Fitch protested, "But I did, captain! Honestly I did."

"Silence!" ordered his captain. The trooper gave a sullen look and glanced downwards.

The colonel surveyed the man for a moment. "I will not have such tardiness in the regiment, Captain. Charge the man, please, and remand him for my Orderly Room."

Trooper Fitch looked on in dismay, for he knew that he was in trouble.

Captain English pointed at Fitch. "You heard the colonel, Fitch. Get that saddle off your horse and take him back to our lines. Give him a good rub down."

Trooper Fitch said, "Yes sir," a note of resignation evident in his voice.

"And damn well make sure you picket him properly this time!"

Quickly Fitch removed the saddle whilst the other trooper led the still shaking and blowing horse away, Fitch dejectedly hurrying alongside him.

The other trooper whispered quietly, "Twern't your fault, Albie. I saw you tether the bugger up proper, like. She must have worked herself loose or something."

Fitch screwed his eyes up in dismay. "I know that I picketed my 'orse up proper, Ernie. I just can't work out how she managed to get herself free."

The other man, Trooper Summers, smirked behind the neck of the blowing horse he was leading. "There, you bugger!" he thought. "That be the first part of the payback for having my missus behind my back!" It was he who had secretly released the animal from the heel rope, and suddenly striking the animal on the nose he had started it out on its frightened run. Ernie poked his head out from around the horse's neck and said in a confidential tone, "Don't you worry about it too much, Albie. I'll tell the captain I saw you tether it up properly."

Albert gave a wry smile. "Thanks, mate," he said.

"Not at all, Albie. After all, that's what friends are for, isn't it?"

Albert smiled. He was lucky to have such a good friend. He had failed to notice the note of irony in Ernest's voice and the self-satisfied smug look that was upon his face.

During the time of the one hour's rest the colonel had carefully studied the map with his adjutant. The decision was now to take the regiment the twenty miles or so to the village of Amesbury. There they would make camp for the night. The regiment would ride for another 2 hours before stopping again. The adjutant rode off with one of his headquarters corporals to gallop on ahead to Amesbury to secure billets for the officers and to find a location to bivouac the regiment.

The colonel had called a quick orders group and had given a brief outline of the regiment's continued move. These quick orders groups were a regular feature of the North Somerset Yeomanry as with any fast-moving cavalry regiment things could change at a moment's notice and all the key officers would need to be kept informed. At the same time, he received a report from the squadron commanders of how their men were faring. Except for the death of the "A" Squadron horse, only six horses needed re-shoeing, although 2 of them had since gone lame. All in all, the colonel was quite pleased with the way the move was going, and he told his officers so.

He had decided that after the next 2 hour stopping point had been reached, the rest of the way to Amesbury would be used as a tactical exercise. To that end, "B" Squadron was tasked with sending out reconnaissance patrols from there onwards until they reached their objectives. Lieutenant John Davey, the officer commanding "B" Squadron, rapidly made notes in his brown army issue notebook. He already had it in his mind that the patrol would be led by Serjeant Reginald Watts. He was a good senior non-commissioned officer and he knew that he could be trusted with this mission.

Normal good army practice was to give junior officers the opportunity to undertake the role of officers higher up in the chain of command. This was so that if a senior officer became a casualty then a junior officer could quickly step in to fill that role. The officer commanding "C" Squadron, Lieutenant Liebert, was temporally appointed as adjutant for the remainder of the move to Amesbury. Colonel Glynn mounted his horse and stretched himself in the saddle. "Get 'em moving, adjutant, if you please."

Lieutenant Liebert felt himself to be quite important at last as he easily assumed the mantle of the adjutant. With a brief flurry of orders, the regiment quickly mounted and were on their way once again. Within ten minutes they had already overtaken the farrier's wagon that had trundled on ahead of them. There was some good-natured cat-calling between the passing troopers and the farrier's men as each troop rode by, but each cavalry man knew the total dependence that they had on him and his team. The farrier was smoking a huge cob pipe as the men passed him by and good naturedly acknowledged them as they fox-trotted past.

3½ hours later, and having crossed part of Salisbury Plain, the North Somerset Yeomanry entered the small Wiltshire town of Amesbury, some 30 miles or so distant from Bradford on Avon. The adjutant rode out to meet them with his small group of men. With the colonel's approval, he led the regiment to a salient of land that was bounded on each side by the River Avon and slightly to the left of the village. The colonel nodded in approval, for the duty squadron would only have to physically guard the landward side of the salient. The river would act as a natural boundary to contain his Yeomanry and would only need to be patrolled at irregular intervals.

"Give the guard duty to "B" Squadron will you adjutant," said the colonel in a conversational tone. He then added in a tired voice, "I hope that you have found us a nice billet?"

The adjutant smiled. "I couldn't have found a better one for you, sir," he responded. "The regimental officers and yourself are to be the welcome guests of Colonel Sir Edmund and Lady Florence Antrobus for the night in Amesbury Abbey. A lovely couple sir, and they insist that all the regimental officers stay overnight with them. Their son, Edmund, is a Lieutenant of the Grenadiers. He happens to be home on leave from France at this very moment."

"Good. Well done, Stanley," he acknowledged.

The adjutant called back over his shoulder, "Corporal Cleall!"

Alf Cleall, who had gone ahead with the adjutant in advance of the main body, nudged his horse across to the adjutant. He saluted the colonel. "Yes sir?"

"Escort the colonel to the abbey will you."

"Yes sir." He looked at his commanding officer and said, "If you would care to follow me, sir. It's a scarce 10-minute ride to the abbey." He pointed across the river. "You can see the place from here, sir." The colonel looked across the river and saw the house and nodded his acceptance.

After a few minutes riding and after crossing the river by the road bridge, the imposing abbey building came into view. The colonel was expecting it to be looking something like a church, so he was taken completely by surprise at the sight of a large country house. He was greeted with the vision of six imposing white Romanesque type columns at the very front of the house and surrounded by very beautiful parklands. The 2 men trotted to the front of the mansion and dismounted. A groom came dashing out from around the side of the house and took the reins of Elizabeth from the colonel.

Dismounting, the colonel gave himself a good stretch. It was a long time since he had ridden such a distance. As if by magic a liveried butler appeared at the top of the steps that led up to the front door. As he walked up the steps towards him the colonel heavily slapped his riding crop against his trousers, knocking out some of the dust from the day's ride.

The manservant bowed his head and said in a deep sonorous voice, "Welcome to Amesbury Abbey sir. I have your room waiting you and your valise is already here. I have taken the liberty of running you a warm bath. Once you have refreshed yourself sir, Colonel Sir Edward and Lady Florence have requested your company for sherry."

The colonel beamed. "Lead on man," he said. "A hot bath is something I am really looking forward to."

Alf Cleall, completely forgotten, wheeled his horse around to trot back to the bivouac area. No feather down bed for him tonight, just the hard ground and his blanket to wrap himself up with, covered by his tarpaulin sheet. He looked up at the sky. At least it was going to be a dry night, he thought. He smiled as he thought of the pleasure of taking a bath in the River Avon. No doubt most of the regiment would too.

Tuesday, 18th August 1914.

Reveille was sounded at 6.30 a.m. and the regiment, having taken breakfast, proceeded to ride the remaining 25 miles to their encampment in Winchester. The journey would take about 4½ hours, including a good rest for the horses.

The colonel had sent word to the Adjutant that the regiment was to be ready to move off at 9 a.m. and when he arrived the Squadrons were already formed and waiting to go. He quickly held another "O" Group with his company commanders, but little did they know that they were in for quite a surprise.

At dinner the previous evening he had a private meal with his hosts and their son, Lieutenant Edward Antrobus, and a particularly pleasant evening it was too. The colonel, over a port, had outline his proposed route to Lieutenant Antrobus and picked his brain for any local knowledge of hazards that might spring up over the next 25 miles or so.

Lieutenant Antrobus thought for a moment and concluded, "You might have a problem at Stockbridge, where you will have to cross the River Test by a 3 arched stone road bridge. It is quite narrow there and I would advise you to request the Military Police to be in attendance so that the transition will take place without any problems. It is also a frequently used drove way, and believe it or not, you often encounter large flocks of sheep being driven along it, coming over from Wales and going to London."

"Excellent advice, Edward. I will take that."

"If you wish colonel, I can ring ahead tomorrow morning. We have a company of Grenadier reinforcements training down there at the moment and we also have a Military Police detachment in situation. Would you care for me to make the arrangements for you?"

"Oh rather!" he enthused. "I'll brief my officers accordingly tomorrow morning."

"One other thing, colonel," he said, a wicked twinkle in his eyes. "Would you like me to spring a surprise on your leading troops?"

"What sort of surprise?

Edward pointed at the map and said, "Once you have safely negotiated the river obstacle, I notice that you have to pass below Stockbridge Down." He pointed the place out on the map. "It is quite high," he continued, "and it has a good commanding view of the countryside around."

"I see that," replied the colonel.

"Well, we already have established an observation post on the hill, just as the enemy would do if you were in France. My men will see you coming a long time before you see them."

"And?"

"We have a plentiful supply of blank ammunition. Would you like my men to spring an ambush on your so you can see how they react?

The colonel gave a boyish grin. "Capital! What fun! Yes, yes, Edward, I would love you to do that!"

Lieutenant Antrobus smiled. "It will do my men good too! There is nothing like an unexpected event occurring to make the men's adrenalin level rise beyond expectation! I will warn them to be on the lookout for enemy cavalry, that should sharpen them up!"

The colonel laughed.

They reached Stockbridge without incident. The leading squadron, "C" Squadron, were stopped by the Military Police just before they got to the bridge and sure enough, by happenstance, a huge flock of sheep were being shepherded across the bridge. The colonel smiled ruefully to himself. Thanks to the advice of Lieutenant Antrobus, the mayhem that would have ensued had they met the sheep at the bridge was avoided. The colonel halted his regiment and called for an "O" group of his officers.

"Adjutant," he said. "On completion of this "O" group please go with your servant ahead of us to Winchester and to our encampment. Please ensure that we have guides ready to meet us at Sparsholt and lead us in to the bivouac area."

"Very good sir."

"Gentlemen," continued the colonel. "Once we have cleared Stockbridge, I want you to ride tactically to Sparsholt, following the line of the road that leads down to it. There we will revert to normality and be taken to our campsite by the guides. "B" Squadron will lead, followed by my tactical headquarters, then "A" Squadron followed by "C". Is that clear?"

The officers responded with a "Yes Sir," for the 4 or so miles ride to the village looked easy enough.

"One more thing gentlemen," he added, an impish grin appearing on his face. "As I have said, we are moving forward tactically to the village, so expect anything to happen. If anything does happen, I would expect you to react to it!"

A military policeman approached. The serjeant waited a moment before reporting to the colonel that it was now safe to move on. They would lead the way through Stockbridge on their motor-cycles, for already an excited crowd were gathering along the High Street and starting to line each side in expectation. The riding through the town of a whole regiment of Yeomanry was an unexpected event and they were determined not to let the opportunity slip by them without the men getting a rousing reception.

The regiment passed through the place and the welcome they received almost outdid the farewell they had at Bath. Excited children ran alongside the trotting horses, and one game lad kept up with the colonel and his headquarters until they reached the outskirts of the place. The colonel grinned and flicked him a silver sixpence, and the excited boy caught it before it hit the ground. "Well done youngster!" encouraged the delighted colonel.

They reached the outskirts of Stockbridge and with a cheery wave the military policemen accelerated their motor cycles and left the regiment behind. The Yeomanry now shook out into their well-practiced tactical routine. Out went the scouts and the colonel watched in anticipation.

The ground was quite undulating, but mostly they were riding uphill. It was a lovely summer's day and the sun shone quite brightly from their right-hand side as they moved forward in a generally easterly direction. Very soon Stockbridge Down appeared on their left, the higher ground commanding the view. The colonel waited expectantly, for although he knew what was going to happen, he did not know how or when. He did not have long to wait.

The chattering of a Maxim machine gun suddenly erupted from the hill. Glancing up, the colonel saw some raised earthworks on which the weapon and about 20 rifles had suddenly appeared, pouring fire down upon them. The colonel thanked God that they were using blanks, for had they been real bullets the regiment would surely have taken casualties.

Lieutenant Liebert responded magnificently. "Squadron – draw rifles!" he screamed at the top of his voice and wheeled them around to charge the unexpected ambush. His squadron automatically broke into 2 parts, he led on the left and the Squadron Serjeant Major on the right.

The colonel broke through on Elizabeth and at the gallop. "For exercise, for exercise, for exercise," he yelled.

The Squadron commander understood perfectly well. He pointed his sword towards the enemy and shouted "Charge!" 120 horses thundered forward with the Bugler blowing for all his worth. The colonel got caught up in the excitement of it all and, drawing his sword, joined in with the charge.

The colonel had developed a tactic of a pincer like movement for each squadron. The first attacking squadron would break to either side of the enemy troops, and, much to his delight and without any orders having been issued to him, the squadron commander of "A" Company automatically led the charge towards the very heart of the enemy position. The colonel hoped that, with the advent of the dreaded machine gun, this new tactic of his would reduce the amount of firepower directed at the main assault force.

As the horses galloped up the hill a figure appeared on top of the earthwork, waving a white flag. Lieutenant Liebert saw the action and shouted at the top of his voice, "Squadron! Break! Break! Break!". The gallop was immediately brought down to a trot and they passed each side of the machine gun position.

The colonel arrived to speak to the officer concerned. "Ah! Edward! I did not expect you to give up some of your leave to take part in the action."

The young officer grinned. "You couldn't expect me to miss out on the fun, colonel?"

Glynn laughed. "No, my boy, of course not!" How did it look?"

Edward grinned. "Scared the hell out of me, sir, and I knew they were coming."

Colonel Glynn smiled. "Good, good," he enthused.

Lieutenant Liebert arrived and halted his horse by his colonel's side. "Ah Frederick," he said, "I don't know if you already known Lieutenant Antrobus, with whom I had the pleasure of dining and plotting with last night."

Lieutenant Liebert saluted with his sword and Antrobus returned the compliment. "Pleasure to meet you," he said.

Liebert grinned back at him, "And the same, old boy," he replied.

The colonel spoke. "Well done, Frederick, now get the squadrons back in order for me on the road would you please." The lieutenant saluted and rode away.

Within the hour they arrived at the village of Sparsholt, just on the outskirts of Winchester. 4 guides were waiting for them, one for each squadron and one for the Headquarters elements. They were led to their allotted positions in the Bell tented barracks that was to be their home for the next few days and settled themselves in to an increased tempo of a training regime.

Wednesday, 19th August 1914 to Thursday, 27th August 1914.

A large house had been taken over for the regiment on the Wednesday and was serving as its headquarters. It even had 2 telephones connected for ease of communication. Despatch riders regularly arrived with orders from the brigade as to precisely what training the men had to carry out. So far most of it had been drill and riding, practising charges and the like. The war was reaching something of an impasse although it was rumoured that the Germans were massing their forces near the town of Mons, in Belgium, and that some heavy fighting was to be expected.

Midway through the morning the adjutant rapped urgently upon the colonel's door. "Come in," he bid.

The adjutant entered. "Sir, I am terribly sorry to say that I have discovered something rather disturbing."

The colonel arched an eyebrow and said, "Really?"

The adjutant nodded. He put his hand into his pocket and placed some revolver bullets in front of the colonel. Colonel Glynn picked one up and examined it. "Dum-dums!" he said disapprovingly. The adjutant nodded.

"Where did you get them?"

"I took them off one of the younger officer's sir," replied the adjutant.

"I hope you gave him a flea in his ear, Stanley. These bullets are totally illegal."

Captain Bates said, "I think it is mostly the younger officers who have made some dum-dums sir," explained the adjutant. "With your permission I would like to put it on Regimental Orders that on no account are bullets to be converted into them. Do I have your authority to do so?"

Glynn nodded. "Of course you do." He thought for a moment and lit one of his cheroots. "I think, Stanley, that on the face of it you should get all of the young officers together and muster their ammunition."

"Yes sir."

"If you are to find any more, you are to confiscate them immediately."

"I understand, sir."

"Good. Let the quartermaster know how many rounds you have confiscated. Make sure he issues replacement rounds to the officers concerned, but he is to charge them the cost of each bullet. Not only that, each officer in possession of an illegal bullet is to pay £2 each into their squadron welfare fund. Will that do?"

Bates nodded. "Yes sir. I don't think that we'll have any troubles with dum-dums once that has been done."

"Excellent! See to it then, Stanley."

"Yes sir."

On the Saturday of the 22nd August the regiment were given orders to leave Winchester with each man carrying 100 rounds of Mk VI training ammunition. For operational purposes the ammunition used by the British Army was the Mk VII and this had the tendency to expand inside a target, although according to the Hague Convention on dum-dum bullets, it was still legal.

The Yeomanry first rode to Petersfield, in Hampshire, some twenty miles distant from their original location. They stayed there overnight before riding on another ten miles for the short move to Midhurst where they encamped once more. These short moves gave the troops plenty of practice in rigging and derigging camps and very soon they became most proficient at it. Another short ride took them to Billinghurst in Sussex where again they made a hasty camp.

There were a few grumbles from the men as they made their way inexorably eastwards, for none of them knew their true destination. Rumours were rife, and one was quickly circulated amongst the men. On the 23rd August the expected battle at Mons had occurred, but the British had fared badly and were now in full retreat. The feeling was that the regiment was moving towards the coast to go to France to help stem the seemingly unstoppable advances that the German's were making. Excitement and expectation amongst them was running at almost a fever pitch.

The next day the regiment rode to Crawley, which was about 16 miles north, north east of Billinghurst. Here they went into prepared tents. The unit managed to get in a full days training during the 2 days they were at Crawley, for the weather was kind to them.

A whole day was spent on the local rifle range and the men were thoroughly tested on numbered targets up to a range of 400 yards. The targets were stationary and the men fired from prepared positions in order to test their shooting skills.

The large bullseyes were on metal rails that lay beneath a large earth embankment and this would protect the men behind it. When the men were ready a signaller, by the use of flags, would communicate with another. This man was well away to the side of the targets and about 200 yards away from the butts. He in turn would relay the signal to the man in the butts, and each time he did the targets would be hauled up and appear above the embankment.

When the firing ceased, the men would lower the targets and search for the bullet holes. Here they would be counted, and the number on each target counted by an officer and recorded. Once that had been done, the bullet holes were covered in paper and glued over, making the target a fresh one so that the whole process could take place again.

When the men were at the 300 yards point from the targets, they would have to undertake what was known as "The Mad Minute". On the order been given of "Rapid Fire", he had to fire 15 rounds at the target to his front. This practice gave the British rifleman and his weapon the ability to fire accurately at their targets. Most soldiers on the receiving end of it thought they were been fired on by machine guns.

At the end of the allotted time, the officers in the butts would give their recorded figures to Captain English. He would then go back to the firing point and tell each soldier, who had been allotted a numbered target, how many shots he had hit the target with. If they scored over 84 hits out of the 100 rounds, they would be awarded the coveted title of "Marksman" and his pay increased by 2d a day, for he was a valuable asset. One man actually had a perfect score of 100 hits.

"Bloody hell, Fitchy," said his chum, Trooper Summers. "I didn't know you could shoot like that!"

Fitch grinned. "Neither did I, Ernie. Still, the extra money will be nice."

Summers grinned and gave his mate a friendly dig in the ribs. "Help you to pay for your fines and kit!" Both men laughed.

Again, the rumour factory went into overdrive. It appeared as if though on the 26th August the British Army had fought a holding action at the battle of Le Cateau. British casualties had been extremely heavy, and for the first-time artillery firing air bursts had amply demonstrated how dangerous this way of using ammunition was in time of war.

At Crawley, and much to the disgust of the officers, the regiment trained in a dismounted role. To their distaste the cavalry men were used liked common infantry and were instructed in how to dig and construct trenches. They were also shown how to make a bunker to protect them from the artillery airbursts that the Germans were now beginning so effectively to use and that the British guns were beginning to copy. The enemy artillery pieces had a distinct advantage over that of the British and Dominions troops, for they were using a new type of recoilless artillery piece. This meant that the barrel recoiled on the gun wheels or mounting so that the weapon did not have to be re-set every time it fired. The British weapons had not yet advanced this far, for the only means of stopping an artillery piece from being thrown backwards by the force of the shot was by the use of blocks or the digging in of the wheels to stop it rolling backwards. Neither of these methods was particularly successful.

Alf Cleall was giving the task of constructing a single dug out that would be deep enough to take a dozen or so men. He did not understand why he was chosen to do so, but as usual he set about the task with a willingness and cheerfulness that was hard to emulate.

6 troopers were allocated to Alf Cleall's working party and they set about the job they had been given. A serjeant of engineers was with them and he showed them how to correctly install the corrugated iron revetments and how to place sandbags on top of the roof of the bunker.

"How effective will this be?" enquired Alf.

The serjeant gave a wolfish grin and gave Alf a huge wink. "I expect you will find out soon enough," he said, a hint of mischievousness in his voice.

When they had finished, the engineer took Alf with him to a spot about 50 yards away from the bunker. He pointed towards the completed structure. "That's the secret of them," he said, satisfied with his work.

"What secret?" enquired Alf.

The serjeant smiled. "You have to keep the top of the bunker level with the ground around it, otherwise the Germans will know that is where you boys will be sheltering when the shrapnel starts flying."

"I still don't see what the secret is," replied Alf, scratching his head.

"Ah, if the Germans know you are hiding in the dugout while the shrapnel is flying, they'll suddenly switch shells to high explosive."

"So?"

"The dugout will protect you from shrapnel, but not from a direct hit from a high explosive shell."

Alf nodded. "Ah! Now I understand."

As both men looked on, straw dummies were stood up in rows around and about the newly completed dugout. Alf Cleall looked curiously at the engineer serjeant who gave him back an enigmatic smile.

The adjutant beckoned Alf towards him. "How confident are you of your handiwork, Corporal Cleall."

"Why, totally sir," he replied, somewhat confused by the question.

The adjutant nodded. "Good," he said.

The colonel walked across to the adjutant with all the regiment's officers dutifully walking behind him. Alf immediately sprang to attention. "Relax, Corporal Cleall," he said. "Pay attention to what is happening as you are going to play a major part of it." Alf frowned.

The adjutant stepped forward, an impish smile playing across his face. He held his forage cap out. "Gentlemen," he explained. "We are now going to have a little raffle."

"Oh, I say," cried Captain Lubbock. "What can we win then, adjutant?"

The colonel responded with a little laugh. "There really is some sort of prize, gentlemen, I can assure you," he said. "Explain it please, Stanley."

Captain Bates grinned. "In my hat, gentlemen, there are pieces of paper. There is one for each of you. If you draw a piece of paper with a cross on it, go over there and stand next to Corporal Cleall."

The colonel grinned and walked over and stood next to Alf Cleall. Curiously, the officers picked bits of paper from the adjutant's upended cap.

"Ah!" cried Lubbock in excitement. "Looks like I've won whatever it is!"

The Officer Commanding "B" Squadron, Lieutenant Davey, groaned as his paper produced a blank. "You are always lucky, captain," he complained.

When the draw was over the colonel addressed the group of officers and Alf Cleall. "Now gentleman, time for me to tell you what it is all about." The colonel pointed towards a hill in the distance, some 600 yards from where the officers were standing. A white flag flew at its crest. "Shortly the adjutant will take the unit up to the flag. There they will watch a demonstration to be put on by our artillery. The artillery will be laying down a bombardment of airburst shells above the structure that our experienced and able Corporal Cleall has just constructed. I am assured by the engineer serjeant that Cleall has made a perfectly good job of it and there is no fear of any shrapnel penetrating the dug-out. However, the effects on the dummies will be there for everyone to see." The colonel quietly said to Bates, "When the shelling has ceased, Stanley, bring the regiment down so they can see for themselves the effect of an air burst."

"Very good, sir!"

The colonel addressed the officers and Cleall. "We, gentlemen, shall we experience the engineer serjeant's and Corporal Cleall's handiwork at first hand." The colonel waited for a moment to let his words sink in. Several officers glanced nervously towards each other. The colonel grinned and made a dramatic statement. "Those of you lucky enough to have drawn a piece of paper with a cross on it will be with me in the bunker when the shells start exploding.

"Bloody hell!" exclaimed Lieutenant Gibbs, one of the officers who had drawn such a piece of a paper with a cross on and was to go into the dugout.

"I hope not," replied the colonel, smiling. "I really would like to come out of there in one piece." The colonel glanced at his watch. "It is now 2.50 p.m., gentlemen. At 3 p.m. precisely the artillery will send thirty rounds of airburst shells above our dugout over a 2 minute period. A minute after the last shell explodes we shall come out." The colonel turned to his adjutant. "After that minute is up, adjutant, bring the regiment down on to the position will you please."

"Yes sir!"

"Well gentlemen. Is everything completely understood?" The surrounding officers nodded their heads. Several looked apprehensive whilst the younger officer's faces became flushed with excitement. It did not bother Alf Cleall, for he had been under fire before. "Very well then gentlemen. Time to get under cover I think." The colonel led the way towards the bunker and a grinning engineer serjeant followed on behind them. It was his job to make sure that all the officers remained safe.

At precisely 3 p.m. the shelter shook violently from the impact of the airbursts. For the inexperienced officers in the bunker, the noise from above was astonishingly loud.

They could quite clearly hear the crack of the shells as they exploded above their heads. To them it sounded like a continual roar of thunder. Pressure waves from the shells sometimes penetrated the bunker. The engineer serjeant had already advised the officers to plug their ears with their fingers.

The men in the dugout were silent. For most them this was the very first time they had been on the receiving end of an artillery barrage, albeit a short one. Lieutenant Longrigg uttered what he thought was a silent prayer and was somewhat astonished when someone added an "Amen" at the end of it.

The colonel was quietly studying his pocket watch, taking no notice of the sound of the exploding shells. There was an unusually heavy explosion above them and the little oil lamp swung alarmingly on the overhead beam which seemingly protested in agony and made the noise of a large crack. Dirt flowed down from the roof, just missing Corporal Cleall's face. A note of alarm sounded around the dugout.

"Steady men," assured the colonel in his calm voice.

The engineer serjeant grinned. "Bit close, that bugger!" he grinned. He took out his penknife and began to pare one of his fingernails.

Just as suddenly as it had begun, the barrage ended. A physical sigh of relief could be heard in the semi darkness. After what seemed to be an indeterminate time the colonel said, "Right gentlemen. That's it. Follow me out."

The colonel led the way with Corporal Cleall following closely on behind him. A scene of utter devastation met their eyes. Of the straw dummies that had been scattered around, very little was left. Pieces of smoking shrapnel littered the pockmarked ground around the dugout. Alf walked on to the top of his handiwork and noted a large crater a couple of inches deep.

A grinning engineer serjeant walked over and pointed it out to him. "That air burst should have gone off at about 30 feet above the dugout," he explained. "It were more like 3 feet when it did," he added.

Alf nodded. "We felt that bugger alright. In fact, I thought he was coming in!" Both men laughed.

The unit moved down from the hill and towards where the bombardment had taken place. The flushed faces of the newest officers to join, Lieutenants Wills and Fry had been replaced by a whiteness of reality. They had never experienced artillery fire before. The colonel looked at them and inwardly smiled to himself. That short experience would be an invaluable lesson to them both. He looked at Lieutenant Horner who was coolly examining the top of the dug-out with Corporal Cleall. He looked nonplussed about the whole affair and the colonel noted him down as an officer with a cool head.

Friday, 28th August to Sunday, 6th September 1914.

They had made the short journey to East Grinstead where the regiment was to stay for a week to undergo more training. Alf Cleall sat in the bar of the Dorset Arms Hotel, the public house that had been allocated for the enlisted men to use. The sergeants were using the Prince of Wales Inn as their mess. Local leave had been granted up to 10 p.m. each night and by this time the soldiers had to be back at their tented accommodation which was scarcely more than half a mile away. Alf Cleall had been given permission by the adjutant to help out behind the bar as the owner did not have the staff to cope with the influx of men. He had also been made responsible for the discipline of those who were using the place. Because of this, he had been given the same permission as the Sergeants' Mess in that he did not have to be back in camp before 11 p.m. each evening.

He certainly found no problem with this, and as R.S.M. Shakespeare was also billeted there he made sure that the men behaved themselves properly. On the first night that Alf helped the beaming owner approached him. "Alfie, I wish you could be here on a permanent basis," he said.

Cleall laughed. "Nice hotel," he said. "I notice that you got one of them new-fangled Automobile Association signs hanging outside. What's that for?"

George Rowe smiled. "Well, passing motorists see the sign and they know, if they are a member of that organisation, that we have superior accommodation on offer. So, they stop and use the place."

Alf nodded and made a mental note to find out more about it for his hotel back in Bath. They had several lodging rooms there and as far as he could see the day of the motor car was arriving very fast. Soon there would be very few horses used for getting around in. "Think I might like to get one of them signs for my pub," he said.

"You own a pub?"

Alf grinned. "Aye," he said. "Not so grand as yours, mind, but a nice hotel all the same."

"Who's running it now then?"

"My missus and my brother." He was quiet for a moment before he added, "I do hope everything is fine there."

George Rowe grinned. "I'm sure it is," he said. Then as an afterthought he said, "Does your pub have a telephone?"

Alf grinned. "I know we be up from Zummerzet," he replied, "but we do have some telephones down there. I had one put in a couple of months ago."

The hotel owner called across to the other barman who was busily pouring some beer into a tankard. "George!"

George stood up from his bending position by the cask of ale, a half-filled tankard in his hand. "Yes?"

"Look after the bar by yourself for a moment. I won't be long." He turned to Alf and grinned. "Follow me," he said mysteriously.

The men left the bar and trudged up the stairs to the owner's suite. George Rowe inserted a large key into the door and unlocked it, beckoning to Alf to follow him. On entry Alf noticed that it had 3 rooms. There was a surprisingly spacious office come sitting room and the other 2 were a purpose built indoor toilet with a bath and a bedroom. George pointed to a desk upon which was placed a telephone. Turning to Alf he handed him his key and said, "Take ten minutes and telephone your wife." He smiled and walked out of the room.

In the officers' mess, the night was a gay one and the drink flowed freely. The effects of the war were already being felt and the regiment had received a motor cyclist dispatch which had promoted quite a few of its officers with effect from the following day, the 29th August. And the officers made the most of it. The champagne and port flowed like water and many a young officer would regret his next mess bill.

Captains Huntley G. Spencer, Henry B. Matthews and Geoffrey Lubbock were all promoted to the esteemed rank of major, which delighted the colonel. In addition, Lieutenants Eustace L. Gibbs, Walter S. Batten Pool and John S. Tyssen at last received their full captaincies. Lieutenant Liebert was promoted to captain but from a later date.

The younger officers were not forgotten either. Second Lieutenants John S. Davey, Alexander B. Mitchell, George E. Longrigg, Guy M. Gibbs and Alexander Noel Bailward were all promoted to full lieutenants.

What no-one was aware of was that the number of officers promoted reflected the massive losses that the officer corps was beginning to take. Rapid promotion during wartime was beginning to be the norm.

The regimental tailor increased his holdings of chevrons and officers rank insignia, for he did not want to get caught out in the future.

Some of the men's families had taken lodgings in East Grinstead, and with the adjutant's approval they could visit their husbands on the base. S.Q.M.S. Crammond, of "A" Squadron, was a very happy man, for his wife and child had taken lodgings nearby and were visiting him on the camp.

The day should have been a happy and glorious one, and his little 8 years old daughter was, without doubt, one of the favourites in the regiment. She could do as she pleased and go anywhere in the camp, but she could be usually found down by the horses as she had a fascination for them.

She had gone to the Serjeants' Mess to scrounge something to eat from the willing chefs. This time, when she got to where the cooks should have been, they were all outside having a cigarette and a general natter.

Little Lucy Crammond wrinkled her nose up at the smell of something that had a delicious aroma and naturally she went to investigate it. Being a child, she reached up to pull a large pot towards her.

There was a horrendous scream and when the cooks ran in, she lay on the floor, unconscious. She had been covered in the boiling stew, causing her severe burns. The doctor was hastily summoned, along with her father and mother. There was nothing the doctor could do for her, other than douse her with cold water and the cutting away of the clothing that came away with her skin. She was swiftly conveyed by motor ambulance to the General Hospital at East Grinstead for further treatment. After that episode, family visits were curtailed by the colonel.

Monday, 7th September to Friday, 11th September 1914.

The North Somerset Yeomanry returned to Kidbrook Park and quickly settled down into the mundane life of cavalry men living in the field. Each day took on the monotonous routine of daily parades, drill and horsemanship. The unit was rapidly making the transition from being a regiment of part time territorial soldiers into that of a full-time unit. The regiment, like any regular battalion, found themselves having to deal with disciplinary problems on a more regular basis, although most of them were mundane.

R.S.M. Shakespeare perused the list of defaulters that he was holding in his hands. He was whistling a tuneless air that suddenly stopped as he spotted the now all too familiar name that seemed to thrust itself out to him, Trooper Albert Fitch. The charge against him this time was that of "losing his equipment." The charge was not all that serious and was usually within a company commander's powers to deal with. What was serious was this was the third charge that Trooper Fitch had found himself on in 2 weeks, each for the same type of offence.

Albert Fitch sat on the edge of his canvas cot; his head held dejectedly between his hands. Trooper Ernest Summers looked towards him in a sympathetic way and said, "Cheer up, Albert. It could be worse!" He put his head down and continued to polish his boots.

Albert groaned aloud and said, "I dunno, Ernie. Sometimes I think that I am losing my mind, or something like that. I just seem to be losing things all the time."

His comrade laughed. "Perhaps you've got something else on your mind, Albie."

The young soldier shook his head. "Nah!" he said. "I've got nothing else on my mind. I am just getting bloody careless, I suppose."

Ernie gave a little chuckle and said, "Perhaps you need a fine woman to rut with."

Albert looked up, blushing red and said sharply, "What do you mean by that?"

Ernest stopped polishing his boots and fixed Albert with a stony stare. "Perhaps you need to find yourself your own woman," he said deliberately, choosing his words carefully.

Albert suddenly went a deathly pale and felt as if a cold hand had suddenly reached into him and clutched his heart. "The bugger knows!" he thought quickly to himself in alarm.

The older soldier put his boots down. Carefully replacing the lid back on his open tin of dubbin, he opined, "What I mean, Albie my boy, is that it's time you found yourself a regular girlfriend, like. 'Bout time you started to think about it, my pigeon."

Albert gave a silent sigh of relief to himself as he suddenly realised that Ernest meant nothing by his remark. "You're be getting jumpy Albie me lad!" he thought grimly to himself. Standing up, he said, "Perhaps you are right, Ern."

Ernest looked at Albert, a quizzical look playing across his face. "Going somewhere, me laddo?" he enquired.

The young man nodded. "Got to go over to the quartermaster's stores and pay for a replacement belt," he explained glumly. "I am beginning to think to myself that I be starting to pay the army just to have me!"

"Well then, don't you lose that bugger as well!" cautioned Ernie, a smile upon his lips.

Albert shook his head in disbelief. "I just don't know how come I lost it, Ernie," he said in an aggrieved tone. As an afterthought he added, "Do you think that some beggar has it in for me?"

Ernest gave a laugh. "You can stop thinking like that, Albie. You're the most popular bloke in the squadron, by my reckoning."

Albert shrugged his shoulders. "Ah well, Ern," he responded. "No point in crying over spilt milk, is it?" He put his forage cap on. "All the same, I would dearly love to know what happened to it." He gave him a friendly wave and walked out.

After he he'd left, Ernest took out his pipe and slowly filled it with tobacco, a self-satisfied smirk playing across his features. Without thinking, Ernest thought aloud to himself, chuckling as he did so. "Try looking in the bottom of the river, you bastard!"

He reached under a pillow and pulled out a sealed envelope. This morning, and as the senior trooper in charge of his tent of six men, he had collected the mail for each man. He had faithfully carried out his duty and most of the soldiers had an unopened letter placed upon his pillow. One of them was lucky enough to have a large paper wrapped parcel as well.

The letter addressed to Trooper Albert Fitch carried the all too familiar handwriting of his wife. The curious way in which she put a double-bar on the letter 't's had easily given her away. At first, he had almost exploded in outright anger, but instead his mind had slowly but surely turned into an even more controlled and fierce burning desire for revenge. As he started to grow colder towards his spouse, the love that he had carried for her for so long rapidly dwindled into nothingness. He began to explore in his mind the ways in which he could cause her the most hurt. He already had an idea about that. As for Fitch? Well, as far as Ernie was concerned, he was already a dead man. Where and when he killed him was another matter.

Slowly he slit the correspondence open with his bayonet tip. The contents of this missive, he grimly thought, could even expedite his comrade's death. Laying down his bayonet, he carefully opened the neatly folded three paged illicit document and he slowly began to read it. A tear began to roll down his cheek as he did so.

The colonel acknowledged the adjutant and R.S.M. Shakespeare with a nod as they both formally saluted him. "Good morning, gentlemen," he said. "Nothing too difficult for me, I trust?"

The R.S.M. dutifully passed the list he held across to the colonel. "We have just 2 defaulters, sir. One is on a charge for absence and the other for losing his equipment."

The colonel took the proffered list and frowned. "Why am I dealing with an individual's equipment loss, R.S.M.? That's delegated to company commander's, surely?"

The adjutant intervened. "You are quite right, sir," he said. "But this is the third time that Trooper Fitch has lost some equipment in as many weeks."

"Fitch? Wasn't he the bounder who let his horse stampede through the camp?"

"The very same fellow, sir," agreed the adjutant.

The colonel grunted. He looked up at the R.S.M. and said, "Any suggestions, Mr. Shakespeare?"

The R.S.M. said immediately, "7 days Confined to Barracks and 7 Extra Drills, sir!"

"Extra Drill, R.S.M? I agree to the 7 days C.B., but why the Extra Drills?"

"Because it means that before he does his drill, he will have to lay out his kit at the guardroom for the Duty Officer to muster. Not only will that will teach Fitch to look after his kit but will also remind the duty officer of the equipment his men should be carrying with them!"

The colonel beamed at the adjutant. He looked at the R.S.M. and said, "Excellent suggestion, Mr. Shakespeare. We will have Fitch in first." With a smile on his face the colonel said, "March the guilty man in, R.S.M."

Saturday, 12th September 1914.

Corporal Alf Cleall stood nervously outside his commanding officer's office in the proper "at ease" position, his hands clasped firmly behind him and with his feet placed about 12 inches apart. He had no idea why Colonel Glynn had sent for him. From inside the office he could hear a suppressed murmur of voices. No doubt the colonel and adjutant were discussing something important, he thought. He heard a distinct laugh that he recognised immediately as that of the R.S.M.'s. Whatever they were talking about seemed to be causing them some mirth.

All went quiet as the door to the colonel's office was suddenly pulled open and the imposing figure of the R.S.M. filled the doorway. "Corporal Cleall!" he ordered.

Alf Cleall sprang immediately into a rigid position of attention. "Sir!" he replied.

"Report yourself to the commanding officer!"

Alf inwardly gave a huge sigh of relief. Being told to report himself to the commanding officer rather than being bustled in at double time by the R.S.M. meant that he was not actually in trouble. He marched the 5 paces required into his commanding officer's office before halting and, throwing up an immaculate salute, remained at a rigid position of attention.

The colonel finished writing something and then looked up from his desk at him. His neutral face suddenly turned into a frown. "R.S.M.?" he asked calmly. "Why is Cleall improperly dressed?"

The R.S.M. gave Alf a hard look. "I'm sorry, sir, I never took the time to inspect him before he came in." Mr. Shakespeare shook his head sorrowfully and said, "What have you to say for yourself, Cleall?"

Alf was absolutely lost for words, for the one thing that he always prided himself on was his immaculate appearance. He felt mortified that his commanding officer had detected a deficiency in him that he had failed to recognise. He bowed his head in shame. "Nothing to say, sir," he muttered contritely.

The colonel laughed and pointed at his chevrons. "You've got the wrong badge of rank on, Cleall!"

Alf failed to comprehend the colonel's comment. He glanced quickly down at his stripes and said in a confident voice, "I beg your pardon, colonel. I have my corporal's stripes sewn on correctly, I am sure of it!"

"Oh yes, Cleall. No doubt about that!" said the colonel. He waited for a moment before saying with a mischievous smile, "The only thing is, Cleall, is that they should be serjeant's chevrons."

Alf was confused. "I am sorry, sir," he apologised. "I just don't understand what's happening."

The colonel's smile broke into a broad grin. "Then let me make it crystal clear to you, Cleall. As of this very moment you are promoted to serjeant. Dismiss!"

The R.S.M. ordered, "Corporal Cleall promoted serjeant with effect from 12th September 1914. Salute! About turn! Quick march!"

Cleall reacted automatically and marched out of the office. As he reached the doorway the R.S.M. said, "Wait for me outside my office, Serjeant Cleall." The door closed behind the newly promoted senior-non-commissioned officer.

The colonel and the adjutant were both grinning like Cheshire cats. "How did we do, Mr. Shakespeare?"

The R.S.M. chortled at the colonel and the adjutant and replied, "Perfectly, sirs. Charlie Chaplin and Buster Keaton couldn't have put on a better act! Poor old Serjeant Cleall looked like a horse had just kicked him in the head. I don't think the fact that he has just been promoted has sunk in yet."

The adjutant chuckled. "The colonel has been looking for some time to promote Cleall," he said. "Please make sure that you tell him that both the colonel and I are both extremely pleased about his well-deserved promotion to serjeant."

The R.S.M. saluted. "I'll tell him that with much pleasure, sir."

The R.S.M. beckoned Cleall into his office. "Close the door, Alfie, and sit down." The newly promoted Serjeant Cleall did as he was bid. The R.S.M. wrote out a chit and passed it to him. "When we are finished here, Alfie, take this down to the quartermaster's stores to draw your allocation of stripes and a Senior N.C.O.'s red sash. Make sure that you get a ticket from him for the master tailor. He will immediately sew a set of chevrons onto one of your shirts so that you can straight away get into the correct uniform that befits a newly promoted serjeant. Then I want you to go to the Sergeants' Mess Manager and get your Mess accommodation sorted out. Make sure that you have moved into the Mess by 3 p.m. this afternoon. Any questions so far, Alf?"

Alfie sat quietly for a moment, a broad grin appearing on his face. "It's right then, sir," he said. "I really am to be a serjeant?"

The R.S.M. nodded and said, "Without a doubt, Alfie my lad, and you should know, despite the bit of fun they had with you in the office, how extremely pleased both the colonel and the adjutant were to promote you. They both send you their heartiest congratulations."

Alfie gulped. "I thank them very much, sir," he said.

The R.S.M. nodded. "Things will change very much for you from now on, Alfie," he said. "For a start," he said, "when we are in private conversation, and as you may have already noticed, I shall call you Alfie."

Serjeant Cleall grinned.

"And just to make sure that you make no mistake, you are always to address me as "sir," even in the Mess. Got that?"

Alfie nodded. "Perfectly, sir," he assured the R.S.M.

The R.S.M. continued. "Life in the Sergeants' Mess is something special, Alf. It has its own set of rules. The Mess Manager will give you a copy to read. Make sure you do!"

"Yes sir!"

"You have the rest of the day off to get yourself sorted out," explained the R.S.M. There came a sharp knock on the door. "Come in!" ordered Mr. Shakespeare.

The door opened, and Serjeant Gibbs marched in and halted. "You sent for me sir?"

"Ah! Charlie! I've got a task for you." He indicated Alf and said, "I want you to take our newly promoted serjeant and run through the "do's" and "don'ts" of mess etiquette."

Charlie beamed at Alfie. "About bloody time too!"

The R.S.M. laughed. "Off you go." He said to Charlie, "Make sure that Alf is in the Mess bar for 4 p.m."

A quizzical look played across Alf's face. Charlie laughed and said, "It is one of the first Mess traditions you are going to learn, Alf. How we welcome a new serjeant into the Mess!"

By 8 p.m. that night a perfectly befuddled Alf was put into his cot by his best pal, Charlie. He had learnt from first experience that the R.S.M. always bought the newly promoted serjeant a pint on behalf of the Mess. Thereafter he was duty bound to drink any drink bought him by other mess members. Alf was a popular man in the regiment and was bought many a drink. He immediately fell asleep in his cot, a bemused smile fixed upon his face. He was a confused and happy man.

Across in the men's beer tent the same could not be said for a brooding Ernest Summers. The letter his wife had written to Trooper Albert Fitch had confessed his wife's undying love for her paramour. In it she referred to some of the intimate sexual pleasures that the couple had frequently indulged in. The references to them had made him blush a scarlet red, although most of that colour was anger. He resolved that tonight he would carry out the first stage of his nefarious plan.

Having finished his hour's extra drill for that day, and having double checked and carefully packed his kit away, Fitch hurried to the beer tent before it closed at 9 p.m. He had just enough money to buy himself a pint - and did he need it! He got his glass of bitter after a short wait and took a deep drink from it. He spotted Ernest on the far side of the big recreational tent and slowly threaded his way through the maelstrom of other soldiers, a few of whom were obviously in a drunken state. One trooper had wrapped his arms around the main pole of the marquee tent, and oblivious to all others was crooning a melancholy and tuneless air to it.

He plumped himself down on the canvas chair next to his comrade and placed his pint pot up on the rough wooden plank that served as a table. He noticed that Ernie was looking very sorry for himself and asked, "What's up with you then Ernie? Something wrong is there?"

Ernie looked around to make sure that no-one else could hear the conversation. "If I tell you something, and it's something very personal, do you swear to keep it a secret?"

"Why Ernie! Aren't I your best friend? 'Course I'll keep anything you say to myself. What is the problem?"

Ernie took a deep breath and said vehemently, "It's her! 'It's the bitch I'm married to. That's the problem."

"The bitch?"

Ernie nodded. "Yes! That bitch of mine, Alice!"

"What! You mean your Alice?"

"Bloody right I do!"

Albert sat quietly for the moment. He never in his life thought that poor old Ernie had the courage to call his wife a bitch, even to him. He took another swig from his pint pot and prompted, "Well? What are you going to tell me?"

Ernie gave Albert a morose look and said, "I had a letter today." He went silent. "From Alice?"

Shaking his head vehemently he exploded, "From that cow! No! She bloody well doesn't write to me!"

Ernie went silent again, prompting Albert to say with a note of exasperation in his voice, "Well?"

Ernest looked Albert in the eye and thought to himself with pleasure of the severe mental wound he was about to inflict upon his "best mate." He savoured the moment and prolonged it by taking another sip of his ale. Wiping his hand across his mouth he said, "Another friend of mine wrote me a letter about Alice," he explained. He went silent again, forcing Albert to be the architect of his own downfall by making him ask for more information.

"And?"

Ernie took another sip of his warm beer. He looked at Albert and said in a sad voice, "I've been told she is having an affair with another soldier."

In a trembling voice Albert asked fearfully, "Do you know who he is, then?"

Inwardly Ernie was dancing in joy, for he could visibly see the terrible effect his words were having on poor Albie. Again, he waited, toying with his supposed friend as a cat does with a mouse.

Albert turned his face away from Ernest to hide his shock that he was feeling at that moment. He found himself some courage and muttered, "Who is it, then?"

Ernest started to fill his pipe, spinning out the time. Albert was in no hurry to hear the awful truth. His mind was racing to think of a suitable response he should give when the moment that his sins were placed before him upon the altar of retribution.

Ernest struck a match and lit his pipe. He puffed furiously at it for a moment or so before he pointed its stem meaningfully towards his friend in a series of short jabbing motions. Albert braced himself to face the expected onslaught of words or physical violence that was about to be unleashed upon him.

Ernest took another sip of his drink and banged his glass down quite hard onto the rough planked table. "It is some bloody Grenadier Guardsman serjeant that be billeted in the pub!" he snarled.

A great rushing suddenly sounded in Albert' ears as he realised that he had not been found out after all. It felt as if a weight had suddenly been removed from his shoulders. This sudden relief was quickly replaced by one of sheer anger as he suddenly realised that Alice had been unfaithful to him as well. He snapped angrily, "The bitch!"

Ernest agreed. "The bitch!"

Albert was at a complete loss for words. He didn't know what to say. Finally, he came up with, "Are you certain?"

Ernest nodded. "Oh aye, I am certain of it. The brazen cow is even walking arm in arm with the bugger down to the pub."

"The cow!" exploded Albie, but not in sympathy with his chum but more in an acute sense of betrayal by Alice. He had been expecting her to write to him at some stage and Ernie's words had now explained to him why he had not received a letter from her.

Ernest was inwardly rejoicing in the hurt and turmoil he could sense in Albie. He had to mentally stop himself from saying, "Now you know how it feels, you bugger!" He stopped himself from smiling and played his final fatal card of the evening.

"Oh well, it doesn't really matter too much, I suppose," he said, in the best voice of helplessness he could muster.

Albert spoke in the voice of an outraged man. "What do you mean? Of bloody course it matters! If it were my missus buggering about with some other sod, I'd kill the bastard!"

Ernie could not help but grin and said, "He is already a dead man, but he doesn't know it yet."

Albert frowned. "What do you mean?"

Ernest said softly, "If I tell you, you'll have to swear to me to keep it secret for the rest of your life?"

"You know that you can trust me, Ernie."

"Then swear!"

Albert looked at Ernie intently. "I swear!"

The old soldier shook his head. "That's not enough, Albie. You have to swear to me on your mother's life not to tell!"

"Bloody hell, Ernie! I swear on my mother's life that I am not going to tell anybody anything!"

Ernie nodded and went quiet. He was surprised at how easy the lie had come to him. He said in a confidential tone, "I haven't touched me missus for over eight years, you know. Not since she got that terrible disease."

Albert sat bolt upright in a blind panic. His face went pale and, in his shock, he accidentally knocked his remaining beer over. Ernie pretended not to notice. "What disease?" he asked, his voice quavering in a terrible expectation.

Ernie made a great play of looking secretively about as if he was making sure that no-one was listening. He said thoughtfully, "Doctor did tell me the name, but 'twas too bloody difficult for me to remember." Milking the moment, he spun the time out for another few seconds before wrinkling his forehead and saying with a sigh, "I think it ends 'yphillis' or something similar. I'm not too sure about it." Ernie looked out of the corner of his eye at Albert and nodded. "All I know is that she is what they call a "carrier" or a little like that!"

In a deathly voice Albie asked the question that he didn't want to, but he had to know. "What do you mean, "carrier"?"

Albert feigned an angry voice and said, "It means that she won't suffer from the disease, like, but any bugger who has some rumpty-tumpty with the bitch will. That be why I had to stop having personal relations with her."

Albert thought for a moment that he was going to faint. He said hopefully, "You can't be seriously telling me that every bugger who touches her would get infected though, surely?"

The old trooper nodded. "The worst thing is it takes some while for the disease to show." Ernest expounded, "It becomes a mental disease, like. It sorts of addles your brain without you knowing it. You don't notice it happening, but other folks do."

Albie said fearfully, "And what are the signs?"

Ernie shrugged. "Doctor told me that I had to look out for the first signs, such as putting things down and forgetting where I put them, you know, little things like that. Then it gradually gets worse. You start to forget where you are and things like that. Eventually you forget who you are. It's then they shove you into the loony bin. After about six months you forget to breathe, and you just die."

Albert gave a strangled cry and jumped to his feet. "I feel sick!" he cried. Jumping to his feet he placed a hand over his mouth and ran pell-mell out of the tent. Alfie could hear other troopers laughing at his plight, and if Albie could have listened hard enough, he would have discerned that the loudest laugh of all was Ernest's.

Sunday, 13th September 1914.

There was an unexpected sharp rap on the door of the cottage where Alice lived. She was upstairs at the time and looked out from her bedroom window to see an army officer standing outside. He impatiently knocked on the door again. She gave a frown and ran down the stairs, her footsteps echoing in the almost empty house. She opened the door, wiping her hands in her apron as she did so, for she had been dusting.

"Mrs Summers?"

"Yes."

"I am Captain Smith, the billeting officer for this area."

"Billeting Officer?"

"Yes. You would have seen the poster on display in the Post Office that I would be going around and allocating billets to men."

"What do you mean, billets?"

Captain Smith was carrying a wooden millboard in his hand. On it he had the names of other households that had numbers marked against them.

"There is a new army regiment moving into the area for training purposes, and you are required to billet, or perhaps as you would better understand it, to accommodate, however many men I decide upon."

"Well I don't know about that," she said indignantly. "My husband wouldn't allow it you know!"

The army officer grimaced, for he was used to obstacles regarding billeting issues been thrown in his way. "You and your husband have no choice in the matter, madam. It is the law."

"Humph!"

"Never mind the display of indignation, Mrs Summers. The law is the law. Do you mind if I come in and check your house so I can see how many soldiers you can accommodate?"

She answered in an indignant tone, "Yes, I do mind. You can't come in!"

This brought back a provoked reply from the officer. "You have a choice, madam. Either I come in and allocate you the number of men I think suitable, or I will just mark you down to accommodate 6 men!"

Alice was quiet for a moment. "Then you had better come in," she obliged sullenly.

The captain nodded and walked in and Alice showed him around the cottage. She had 2 bedrooms upstairs and 2 rooms downstairs. The billeting officer nodded his head and wrote something down on his millboard. After walking around the cottage he finished up in the kitchen. He put a tick in one of the boxes. "Right," he said firmly. "You have a nice little cottage here, Mrs Summers and I shall be placing 5 men in here. The serjeant is to have the upstairs room and the 4 other ranks the front room."

Alice put her hand to her mouth at the thought of 5 soldiers being lodged in her house. "Am I supposed to feed them as well? I don't have any money!"

The captain took out a sheet of paper and handed it to her. "All the details are contained in this."

Alice blushed. "I can't read."

The captain nodded. "You will receive 9d per day for each of the soldiers billeted in your cottage. For that 9d a day you are to provide them with candles, vinegar, salt, the use of the fire and the use of your cooking utensils for dressing and eating meat. The serjeant will provide the food for the men for their evening meal."

Alice's ears pricked up. "9d a day! Each?"

"Yes, 9d a day, or, in total, 3s 9d a day for billeting."

Alice frowned as she tried to work out in her head how much that it was a week she would be getting. The captain could see what she was trying to do, so he told her. "That means you will be getting 26/3d a week to accommodate them," he said.

From at first hating the thought of it she suddenly realised the financial implications of it all. Money was tight for her, for apart from her earning odd sums of money doing laundry and cleaning jobs, her sole source of income was the measly 3s 6d she received each week from Ernest from an allotment of his pay.

"When does all this start?" she asked sweetly.

"Tomorrow!"

"Tomorrow!"

"Yes Mrs Summers, tomorrow. A serjeant plus 4 men will arrive here sometime late tomorrow afternoon. You will need to make space in your front room for the soldiers to be able to put up their cot beds. They can help you move your belongings around in order to create the space."

"How do I get paid?"

The captain signed a certificate and handed it to her. "Go down to the Post Office tomorrow morning and hand it to the Post Mistress. She will make out an identification card for you. Your billeting money will be held by her and she will tell you when you are to go to the Post Office to collect your money. That will happen every Saturday without fail so you can collect your first payment next week. Now then, Mrs Summers, is there anything else I can help you with as I need to be getting on with my duties?"

Alice thought for a moment and said, "So effectively all this will begin tomorrow afternoon, then?"

"Quite correct."

She shook her head in acceptance. "No, I have no more questions. Thank you."

The Billeting Officer left, a satisfied smile on his face.

Monday, 14th September – Monday, 26th October 1914.

The regiment was now at full complement and a reorganisation of duties had taken place. The colonel asked the adjutant to put the officer positions and duties into the Daily Routine Orders, knowing that Brigade would get a copy of them. The typewritten orders began:

"Officer Locations.

Commanding Officer – Lieutenant Colonel G.C. GLYNN DSO
Second in Command – Major A.H. GIBBS
Captain & Adjutant – Captain S.G. BATES
Machine Guns – Major H.B. MATTHEWS
Transport – Captain H. BROOKING
Squadron Captain – Captain C.W. EDWARDS R.A.M.C.
Veterinary – Captain R. RAWLING R.A.V.C.
Lieutenant & Quarter Master – Lieutenant F.A.B. HOLWELL

"A" Squadron.

Major G. LUBBOCK
Captain R.E. ENGLISH
Lieutenant A.B. MITCHELL
Lieutenant G.E. LONGRIGG
Lieutenant W.D. WILLS
Lieutenant A.N. BAILWARD

"B" Squadron.

Captain F.A.C. LIEBERT
Captain E.L. GIBBS
Lieutenant J.S. DAVEY
Lieutenant G.M. GIBBS
Lieutenant R.C. GIBBS
Lieutenant L.C. GIBBS

"C" Squadron.

Major H.G. SPENCER
Captain H.H.S. TYSSEN
Lieutenant A.H. GARTON
Lieutenant E. HORNER
Lieutenant R.A.B. CHRISTIE
Lieutenant C.T. O'CALLAGHAN

Reserve Squadron
Captain W.S. BATTEN-POOLL
Lieutenant L.H. FRY"

Training of some sort of the other was taking place on a daily basis and the men swiftly fell into the regular, and to some, almost boring routine. Most days were the same, commencing with physical training before breakfast and then usually on to drill. This was interspersed with looking after the horses and exercising them. Very little seemed to focus on what they would actually be doing if they ever got to France.

The war had now become a war of attrition and the casualties taken by both sides were exceedingly high. The British Army was falling back, in good order, towards the coast of France. If you could believe what the newspapers were saying at the time, the whole purpose was to extend the enemy lines so that a decisive and final blow could be made against the enemy. It would be all over by Christmas.

The biggest event during this time was the court martials of Troopers Haskell and Simmons. Both men had absented themselves from the Yeomanry on the very day that the regiment had ridden out of Bath on the 17th August for the ride to Winchester.

On Saturday, 10th October 1914 both men paid the penalty for their folly, for they had been quickly apprehended by the City of Bath Police Force. This was the first court martial in the North Somerset Yeomanry since the Boer War, and everyone was curious to know what the penalty would be. They would not be long in finding out, for at the trial both men had pleaded immediately guilty. The President of the Court Martial, a full colonel, sentenced the pair to 40 days field punishment number 1 with 47 days loss of pay.

Field Punishment Number One was introduced after flogging was outlawed in the British Army and Haskell and Simmons became the first 2 men of the North Somerset Yeomanry to be sentenced to it during this war. Both convicted men were placed in fetters and handcuffs and attached to a fixed fence outside to the main eating marquee from 1800 hours to 2000 hours each day for a maximum of 3 days out of 4. They were in full view of the whole regiment and that added to their resentment.

The punishment was applied with their arms stretched out and the legs tied together, known by the troopers as "a crucifixion" because of the position they were restrained in. They were there as a living example to all the soldiers as the punishment for absence and would do so for the next forty punishment days at the same time, regardless of the weather.

On the 15th October 1914 the regiment sadly had to say goodbye to the popular Lieutenant Horner, for he had been selected to be transferred to the 11th Reserve Cavalry, based at Tidworth. He had been given the role as a training officer in that unit, for newly enlisted men would be sent to the Reserve Cavalry to commence their basic training. The 11th were to be responsible for the training of men who would then be drafted on to the 10th and 18th Hussars, Hampshire Yeomanry, North Somerset Yeomanry and the Wiltshire Yeomanry. Each of these units had to attach an officer to act as selection officer for their intended reinforcements, an important position.

The colonel had given some considerable thought to it and had at last decided upon Lieutenant Horner. He would be sorry to lose him, for he was a good officer, but he could see that he had a bright future in the army in front of him, and a move to training men for his regiment would be beneficial for all of them.

Alice looked out of her window to see an army lorry squeal to a halt. The driver of the lorry and a serjeant alighted from it and the 2 men walked around to the back of the truck.

The Serjeant called out, "O.K. lads! We are here. Get everything unloaded." He then turned around and walked down the front path to the front door. He was about to knock on it when it was suddenly opened to greet him. To his surprise he saw a good looking woman in front of him. "Mrs Summers?"

Alice smiled sweetly at him. "That's me."

The serjeant put out his hand to shake hers, saying, "I am Serjeant Willcox, of the Royal Garrison Artillery. Myself and 4 other soldiers have been billeted here."

"Yes, I know." Her heart skipped a little, for the serjeant was a very handsome man and she felt immediately attracted to him.

"May I come in and look at the rooms?"

"Of course, serjeant. Please come in." The serjeant stepped inside into the medium sized room and saw at once that Mrs Summers had spent some time in making space for them.

"I know that we are welcome here, Mrs Summers, but I shall do my best to work in with your routine so that we give you the minimum amount of bother."

"I don't expect any bother at all, sergeant. Make yourself at home."

He grinned back at her, the whiteness of his teeth set into the dark features of his face reminded her of a handsome gypsy prince. "Thank you, Mrs Summers."

Alice shook her head and said, "You must call me by my first name, Alice."

"Alice? What a beautiful name. My name is Albert."

Her heart skipped another beat, for she now knew that she was going to enjoy the presence of menfolk around her house once more. A figure appeared in the doorway, carrying some canvas cot beds. "Where do I put these, sarge?" he enquired.

"This will be your room, Fred. Get it set up please." The soldier nodded.

Albert looked at Alice and said, "I believe that I am to have a separate room?"

She nodded. "Follow me, Albert," she invited, and led him up the stairs. Already her mind was beginning to dwell on the future.

Tuesday, 27th October 1914.

It was a standard day and the officers and men went about their routine training. As each day slowly progressed they were becoming more and more proficient at being soldiers.

On the day war was declared each man had ceased to be a territorial soldier and had been embodied into the regular army on the 5th August 1914. This meant that his pay was increased slightly, but also that those former territorial soldiers were expected to attain the standards of a regular soldier.

The men were far fitter than they had been before they were mobilised, and they seemed to have physically and mentally grown. An unannounced visit by the brigadier to the North Somerset Yeomanry, which in the past would have thrown the unit into a flurry, went as smooth as clockwork.

Serjeant Cleall had happened to be the Orderly Serjeant of the Day, and from the guardroom had noted the approaching brigadier general's car flying his pennant, flanked by 2 Military Policeman on motor-cycles. In a flash Cleall had dispatched 2 runners to locate the adjutant and colonel to inform them of the unexpected arrival, and at the same time had turned out the guard to greet the surprised brigadier general with a general salute of 'Present Arms.' The delighted brigadier general Ashley-Cooper had taken the time to get out the car and to inspect the guard. Cleall was made a happy man, for this meant that the runners he had despatched had more time to locate the colonel and the adjutant, which luckily, they did.

Standing on the running board of the staff car, Serjeant Cleall personally conducted the commander of the 2nd South Western Mounted Brigade to the headquarters office, where Colonel Glynn and Captain Bates were already waiting expectantly.

The brigadier general entered the Commanding Officer's office and shook hands with the colonel and the adjutant. He had a broad smile on his face that both officers could not but help notice.

There was a sharp rap on the door. "Come in," ordered Colonel Glynn.

His manservant, Adams, entered the room bearing a silver tray laden with the paraphernalia required for tea. "Would you like a cup of tea sir?"

"Oh rather," he replied.

Adams poured out three cups of tea and added sugar and milk to the obligatory quantity for the colonel and the adjutant. He added 2 teaspoonfuls of sugar to the 9th Earl of Shaftsbury's teacup and passed him his drink. He raised an eyebrow in a curious manner and waited for Adam's to discreetly leave the room.

"Good man there, colonel. How did he know how many sugars I take in tea?"

The colonel laughed. "That is why he is my servant sir; he simply knows these things.

93

"Well, I will get straight to the point of my visit. I expect that you are curious to know what it is all about?"

The 2 officers exchanged glances. Smiling, the colonel said, "You do not have to have a reason, sir. You are always welcome to visit my regiment at any time."

The brigadier general took a sip of tea and carefully placed his cup and saucer down on the table. "Do you think you are ready for war, Glynn?"

"Yes sir," came the immediate response.

The brigadier general reached for his cup of tea and took another slow sip from it. He seemed to be making up his mind about something. He nodded. Looking directly at the colonel he raised the question he had on his mind. "How do you think you compare to a regular unit?"

Glynn responded immediately. "On a par, without doubt, sir." Then he quickly added, "As a matter of fact, I would say that we are probably much better than some of them, but that is not meant to be taken as a derogatory remark."

The brigadier general stroked his chin. "You know that most of the regular soldiers do not take kindly to Yeomanry. In their eyes territorials are simply not up to the mark. There is also a worry in higher echelons as to how they would react under battle conditions. The territorial units are, at present, considered by Lord Kitchener not to be an effective military force. Those few units we do have in France at present are deployed in garrison duties in order to free up regular units from non-combat duties."

Captain Bate's eyes sparkled with mortification and he interjected, "Do you mind if I say something, sir?"

The colonel looked at the brigadier general who nodded his assent. "Please feel free to do so, Stanley."

Bate's thought for a moment, formulating his words, before saying in an passionate manner, "I am a regular soldier sir. I have been with the North Somerset Yeomanry for some considerable time. The speed of their transition from being a territorial force to being as good as a regular unit has been quite remarkable. In fact, sir, if you were to send me back to my old regiment I would feel quite peeved at you in doing so."

The colonel smiled.

Captain Bates continued enthusiastically, "This is a wonderful regiment that many regular units would be glad to have by their side. They are just as professional, and more to the point, they have that certain feel, that confident elan about them that would equal that of any Hussars regiment that I can think of."

The brigadier general thoughtfully stroked his chin. "I can tell you now, gentlemen, that mine is not just a casual visit." Putting his hand into his pocket he pulled out a brown envelope with the words "Most Secret" stamped across them. He handed it to the colonel.

"May I open it?"

"Please do."

The colonel took his paper knife from off his desk and carefully slit it open. Inside was one brief sheet of paper. He read it and then handed it to his adjutant. Grinning broadly, he said, "We won't let you down sir.

Rising to his feet the brigadier general replied with feeling, "I know you won't." Both men shook hands and, calling for his driver, he left the room.

After he had gone the colonel went to a closed cupboard and took out a decanter of port and 2 glasses. He placed them on his desk and swiftly filled them both. Taking a sip, he passed one to his adjutant. "Read me that line again Stanley, if you would please."

The adjutant grinned. He said in a formal tone, "The Regiment has been selected for service in France. On receipt of this order the unit is to be notified immediately and are to be ready to transit to France as reinforcements as from the 2nd November 1914. Expedite."

The colonel nodded. "I think that the brigadier general was intimating to us that although we are going to France that we won't be going into the front line."

"That's the way I read it too, sir. They have been practising us rather a lot in trench digging recently, so I suppose that is the task that we will be carrying out."

The colonel agreed. "Still," he replied. "We will be within the sound of the guns and modern warfare is such that you never know what will happen. At least by being over there we will have a better chance of having a go at the enemy.

The adjutant smiled broadly. "I hope we do sir."

The colonel made his mind up. "What time is it?"

The adjutant took out his half-hunter gold watch, a present from his fiancee, and glanced at it. "Coming up to 11 a.m. sir." Anticipating the colonel's next question he quickly added, "There is one squadron out of camp, due to arrive back in for lunch at 12.30 p.m."

The colonel tweaked his moustache. "At 12.45 p.m. I want all the men formed in a hollow square on the parade ground. I intend to deliver this important announcement to the regiment myself. Keep its purpose quiet for a moment, if you please."

"Of course, sir. Should I send a messenger to "A" Squadron to ensure that they return here promptly for 12.30 p.m.?"

The colonel nodded his approval.

At 12.45 p.m. the whole regiment formed a hollow square on the parade ground. A raised dais had hastily been improvised and stood awaiting the colonel. The men did not have long to wait, for he soon arrived with his adjutant.

R.S.M. Shakespeare called the men to attention as the colonel approached, and waited his moment. The colonel stood on the dais and the adjutant stood beneath him, facing the R.S.M. Mr. Shakespeare marched forward and halted smartly in front of the adjutant, and saluted.

"Sah!" he barked out in the very best R.S.M. fashion. "The regiment is formed in hollow square and at your disposal. All officers and men, apart from the 6 men on guard duties and 2 prisoners, await your orders."

The adjutant returned the salute and said, "Thank you R.S.M." Mr. Shakespeare stood his ground as the adjutant did an about turn and saluted the colonel.

"Sir! The regiment is formed and is at your disposal."

The colonel nodded. "Thank you adjutant, stand the men at ease please".

The adjutant saluted again and once more performed an about turn. He took a deep breath and shouted, "North Somerset Yeomanry, stand at - ease."

There was a sharp thud of almost perfect timing, and the regiment was stood at ease.

The colonel smiled. "Break ranks lads, and move forward to gather around me."

There were some surprised looks when he delivered that sentence, but immediately the men and officers broke ranks and gathered closely around him. An expectant hush fell over them.

"Well boys, we have received the best of news, and news that I am sure you will be very glad to hear. Very soon we will be going to France." An excited buzz ran amongst the men as the R.S.M. quickly demanded, "Silence in the ranks." The men quietened. With twinkling eyes he nodded at his adjutant. "Read the letter please."

Captain Bates got up alongside the colonel on the dais and from his tunic pocket produced and envelope from which he took out the letter. He read: "The Regiment has been selected for service in France to embark at early notice." He waited for a moment for the message to sink in before he continued. "The C.O. has also received a letter from our Brigadier General, The Earl of Shaftsbury, as follows:-

"My heartfelt congratulations upon the distinction conferred upon you, and your gallant regiment. It will be sad here without you, but we must hope to meet again before long across the water."

The colonel has responded with the following: "The Commanding Officer knows the Regiment thoroughly appreciates the honour of having been selected, and wish they had been able to go under the brigadier and with the brigade."

The colonel waited again as a little buzz of excitement ran around the men gathered before him. "What I am about to tell you is most secret, and you are only hearing it because as of this moment every single one of you is confined to camp and is not to proceed outside its boundary. Those officers and S.N.C.O.'s billeted outside of the camp are, after this parade, to go directly to their civilian billet and remove their kit and personal items. The Quartermaster will establish extra tents as needed. None of what I am saying is to leave this camp. I will deal with any breach of this most severely."

The colonel waited a moment before saying: "This next week will be the most crucial one for all of us. The bare essentials are these.

The transport and horses, under Captain Brooking are to proceed to East Grinstead station at 7.30 a.m., Thursday the 29th October.

The regiment will follow on Monday 2nd November in 4 special trains and will proceed to Southampton to embark for France, arriving there the following day."

A sudden and involuntary cheer escaped from the lips of the men, again forcing the R.S.M. to demand silence. The colonel smiled again. "As you see, there is not much time left." A tittle of laughter ran amongst the gathered men. The colonel became serious. "Each of you is to write a letter home to your loved ones, explaining the short notice you have been given and that by the time your loved one gets the letter, you will be in France." The colonel nodded directly to his officers in front of them. "You, gentlemen, are now to officially censor each of your men's letters from here onwards. The unit post box is now sealed, and under my orders has been removed. Once you have censored the letters you are to seal them and bring them to the adjutant, who has made arrangements to have them all posted on the 4th November.

Of one thing that I am sure of is that the regiment will give a good account of itself. You have the honour of being one of the first territorial regiments to help our regular soldier comrades, and I know each and every one of you will do your duty." He waited for a moment before he said, "Are there any questions?"

All went silent, and the R.S.M. thought that he would ask the question that the men would want answered. "Are we going to join the fight, sir?"

The colonel grinned, for he had anticipated that. "Probably not, R.S.M. It looks as if we will be used to dig trenches so our regular comrades can be released to go forward to repel the foe." He could sense the despondency that was quickly forming around the men so he added, "However, if we are close to the Front line there is always a strong possibility that we will be used in the fighting role." He waited for a moment before saying, "That will be all. Adjutant!"

Captain Bates called aloud, "Re-form hollow square!" The men scurried about to restore the square and quickly did so. The colonel was pleased with the result. "Carry on," he ordered.

"Very good sir." The adjutant called the men to attention and saluted the colonel as he stepped off the dais and walked away.

Addressing the officers, who were formed in a separate block away from the men, he said, "All officers are to be in the officer's mess at 2 p.m. for a full briefing of the timings from me. Fall out the officers."

Major Lubbock, who was in charge of the officers, gave the order of "Fall out the officers," who immediately sprung to attention, saluted, and left the parade ground, the younger amongst them talking excitedly to each other.

Wednesday, 28th October 1914.

The day started at 5.30 a.m. as the bugler sounded the reveille. Men spilled hurriedly out of their tents, rushing towards the ablutions and the tubs of warm water placed there by the army cooks. The first ones who arrived would get the clean water, so there was a certain urgency about them.

Having washed and shaved the men returned to their tented accommodation to indulge themselves with a cup of tea. Today would be a day of pure work details for them and all training had been cancelled; even the 20 mile-route march that was supposed to have happened the following day. All they had time for was the preparation for the regiment's move.

At 6.30 a.m., and in their physical training gear, they fell in on the parade ground for an hour or so of fitness training before breakfast. This ceased promptly at 8 a.m. Returning to their billets they quickly changed into their fatigue uniforms and then raced across to the dining hall tent, taking their knives, forks, spoons, tin cup and mess tin with them. In the large marquee they formed an orderly queue to receive their first meal of the day.

The wooden benches had been set up and placed upon them were large pans of fried eggs, thick slices of bacon, sausages, beans and a hand sized wedge of white bread. Holding out their mess tin before them as they passed along the line of cooks they would get a good portion of each item slapped into it. At the last table stood one of the army cooks in front of a large copper of boiling hot tea. As each man passed by a ladle full of the black liquid would be sloshed into the cup – you had to be sure that you held it level, for if you lost any of the contents it would not be refilled. They helped themselves to fresh milk, although the duty lance-corporal ensured that they took no more than one teaspoonful of sugar for their tea.

The men took their places on rough-hewn benches and quickly ate their meal from the flat tables. As soon as they vacated a place, it would be filled by another trooper.

On completion of breakfast they returned to their tents to make their cots and neatly stow their kit away, for the serjeants would be around soon to hustle them outside and muster them. At the same time, they would inspect the billets and woe betide anyone who left his tent in a mess!

At 8 a.m. they all fell in on the parade ground in their squadrons under the watchful eye of the Regimental Serjeant Major. Normally he would have taken them for an hour or so of drill, but not today.

The men were broken up into manageable sizes for the working tasks that would be allocated to them.

Serjeant Alf Cleall had 20 men assigned to him and was ordered to report to the quartermaster, Lieutenant Howell, for a work detail. When he arrived with the men the Q.M. and his Regimental Quarter Master Serjeant were already waiting for them. Their task was to load the wagons, under their directions, with the sealed boxes that contained all the Yeomanry's equipment.

Each wagon had a number painted on the side. The R.Q.M.S. came over to Cleall and handed him a sheet of paper. "Here you go, Alf," he said. "I want you to load up wagon number 1 with all the boxes shown on the sheet."

"Any particular order?"

"Yes please." The R.Q.M.S. pointed at the paper and said to Alf, "Each numbered box has to be loaded in reverse order. I need you to get your troopers to put boxes 1 to 20 in cart number one, box 20 goes on first, followed by box 19 and so on, until box 1 is the last one to be loaded."

Alf nodded, for he did not need to know what was in the boxes, as the Q.M. and his staff did. To him they were just sealed boxes. He beckoned towards 2 of his working party, Fitch and Summers, and said, "You lads get onboard the cart and load the boxes as they come. The rest of you men, follow me into the tent and start taking them out to the cart that I will show you."

Inside the large tent men of the quartermaster's department swiftly took charge and pointed out which boxes had to be moved outside to the waiting carts and then manually loaded. Alf Cleall stood patiently by the door, ticking off the box numbers on his list one by one and good naturedly supervising the order of the load.

The men worked hard to accomplish their tasks and they needed no urging on. The quicker the job got done, the quicker they finished. Only essential duty personnel would be working and the rest of the regiment had been given the afternoon off by the colonel in order that every man could securely pack his kit and put away or return any item that they did not need. All personal items that were needed in France were to boxed up and put in the safe-keeping of the Quartermaster.

By midday, the loading of 20 wagons had been safely accomplished and the men were allowed to go. The only incident was when Trooper Summers accidentally let go of his end of the box, causing poor Trooper Fitch a nasty cut on the leg in the process. Alf had sent him off to the medical tent as it looked as if it would need a couple of stitches to be put into the wound. "Poor old Fitch," thought the genial serjeant. "If he wasn't losing things he was always meeting with some sort of accident." Fitch now had the reputation of being something of a "Jonah" and Alf had known the other sergeants to winch at the name when they found they had him on guard duty or a working party.

Thursday, 29th October to Friday, 30th October 1914.

The transport, under the able command of Captain Brooking, departed at 7.30 a.m. sharp on the Thursday. The colonel and adjutant were there to see them off, for they would take longer to get to Southampton harbour with all the heavy equipment.

The Yeomanry's final days at Forest Row saw much attention being paid to the horses by the men, for it would be these horses that they would be riding to battle on. The Army Veterinary Corps had arrived en-bloc on the Friday morning and had given all the animals a thorough examination. A very pleased colonel accepted the fact that all the steeds were found to be fit and ready for action. Not even a loose horseshoe could be detected during their unexpected inspection. An "A" report on the fitness of the regiment's horses was well received throughout the Yeomanry and the Brigade.

There was not much left to do now and the men were warned that the canteen would be dismantled on the Sunday morning in preparation for the regiment's move on the Monday. The men accepted this stoically, for they were still confined to camp and it meant that they would have to make their own fun that day and so a sports day was hastily organised.

On the Friday the doctor requested to see the commanding officer regarding one of his cases. The colonel readily acceded and made an appointment for him at 2 p.m. At the chosen time he knocked on the colonel's door.

"Come in, Captain Edwards," he invited.

He entered and the colonel waived him into a chair. "Good afternoon, sir," he said.

"Good afternoon. Is there a problem?"

The medical man stroked his chin thoughtfully. "Not medically, sir, but I think I am detecting the early signs of a mental illness developing in one of your men and I am wondering or not whether we should take him to France."

The colonel's eyes became alert. "Who is the man?" he asked.

The doctor gave a cough and said, "I am afraid that at the moment I am not in a position to breach the doctor/patients confidentiality. All I can tell you about him is that he is a trooper in one of the squadrons."

"So you won't tell me who he is?"

"I am afraid not, colonel. However, should I consider him to be a danger to himself or to others of the regiment I shall have to inform you so that you can decide whether he goes with us or not."

"I think it is much too late now, doctor. Can you tell me what his problem is?"

The doctor nodded. "That I can, colonel. The man believes that he is suffering from syphilis that he caught from another soldier's wife. That trooper is also a member of the regiment, but I have not taken him in for an examination. I have studied both trooper's medical records and they are both very fit men."

"Have you examined the man for the disease?"

The doctor nodded. "Oh yes. It was the very first thing that I did."

"What was the result."

"Physically, he is as fit as a fiddle and there is no sign of the infection in him. That is why I have not called the other man in, for I did not want to make him concerned. He probably knows nothing about his wife's infidelity."

"I see. Why are you really worried about him?"

"As I said, sir, it is not a physical thing with him, but a psychological thing. As you know, psychology is in its infancy and the army are only just beginning to accept it as a medical condition, but under the strictest definition."

"Is the man likely to harm anyone?"

The medical man thought for a moment. "No!" he responded.

"Is the man a lunatic?"

"No."

"Will the man harm himself?"

"I don't think so, but of that I am not sure. I just want you to know that one of your troopers has the potential to turn into a lunatic, and that there won't be anything we can do about it."

"Well, thank you. Will you still not tell me his name?"

"I'm sorry sir, but my Hippocratic oath forbids me from doing so."

"What about the name of the other trooper?"

"Well sir, as it is not a medical matter, but more a pastoral one, I can tell you that the other man's name is Ernest Summers, of "A" Squadron."

"Well, alright Captain Edwards. I will not pursue this any further. Will you ensure that you inform me immediately if there is likely to be a problem?"

"Of course sir."

"Good. Well, off you go then doctor. Would you please discuss this with the padre?"

"Of course sir. Thank you for seeing me." The physician stood up, saluted and left the room.

The colonel frowned. The last thing he wanted was a lunatic in their midst.

Saturday, 31st October and Sunday, 1st November 1914.

In the headquarters the adjutant checked his last typed instructions for the clerk to place on the regiment's daily orders board. He knew that these would be eagerly awaited by the men as they contained the final details of the move. He read them through again, just to make sure that the clerk had not made any errors. They stated:

"1.   Proceed to East Grinstead to entrain for Southampton in the following order:

C Squadron	7.30 a.m.
B Squadron	9.30 a.m.
A Squadron	10.30 a.m.
HQ and Machine Gun Section (Maxims) 1 p.m.	

2.   Haversack and water bottle to be carried on the right side. The runner of the water bottle to be outside the waist belt. The Mess Tin will be fastened through back D of the saddle on the near side. Nosebag fastened through the back D of the saddle and the D in front of the Mess tin to prevent rattling. Saddle sheets folded over the cloak. Blankets to be folded in 4, G.S. Blanket over the horse blanket. Pegs and heel ropes to be fastened on the sword scabbard.

3.   Haversack to contain:

1. Holdall containing laces, toothbrush, Razor, Shaving Brush, Comb, Knife, Fork, and Spoon.
2. Housewife.
3. Towel. Soap."

With a sigh of satisfaction he signed the final set of orders for Forest Row with a flourish. From the morrow the unit would be using a war diary to record all that went on. Just to confirm that he had it ready, he opened his desk drawer to ensure that it was still there. He gave and grunt of satisfaction before closing it and shouted, "Trooper Harding!"

There was almost an instantaneous polite knock on the door and the regimental clerk appeared. He came to a halt in front of the captain and saluted. "Yes sir?"

Captain Bates pointed at the signed orders that lay on the desk. "Put those up immediately," he commanded.

"Yes sir." Picking them up, the young clerk saluted once more and left the office. One copy was to go on the main notice board, one to each of the squadrons, and one each for the officers' and sergeants' messes, and one to Brigade. Outside the front of the office men were already gathering anxiously, waiting to see what their final instructions were to be.

"Make way, make way there," he called, pushing himself importantly though the throng of eager men. Helpful hands willingly cleared a path for him. He took a key out of his pocket and opened the locked glass front of the noticeboard and pinned up the Daily Routine Orders, the last he would do in England.

Back in his accommodation tent, Ernie spoke compassionately to his supposed friend. "Bloody hell, Albie! I am right sorry for dropping my end of the box. How's your leg?"

Fitch gave a mournful glance downwards at his bandaged leg as he lay on the cot that served as his bed. "It's not your fault, Ernie," he said, shrugging his shoulders, "these things happen." He gave a wry grin and said, "It just seems that everything is happening to me and all at once."

Ernest nodded in agreement. "You just happen to be going through a bad patch, Alb; it will pass."

"I hope so. Still, what can possibly go wrong now. Tomorrow we head for France and perhaps our first real taste of fighting!"

Ernest nodded. "Are you scared?"

Albert took a moment to think, his brow furrowing in deep concentration before he replied. "I don't know, I sort of think that I am looking forward to it. You know, a new country, new people, seeing what the war is really like."

"Aren't you afraid of being killed?"

Fitch sat up from his cot and placed his feet on the floor. "The way my life has been going lately, it won't really matter, will it? People already have me marked down as a "Jonah" and don't really want me to be around them." He put his trousers on and slipped his braces over his rough woollen shirt. "If I didn't have you as my friend, Ernie," he said, a serious note evident in his voice, "I don't know what I would have done." He put his tunic on, for shortly he would have to go on defaulter's parade. He looked his friend straight in the eye and said with feeling, "I've never said this to you, didn't think I needed to, but there is something I have to say."

"And what's that?"

Albert stuck out his hand and grasped the surprised Ernest by his, and shook it, vigorously. "Thank you for being my friend, my only real reason to keep going."

Ernest suddenly felt extremely guilty.

Monday, 2nd November 1914.

The move to East Grinstead railway station took place smoothly and in the sequence laid down on the published daily routine orders for Saturday. These instructions had been duly broken into their constituent parts by the squadron commanders and so on down along the chain of command. Everyone knew exactly where they had to be and at what time.

The colonel and the adjutant were at the main gates of the camp to watch "C" Squadron canter out from Forest Row for the move to the train station for the 40 minutes or so required to get there. Military Police on motor-cycles led the way.

As they trotted out of the encampment, their squadron commander, Captain Liebert, ordered an "Eyes left" and saluted the colonel as his squadron passed by. The colonel returned the acknowledgement and called out cheerily, "Have a good and safe journey men!" He felt very proud of his Yeomanry as they rode by, for they looked exactly what they were, every inch a fighting outfit.

The Squadron Serjeant Major of "C" Troop had unexpectedly gone down during the night with acute appendicitis and had been rushed off to hospital for emergency surgery. The adjutant had already dispatched a telegraph to their new Brigade Headquarters and had asked for a replacement to join them immediately upon their arrival in France.

Finally, the 2 wagons containing the company stores drove past. They would take a couple of hours to travel the 8 miles, but that was all the better. It would give "A" Squadron the time to get their horses onboard the train and settle the men down.

The colonel left just after 11 a.m. and made his way to the station, leaving his adjutant to finally hand over Forest Row to a detachment of the Sussex (Garrison) Battalion, soldiers that were too old to go on active service. They had taken over the guard duties at the camp on the Sunday at noon, leaving the regiment free to carry out its business of the move.

The headquarters and maxim gun sections were the last to leave, and as they left the adjutant gave the keys of the office safe to the elderly captain who was in charge of the detachment. It felt odd leaving the place, but there it was. He formally saluted the captain of the Sussex Regiment and said, "Here is the orderly room safe key, Thomas, hold it for the next regiment who comes here."

The captain returned the salute and took the key. "Good luck Stanley, to you and your men," he said. Ceremoniously he added; "I have the camp!"

"Thank you." He took the reins of his horse offered to him by his batman. They were the last 2 men of the North Somerset Yeomanry to leave Forest Row.

30 minutes later they were at the train station. Dismounting, the adjutant handed the reins of his horse to his servant. He would look after it and ensure that it went aboard the train safely.

Serjeant Bristow suddenly appeared in front of the adjutant. He had halted smartly and had thrown up a textbook salute. Captain Bates smiled, for he liked Bristow enormously. A natural athlete and a born soldier, big Serjeant Bristow was popular with everyone, officers and men alike.

"Sir," he said. "The colonel instructed me to keep an eye open for you when you arrived and escort you to his carriage."

The adjutant smiled. "Thank you, Serjeant Bristow. Lead on please." Bristow marched off down the platform, the adjutant following dutifully on behind. The middle carriage of this special train was reserved for the regiment's officers, with one complete compartment reserved for the colonel and the adjutant. Arriving at this carriage the serjeant knocked on its door before opening it.

Inside the colonel was writing something in his personal diary. He looked up and beamed a smile at his adjutant. "Ah, Stanley!" he welcomed.

"Good afternoon, sir."

"All well?"

"Yes sir. The camp is now in the safe hands of the Sussex's. Everything proceeded smoothly and without any problems at all."

"Good. The station master has just been to me to say that everything is proceeding to plan and there are only the headquarters and machine guns to load now."

"Excellent."

The colonel turned to his diary and started to write once more whilst the adjutant selected himself a place to sit. After about 10 minutes there was a rap on the carriage door and the adjutant looked through the window to see his servant. He beckoned to him.

The door opened and the batman saluted. "All done sir," he reported, indicating to him that his horse and equipment had been safely loaded.

The colonel looked up and smiled. "How is it going back there?"

Trooper Arthur Bush replied, "Extremely well sir, although the earlier arrivals are getting a bit restless, I think."

The colonel nodded. "That's not surprising. They have been here some while now. Go and find Lieutenant Holwell and tell him that the colonel requests he reports to him."

"Very good sir." The batman saluted and left.

Within 5 minutes a breathless quartermaster arrived and reported to the colonel. The colonel eyed him up and down and said, "How much longer are we going to be, Holwell. Some of the animals are getting restless."

The quartermaster gulped a little and said, "We are almost ready, colonel. The last of the horses have been put into their compartments and my staff are just doing a final check of the area. We should be ready to go in about 15 minutes."

The colonel nodded. "When you are ready, come back to me and let me know."

The relived quartermaster gave a hardly disguised sigh of relief. "Of course, sir."

After he had gone the adjutant said, "I know you don't think much of him sir, but I think that he has proved himself over the last few weeks."

The colonel grunted in annoyance. "Damme if you aren't right, Stanley. I can't help but dislike him, but to be fair, he has proved himself somewhat in the last few weeks."

"Perhaps a word of encouragement to him sir?"

The colonel frowned.

15 minutes later the quartermaster returned to the carriage with the stationmaster in tow. He reported to the colonel, "Everything and everyone is loaded sir. With your permission, I should like to tell the stationmaster that we are ready to proceed.

The colonel looked to the adjutant, who gently nodded his head. The colonel unexpectedly smiled at the harassed quartermaster, the architect of the successful logistical move. "Yes please, Arthur," he said.

Lieutenant Holwell eyes opened wide a little, surprised by the fact that the colonel had called him by his first name for the very first time. He saluted, and as he was about to leave the colonel added, "Thank you, Arthur - and your men - for the job you have done today, and in the past. It is of no small matter that it is because of you and your department that the move has been so successful."

A beaming quartermaster saluted the colonel and left him, talking earnestly to the station master beside him.

The colonel looked at his adjutant. "Will that do, do you think?"

The adjutant grinned in a boyish way. "Without a doubt, colonel."

A minute or so later the stationmaster stood outside the carriage and held his green flag up high. He looked towards the colonel who nodded his assent. The station master furiously waved his flag and blew his whistle. With a hiss of ejected steam and with a juddering start, the first of the trains carrying the North Somerset Yeomanry slowly rattled out of the station, gradually gaining momentum as it headed towards the docks at Southampton. From somewhere a faint sound of cheering could be heard. The colonel smiled.

The adjutant took out his war diary, and using a pencil made his first official entry into it. "Monday 2nd November 1914.

Forest Row.

The regiment, strength 26 officers, 1 warrant officer and 474 other ranks with 500 horses under the command of Lt. Col. G.C. Glynn D.S.O. left Forest Row in 4 special trains to Southampton where it embarked during the evening on S.S. Rosetti."

The journey took a little longer than expected as on 2 occasions the 4 special trains had to stop to allow others priority on the line. Eventually they reached Southampton some 3 hours later, at approximately 4 p.m. The trains went straight into the docks where their transport ship, the S.S. "Rossetti" lay alongside waiting for them.

By the time the colonel and the adjutant had got off the train, the horses were already starting to be led off their carriages and straight onboard the ship up a specially constructed wooden ramp that took them right into where they would be stabled for the short voyage.

The colonel and the adjutant were met by Captain Brooking, who had previously gone on ahead with the regiment's transport. He was already settled in and he conducted them to their quarters. They were lucky in that they both had single cabins, but the remaining officers were in 6 man billets whilst the men were split up by squadrons and in close proximity to each other.

Each squadron was conducted by a guide and taken to the huge mess decks so that there was no possibility of men wandering aimlessly around the ship. As each mess deck was filled a serjeant was left to supervise it, with strict instructions that the men should stay in their bunks until supper time, which would be announced later.

When the colonel entered his cabin he found that his batman, Trooper Adams, was already there and unpacking his bag.

He waited until Adams had finished and said, "And where is your billet?"

"I'm just down the corridor and through the first bulkhead sir. All the officers' batmen are billeted there."

The colonel nodded. "Good. Fetch me my adjutant will you."

"Straight away sir." Adams left the cabin and closed the door behind him and Colonel Glynn surveyed what he had. There was a scuttle from which he could look out from, together with a table and 2 chairs. There was also a small chest of drawers and a metal wardrobe in which he could hang a few items up. The bed was a rudimentary one with a mattress, sheets, and 2 ship's blankets on top. He noted irritably that he only had 1 pillow. He liked to have 2. There was a gentle rap on the door.

"Come in."

The adjutant entered. "You sent for me, colonel?"

"Ah, Stanley. Take a chair will you." The adjutant sat down and took out his notebook and pencil. "What I would like to do is brief all of the squadron commanders at 7 p.m., so you will have to find somewhere to do that. Secondly, I want the quartermaster to let me know personally when all of the stores and equipment have been loaded."

There was a rap on the cabin door. "Come in," said the colonel.

The door opened and Captain Brooking entered. "Just to let you know, colonel, that the loading is going perfectly well. All of the horses should be aboard within the hour and the company wagons are about to be lifted on as well. All of the men are aboard and safely in their barrack rooms."

"Well done Hugh," he congratulated.

"Thank you, sir. If you are ready, I would like to take you to meet the officer commanding the ship's troops onboard, Colonel Lovat."

"Capital! No time like the present, is there." The colonel and the adjutant both stood up and followed the Officer Commanding "B" Squadron as he led them through a maze of corridors, continually going upwards, until they arrived on the bridge of the ship, where the Officer Commanding Embarked Forces was awaiting them.

After meeting the ship's colonel, a once retired but now recalled to duty officer, he returned to his cabin. He smiled when he noticed that a second pillow had been added to his already made up bed. The deadlight had been placed across the ship's scuttle and tightened down by four brass screws. That would ensure that no light would escape from the cabin during the darkness of the night.

The colonel took out his personal diary and began to record the events of the day. He wrote carefully, for it would be a part of the regiment's history to come.

Tuesday, 3rd November 1914.

The S.S. "Rossetti" slipped away from its berth on the morning tide and was gently shepherded out into deeper water by the 2 paddle tugs that had been assigned to her. Soon she was in mid-stream and steaming down the Southampton Water. With final blasts from their sirens the 2 tugs returned to their next appointment and the pilot departed the ship. They were now on their own.

The adjutant had noted with annoyance that he had written the name of the ship as "Rosetti", with one single "s", but quite clearly her name emblazoned across the front of the bridge was "Rossetti". He had resolved not to change the entry into the unit's war diary, after all, it would be bad form to make a mistake in the very first entry he had made!

As they reached the open sea 2 mean and lean destroyers belching black smoke from their 3 funnels each came racing down towards them. The men of the Yeomanry who were up on deck gave excited yells as the ships dashed past, and then suddenly they both executed a turn at speed, one to port and one to starboard. Completing their manoeuvre, they raced past the troopship and passed one on either side, being cheered madly by the Yeomanry who were waving their caps across to the ships. They vessels slowed down and took up their relative escort positions. They would stay with the S.S. "Rossetti" for the journey to see that she safely made her short voyage, for there was always the danger of a German submarine being present.

"I've never seen anything like it!" commented an excited Alf Cleall to his mate, Charlie Gibbs.

Charlie grinned. "Bloody hell, that was impressive!"

3 other serjeants were part of the small band of soldiers that stood on the upper deck of the ship that was reserved for the S.N.C.O.'s and Warrant Officers. Charlie Gooding, his eyes ablaze with exhilaration, commentated, "Bloody hell, boys! We are proper soldiers now!"

His mate, Serjeant James Bristow nodded in agreement. "Won't be long now then, will it."

"Too bloody soon for me!" interjected Ernie Evans, an older serjeant. His thoughts kept returning to his beloved wife Alma and his children, Ernest and Victor, whom he had left at home back in North Lodge, North Parade, Bath. He suddenly began to feel extremely nostalgic and he looked longingly back towards the land.

Spontaneously, each man suddenly turned to each other and shook hands all round.

Charlie took out his pocket watch and looked at it. "It's 9 a.m. now, lads. It'll take us about 6 hours to get across, hopefully on time."

The Isle of Wight began to gradually slip away behind them and many of the North Somerset Yeomanry casts a backwards glance of what was to be, and unbeknown to them, their last glimpse of England.

Half an hour later, Charlie pointed towards one of the destroyers. "Look," he said. "That destroyer is signalling us. I wonder what that's about?"

Suddenly the ship's siren gave three blasts, and the cry went out – "Action Stations! Action Stations! Embarked forces to emergency stations! Embarked forces to emergency stations!"

"Christ!" shouted Alf. "Grab your preservers and get to your lifeboat station!"

The lead destroyer suddenly threw depth charges spiralling high into the air, and about 30 seconds later huge eruptions of water marked the spot where they had detonated. Someone shouted out, "It must be a submarine!" and any thoughts of not hurrying to their life-boat stations amongst the Yeomanry were instantly dispelled.

Arriving at his appointed place which they had only rehearsed last night when in harbour, Alf quickly counted up his men. There was 1 missing. He couldn't make out who it was, but based on previous history he had a pretty good idea of who it might be. He scanned the faces for Fitch. He was not there.

"Anyone seen Fitch!" he called out in exasperation.

Corporal Tom Brown replied, "He was on the mess-deck just now, Serjeant. I think he was looking for his life-preserver."

"Damn!" said Alf.

Charlie Gibbs, shouted, "Go and get him, Alf. I've got the men covered!"

Alf nodded and dashed though the open doorway and into the ship's main corridor. He cursed his luck that Fitch was in his squadron, for Fitch was a Radstock man but had chosen to join the Yeomanry in Bath rather than Shepton Mallet, although the latter was closer.

He passed some sailors hurrying the other way, and going down 2 sets of ladders came to the mess-deck that he was responsible for. He heard hammering on its closed steel door and faint cries for help emanating from behind it.

The serjeant cursed, for somebody had slammed the bulkhead door tightly shut and you could not get the steel latches open. Looking around, Alf stopped a sailor who was rushing by him. "Help me get the door open," he ordered.

The sailor shook his head. "Sorry mate! I've got a more important duty to attend to."

"I've got one of my men trapped in there," he explained, jerking his thumb towards the messdeck. "The latches are jammed." The sailor quickly opened a box on the bulkhead and said, "Use the axe to knock it upwards!" and then ran off.

Grasping the implement the serjeant gave a couple of hefty knocks to the stuck latches and they came away easily enough. He flung the door open to be greeted by the sight of a miserable Fitch clutching desperately to his life preserver.

"Someone closed the door on me," he explained apologetically.

"Get to your lifeboat station now, Fitch. We'll sort this out later."

The ship gave a violent lurch as made an emergency turn to port and Alf staggered backwards and went flying into the passageway, Fitch landing on top of him. Scrambling to their feet, the 2 men went running up and along to their assigned emergency station. Charlie Gibbs gave a sigh of relief as his friend and Fitch appeared.

The ship was going at its top speed of about 12 knots and was taking evasive action. During the time of his absence below looking for Fitch a third destroyer had appeared and it had also joined in the attack.

Suddenly a white track could be seen racing towards the transport ship and she heeled desperately over to port, the soldiers clinging on for dear life. The ship shuddered and shook as she threw herself into an emergency reverse, slowing down as she did so. With 5 or 6 feet to spare, the racing torpedo sped by and under the bow.

"Over there!" someone called, and suddenly a submarine had seemingly erupted out of the sea, bow first, and making a huge splash as it came back down again. The Yeomanry cheered.

The lead destroyer raced towards the surfaced submarine and brought her deck guns into action, firing her main armament as she did so. The first shot splashed alongside the conning tower as a figure suddenly appeared on the top of it. The next shot hit the submarine and, with a tremendous roar, she exploded amidships, the vessel breaking in 2 parts. Like an inverted "V" she slipped below the surface of the foaming sea, taking her enemy crew with her.

A dark black stain of oil marked the spot where she sank and the lead destroyer slowed down, searching for any survivors or any sign of anything that might have identified their attacker. It did not. Once more a flurry of flashing lights was aimed at them, and almost immediately the engines were brought back into their normal transit speed of 8 knots. The call, "Stand down from emergency stations," was quickly shouted around the ship. The Yeomanry's first taste of real action had ended for the better, and the ship shook with the resounding cheers of the men.

Major Lubbock was not pleased. The fact that one of his men had been almost left behind during the real emergency had reached him. He had his Squadron S.N.C.O's lined up in front of him. "What happened, Serjeant Cleall," he asked.

Alf explained. "When we went to emergency stations, I noticed that Fitch was not there sir, although Corporal Brown had told me that he had seen him in the mess deck looking for his preserver."

Serjeant Gibbs added, "I asked Serjeant Cleall to go below and get him, sir."

Alf nodded. "When I got to the steel bulkhead I found that it was shut tight and the steel handles were rammed down so hard they couldn't be opened by one man. I could hear Fitch calling for help from behind it."

"And then?"

"A passing sailor pointed out the to me where an emergency axe was placed and I used that to knock up and free the wedged bolts."

"How did it get jammed?"

"I don't know sir. All I know is that when the sailors were rushing around shutting the waterproof doors, they must have used a lot of force to slam the latches down."

Major Lubbock looked thoughtful. "It is possible that after the door was closed the lurching of the ship forced it too tight for Fitch to get out by himself. It was just pure bad luck I suppose." The major had made up his mind. "Alright men, we'll put it down as just one of those things and an accident." Major Lubbock gave a little chuckle. "At least we know that Fitch hasn't lost his life-preserver – yet!" His S.N.C.O's gave a laugh in response.

They docked alongside Havre at 3 p.m., the ship filling a just vacated berth, that of a hospital ship. It moved slowly past the S.S. "Rossetti", the large red cross showing plainly on its white side. This was also the first glimpse of wounded soldiers for all of them. They passed close enough to it for them to one of them waving his crutch towards them, and barely catching his words – "You poor sods!"

Once alongside the men of the Army Service Corps and Army Veterinary Corps swarmed aboard to commence the unloading. Surprisingly, although the ship had been put through some violent manoeuvring during the course of the action, none of the horses had suffered any injuries.

The regiment started to disembark, but as the port was smaller it took some time. Squadron Serjeant Major Reeves, of the 7th Hussars, was waiting for them. He was a regular soldier and who already had seen action and he was of an imposing stature. He reported himself to the adjutant who immediately took him along to "A" Squadron. To say that Major Lubbock was delighted to have him was an understatement.

At 6 p.m. the regiment was lined up, by squadrons, and ready for the short ride to Rest Camp number 3 at La Hêve, some 2½ miles north west of Havre. For the first time they carried their rifles at the ready position, the butts of the weapons held in the leather cups on the right hand side of the saddlery. They had practised this method of riding many times, but the difference was that this time the bullets they had charged their magazines with were of the Mk VII variety, the current .303 calibre round of choice for the British Army on active service. The transport wagons were still not off-loaded yet, and that would take another couple of hours.

They moved off, military police on motor-cycles leading the way, for there were strict one-way military routes to follow. This meant that the traffic flow could be maintained at an easy rate and avoided congestion. Some of the civilian population did not like it, as the route was strictly enforced at all times by both the British and French military police, and woe betide anyone who flouted the regulation.

At a steady trot it did not take long for the men to get to the mostly bell-tented area. The officers fared better, for they were put into wooden billets.

Squadron routine quickly took over and the quartermaster allocated each section of 8 men a place in one of the tents. The tents were in rows, and ran in straight lines numbered from A to L, the front tent being numbered as 1, then 2 and then so on until the end of the line was reached. Duckboards were laid down between each row of tents, for each side of them was a taste of what was to come – wet mud. At the far end of the camp and on the outer extremities were the toilet blocks. They were a bit of a luxury as they were arranged as a line of single wooden cubicles, so in this instance men would have some sort of privacy.

In the middle of the encampment were the officers' and serjeants' messes with accommodation. The whole rest camp set-up was complete with a large wooden cook house and stores complex. The regimental headquarters were also there.

By mid-evening the weather turned noticeably colder with the odd flakes of snow falling now and then, but it was far too wet for it to settle. Men from a garrison battalion were carrying out security duties and manned the guardroom, so it made it that much easier for the regiment to get ready for the morning. The Base Commandant, Colonel H.B. Williams D.S.O., would inspect them at 11.00 a.m. in full marching order but less horses. It was felt that after the sea journey the horses needed a little bit of extra time to settle in.

Wednesday, 4th November 1914.

The regiment were standing patiently in the heavy drizzle and the men were getting very cold and wet. The colonel was pleased that they were not mounted as the smell of wet war horses was not one that he cared for very much, despite him being such a fine equestrian. At 11 a.m. the base commandant arrived. At that moment the rain suddenly ceased and the sun burst through what had been a solid block of grey cloud. The effect on morale was tangible and immediate. The colonel called his Yeomanry to attention.

The inspecting officer's motor car came to a standstill and Colonel Glynn walked forward to greet him.

"Morning sir," he said, saluting crisply as he did so.

"Morning Glynn." Colonel Williams smiled and said, "The weather has become kind to you. Welcome to France." The 2 men shook hands.

"Would you care to inspect my men sir? They would be pleased if you did." The colonel smiled, for he was used to handling many regiments as they passed through his rest camps, but this was the first territorial unit to do so under his command.

The colonel was one of the few men who knew the true extent of the casualties at that time, but he was under orders not to divulge them to anyone. In 8 weeks of fierce fighting the regular units were beginning to run out of manpower and now the territorials were being flung in to help fill the gaps. "Heaven help us!" he thought to himself, for he, too, considered the territorials to be "weekend warriors" who would find it hard to measure up to the standards of the regular army.

"Thank you Glynn, I shall be pleased to do so."

"This way, sir," he indicated, pointing towards Major Lubbock, whose "A" Squadron would be the first to be reviewed.

As they approached, Major Lubbock stepped forward and gave the approaching officers a general salute with his sword. "Sir," he said, addressing Colonel Williams, "my squadron is at your disposal." He then fell in behind the colonel as he walked along the front row, stopping occasionally to engage the men in a general conversation.

He then finished with the front rank and moved on to "B" and "C" Squadrons, before finally stopping at the headquarters and Maxim guns section and spoke for some length with Major Matthews, the Maxim's officer. Colonel Williams asked him for his opinion of the weapon and if he thought his men were good enough to go into the trenches with them.

The major looked towards his colonel for guidance, and he nodded in an affirmative manner. "Well sir, to tell you the truth they are an effective weapon, but cumbersome and manpower intensive. But my men are up to the mark on it sir, and can be relied upon to act to the best of the gun's efficiency."

"Efficiency?"

"Yes sir. As you know these weapons have a tendency to jam, and jam sometimes at the most critical of moments."

The base commandant nodded. "I agree with you there," he said.

Matthews explained further and he added, "Before we came here, sir, I ensured that my men had the basic training at Forest Row on the Vickers machine gun, which I know is the weapon of choice out here."

The inspecting officer beamed. He turned to Colonel Glynn and said, "You have some bright officers in your Yeomanry and I am glad that he has just told me what he has." He turned to the Major Matthews and said: "You will be pleased to know that amongst the other cargo being carried in the S.S. "Rossetti" was a consignment of Vickers guns. Later on today I shall try my very best to get you some of them. I hope to be able to replace your maxim guns with Vickers!"

"Oh I say sir," responded the surprised officer. "What wonderful news!"

"That is not all of the marvellous news that I have for you," he said, a mysterious look on his face. "Colonel Glynn," he said, "I am very happy with the state of your men and their preparedness to enter the fray. I have brought with me your next set of orders, which I have been instructed to hand to you personally. Shall we retire to your office?"

Glynn gave a look of surprise. "Of course, sir," he responded at once. "Follow me this way, if you please."

"If would be a good idea if you brought your adjutant with you," he intimated. By way of explanation he added, "It will save you some time later."

"Adjutant, please join us," he called across to Captain Bates.

"Very good sir," came the immediate rejoinder.

As they approached "A" Squadron the colonel called across to the Squadron Commander and his second-in-command. "Major Lubbock, would you please take over." Colonel Glynn was feeling satisfied with his Yeomanry, for the inspection had gone very well. They were walking along the rear rank of "A" Squadron when all that changed.

Colonel Williams suddenly stopped. He pointed towards one of the troopers and with a horrified look on his face said, "My God Glynn! That trooper has only one spur on!"

The adjutant screwed his eyes up in despair and said to the serjeant on the end of the row, "Serjeant Cleall! Take that man's name and report him to me later!"

Serjeant Cleall took one step forward and saluted. "Very good sir!" he called. Walking along the line he came to the trooper's back, and brushing through the line took out his pencil and notebook to take the offender's name. He did not have to ask for it. "Fitch!" he spat. "You are for it now my boy!"

The 2 colonels and the adjutant were sat in the regimental headquarters, enjoying a cup of hot tea. The adjutant had a sheet of paper attached to a millboard and was ready to take notes.

"An excellent inspection, Geoffrey. Your men did you credit. Pity about the last man though."

Inwardly the North Somerset Yeomanry commander was fuming. He would deal severely with the miscreant later. "Thank you, colonel. Now then, what do you have to tell me?"

The colonel pondered for a while and then spoke. "When you left England there was probably some idea that you would not be sent up into the fighting line, but employed on more peaceful duties. Let me dispel that idea very quickly. As I have already told you, your Maxim guns are probably being replaced by Vickers and they should be here soon. Not only that, the 5 unserviceable wagons you have will be exchanged at the same time, so you will need to get your men working to unload these wagons so that they can load the replacements."

The sound of the pencil on the paper seemed to be quite loud as the adjutant made his notes. He continued, "The Germans are advancing far quicker than we anticipated, Geoffrey. We had hoped to give you a months updated training here in France, but that is not to be the case. We are sending you up to St. Omer tomorrow."

Glynn gave a start. "Tomorrow? As soon as that?"

"I am afraid so," he replied, "but from what I have seen of your regiment I am sure that they will take it in their stride." He reached inside his tunic pocket and withdrew a standard army buff envelope, heavily marked in red ink with "Most Secret" stamped on the front and back. "Here are your detailed orders," he said. "Now then, I am sure that you need to crack on and get things moving."

All 3 men stood up together and the colonels shook hands. "Good luck to you and your regiment, Geoffrey, for I think that you are going to be forced into the fight much sooner than anyone anticipated!"

"Thank you sir."

Putting on their caps the officers went outside to where the colonel's staff car was already waiting, its engine running. Shaking hands once more, the visiting officer climbed into the rear seat of the vehicle and ordered his driver to move off.

Colonel Glynn looked towards his adjutant and said, "Come on Stanley, we have a bit of heavy planning to complete."

"Very good sir. I will just send for the quartermaster if you don't mind, he's also got some fast work to do."

The colonel's opinion of his quartermaster had changed dramatically in the last few days, and he added, "I am sure that he is up to the mark, Stanley, but yes, please do send for him. I don't envy him his task."

The adjutant smiled.   It was good to know that the colonel now had complete confidence in all of his officers. The men walked back into the company office where the company clerk, Trooper Harding, was busily typing away. He stood up to attention when the officers walked in. "Harding, go and get the quartermaster for me. He is to stop what he is doing and report to me immediately."

"Yes sir!"

Despite the Base Commandant's promise, the Vickers machine guns were not forthcoming, much to the disappointment of Major Matthews. He did not know that heavy losses of the Vickers machine guns and their complete crews were now taking place on a daily basis at the Front and the ones that had safely arrived on the S.S. "Rossetti" were urgently required to replace them.

Thursday, 5th November and Friday, 6th November 1914.

The regiment did not have long to wait before they moved out of La Hêve. They were ordered to entrain for St. Omer which lay about 190 miles away and close to the Belgium border, north east of where they were now located. They left in 3 special trains between 3.45 p.m. and 6.45 p.m. from Havre. It was a long and tiring journey, and eventually after frequent stops they arrived at the destination late the next afternoon. The men and horses were equally weary, and it was not until 8 p.m. did the regiment get their first hot meal of the day, a basic stew.

They found themselves billeted in a French artillery barracks there so at least had the benefit of being behind stone walls and in comfortable rooms, which was just as well. Outside the rain beat itself down into a body chilling temperature that would quickly freeze a man and could cause frost bite.

The reality of war was forced upon them, for what many took to be thunder turned out to be the sound of the artillery shells exploding. Sometimes the noise would be heard quietly in the background, and at other times it became somewhat louder as barrages at the Front from either side suddenly took on a new intensity.

Serjeant Alf Cleall had the task of supervising the men who were undergoing Field Punishment Number 1, and as soon as they had been fed they were handcuffed into the familiar position of the crucifixion.

There were 3 men on Field Punishment Number 1 now, the unfortunate Fitch being added to the number after being sentenced to 7 days by the furious colonel.   Ernest went by to see his chum and to offer his sympathies to him, but now he took no satisfaction in doing so. He had taken Albert Fitch's spur and had thrown it into the mud, where it would not be found. Suddenly, he began to feel very guilty about it all and resolved to stop his merciless onslaught against him. After all, it was not entirely his fault. No, it was hers, the bitch.

Saturday, 7th November 1914.

The next day the regiment paraded at 10.30 a.m. and marched to its billeting area in and around Esquerdes, a farming village some 4 miles or so from St. Omer, France, in the Pas de Calais Department. It was not too far from the Belgian border. The men were found accommodation in sheds and the horses picketed out in the open on their pegs and heel ropes. The sounds of the guns were much louder now, but the men had begun to ignore them, for they were not causing the regiment any harm.

Some excitement was caused when a German Taube reconnaissance aeroplane, with its black crosses clearly visible on its wings, flew over the area in which they were billeted. It hung around for a moment or so before a lone British aircraft, identified as a Bristol Scout by Captain English, came hurtling down from above it and narrowly missed it. The Taube waggled its wings as the British machine came at him again and turned around, apparently its mission over.

Someone called, "Why doesn't he shoot?" and Captain English nonchalantly replied, "Because they are scout 'planes old boy, and the aircraft aren't armed."

The men watched in fascination as the British aircraft attempted to manoeuvre itself above the Taube and tried to force it down by putting its wheels on the enemy aircraft's wings, but the German pilot was having none of it. At the last moment he would slip aside and after a few more daring attempts, the British pilot gave up. The pilots waved to each other in acknowledgement as they both went their separate ways, honours shared about even in the tussle.

Captain English thrilled at the sight of it all, thinking that the day of the aircraft was being thrust upon them. At that moment he resolved to put in for a transfer to the Royal Flying Corps at some future date.

The men had their first mail delivery since they had left England. Amongst them Ernest, once again, stole the letter addressed to Fitch. There was also a letter addressed to him, and as he passed out the mail to the remaining members of the squadron, he speculated as to who the letter might be from? Some old acquaintance perhaps?

He got back to his tent and sat on his cot before furtively looking about him to make sure that no-one was observing his actions, and lifting up the lid of his wooden trunk, he placed his comrade's letter in with the others that he had already taken. He didn't even bother to read the missive now, for in truth he knew that his marriage to Alice was over. The only question was "when to end it." He was tempted to do it now so that he could stop the allotment of pay that he was sending her, but he had not yet quite made up his mind.

He opened the letter addressed to him and his eyes suddenly took on a fierce and determined look. It read:

"Dear Mr Summers,

It is with a heavy heart that I write to you to let you know that 5 artillerymen have been billeted in your house.   I think it only fair that you, a soldier who is serving our country in its hour of need, should know that your wife, Alice, is now consorting with one of them, a serjeant by the name of Albert Willcox.

Signed, a true friend."

Ernest re-read the letter several times and with a strangled cry threw himself face down on his cot. He stuffed the ball of his fist into his mouth to stop himself crying out loud. "The bitch!" he thought.

Sunday, 8th November 1914.

In the afternoon the whole regiment were sent out to practice digging trenches, their first introduction to the quality of the French soil. Thankfully the rain had stopped and they quickly got into the swing of constructing them. Before they had left England they had practised this several times, so the regiment knew what to do right from the beginning. The men with pickaxes went first, followed by those with spades, who shovelled out the loose earth to form a rampart at the front of the trench facing the enemy. Some of the earth spoils were put into a few sandbags, for there were not many to spare in rear echelon positions, and put around the top of the spoil to form a loophole from which a sniper could fire. Normally it would take up to a day to get a good trench in, and thereafter it would be improved day by day by the men living in them.

For training purposes only, each squadron had to put in 10 yards of revetment, using corrugated iron sheets and metal spikes. Again, these items were needed more urgently at the Front so great care was taken in placing them in, for they would have to be recovered on completion of the exercise for further training use.

The colonel and the adjutant came around at about 5 p.m. to inspect each squadron's work, approving or disapproving as needed. If it was approved, the squadron would remove the precious revetment fittings and then would fill the trench in before returning to the encampment. If it was not approved, the squadron were made to stay there and correct their errors. By 6 p.m. the whole exercise was over, and the men returned for their well-earned supper.

After his field punishment was over, Fitch was released to return to his accommodation. He stopped off in the beer tent to buy one. The men were rationed to no more than 2 bottles of ale in the evening before the "Last Post" was sounded. He spotted Ernie who was sat alone on the far side of the tent. He did not look very happy.

Albert put on a smile and said, "You don't look very pleased, Ernie."

Ernest glanced up at his friend. He wasn't going to say anything, but then he reasoned that it didn't matter anymore. Fitch already thought that his wife was having an affair with another man for Ernie had woven that web of deceit in order to hurt him. He said, "I had another letter today."

Albert sat down and took a deep swig out of his bottle. "Bad news?"

He nodded. "It's her, the bitch!" he said vehemently. He took it out the letter and passed it to Ernie to read. "Bloody hell!"

"Bloody hell is right! It will be when I get home I can tell you."

"Do you want another drink?"

"Can't, I've already used up my 2 tokens."

"Bugger it mate! You can have one of mine!" Albert rose to his feet and went to the bar, spending his token on another French lager style beer that had been made locally. "Here!" He passed the ½ litre bottle to his best friend and a grateful Ernie took a huge swig from it.

Monday, 9th November 1914.

The morning was spent grooming the horses and making sure that they were all fit and ready for when they were needed. Each squadron went for a short ride to maintain the fitness of the steeds and then returned by 11 a.m. It was noticeable, too, that the mounts seemed to have become more at ease with the sound of the continuous gunfire, for they appeared to hardly take any notice of it.

The regiment paraded at 12.30 p.m. for drill under the watchful eyes and control of R.S.M. Shakespeare. All of the squadrons were involved with the exception of Major Gibbs and 1 officer and 2 N.C.O.'s per squadron who were dispatched to the nearby village of Blendecques in France, about 4 miles from St. Omer. They had received orders that they were to help on the following day to dig the defensive trenches that were being put in place by the Royal Engineers. Major Gibbs was made responsible for the detailed planning of the day. His task was to sort out what needed doing and to advise the adjutant accordingly of the manpower requirements.

Back home in England, Trooper Summer's wife, Alice, received some unexpected visitors. A man and woman arrived at her front door without an invitation to interview her.

She answered the loud knock. "Mrs Summers?"

"Yes."

"Wife of Trooper Ernest Summers?"

She gasped, her hand flying to her mouth and thinking they were the bringers of bad news.

The man shook his head and quickly said, "No, no, Mrs Summers. On the contrary, we have some very good news for you. My name is Mr Arkell and this is Mrs Ellis. We are a government agency and working on their behalf. May we come in?"

Mrs Summers opened the door and said, "You had better come in then. I have just made myself a cup of tea. Would you like one?"

The man and woman looked at each other, and the man nodded. Mrs Ellis said, "That would be nice."

"What's this all about?" she enquired. They were sat around her kitchen table, drinking from the beverages that she had just made.

Mr Arkell placed his tea upon the table. "The army have notified us that your husband is now serving overseas and that he has made an allotment of 3s 6d from his pay of 7s 7p per week. Is that correct?" the man asked.

She nodded. "Yes".

Mrs Ellis then joined in the conversation. "New government rules have been introduced to pay a separation allowance to the wives of every soldier who is serving abroad.

That aroused the interest of Mrs Summers immediately. "Really? I have heard nothing about this. How much is it?"

Mr Arkell explained, "That is hardly surprising, but the main thing is that you have to claim your 7s 7d a week allowance."

"How do I do that?"

"We represent the S.S.F.A. and our organisation has been charged with the duty of visiting soldiers' wives and family to help them make a claim."

"Who are S.S.F.A."

"Our long name is really The Soldiers and Sailors Family Association, but we shorten it to S.S.F.A. We can help you with your claim."

"Are you here to do that?"

"Yes," he replied. "But we have to ask you some questions in order to make our decision on the matter to be made to the army. They have charged us with the sole responsibility to make an endorsement of any application," and here the man's voice took on a warning note, "or not to approve it."

"What do you need to know?"

The man looked at his companion before giving a discreet cough and said, "One of the main criteria for the recommendation of a payment of separation allowance is that the woman has to be of a good character."

Alice became a little indignant. "Well," she said, a tint of redness in her cheeks, "I can assure you that I am!"

Mrs Ellis then asked in a quiet voice, "You have 5 soldiers billeted here, I believe?"

"Quite correct."

Mr Arkell twiddled his fingers together. "How are you getting on with them?"

"They are no problem. They are all good lads and the serjeant is very helpful to me. He even gets them to cut up my firewood and tend the garden, if they have the time to."

The pair from S.S.F.A. looked at each other. "Do you mind looking after them?"

Alice shook her head. "No, I don't mind it at all. It is everyone's duty to help our country in her hour of need. My husband is away fighting for his country and I am helping him by making sure that his comrades are being properly cared for."

"Do you do anything more that you should for them," Mr Arkell asked carefully, watching for any reaction to the question.

She nodded. "Well," she said. "They do pay me for doing their washing and ironing, which I don't really mind doing at all, what with my husband being away." She put her hand over her eyes and said in a low voice, "I do miss him so."

Mr Arkell and Mrs Ellis smiled, their moral obligation on behalf of the army now having been successfully discharged. "Thank you Mrs Summers, that's all we require to know," he said.

Mrs Ellis took out a form and said, "Just fill this in, Mrs Summers, and we'll take your claim with us."

She blushed. "I can't read or write," she admitted.

Unflustered, Mrs Ellis took the form and started to fill it in. "That's where we, of the Soldiers and Sailors Family Association come in. We will do it for you. Now then, what is your first name or names?"

"Alice, Mrs Alice Summers." Mrs Ellis commenced to fill in the claim.

The North Somerset Yeomanry paraded at 8.15 a.m. and were wearing their full marching order. They were to move as a dismounted unit and so they marched to Blendecques to provide the man-power required to dig the trenches. There was some grumbling amongst the troopers, for they did not like to be treated as infantry. They were Yeomanry and were supposed to ride to war! Despite this, the regiment arrived at their appointed place by 9.30 a.m. and were immediately set to work by their overseers, the Royal Engineers.

This time the trenches were to be properly constructed and left in place. They were designed to form part of an emergency defensive line should the Germans break through from the Belgian border. The men worked extremely hard and succeeded in digging a trench in some very difficult ground, resulting in everyone getting thoroughly wet feet. They did not mind, for some thought that it might be they who would, at some point, be occupying these trenches, so they made sure that they were constructed correctly.

One of the engineers grinned and, pointing his steaming hot cup of tea towards a soggy "B" Squadron muttered, "Get used to it my boys. Most of the land at the Front is below the water table. Wait to you got to sleep in it!"

They dug with a will until 1 p.m. and then had a brief meal of cold bully beef rations before marching back to Esquerdes, arriving there at 2.30 p.m. Cold and wet, they first had to exercise the horses before they were dismissed so that they could get out of their wet boots.

The unit medical officer, Captain Edwards, went across to see the adjutant.

"What can I do for you, Charles," he asked affably.

"Just to let you know, Stanley, that I have my first case of trench foot."

"Oh! What's that?"

"It's a condition caused by prolonged exposure to the cold and wet and roughly takes about 1 – 12 days to develop."

"What! Have we a case already?"

The medical officer nodded. "I am afraid so."

"What does it look like?"

The doctor stroked his chin. "Well, the best way I can describe it is that if makes your skin on your feet go white and crinkly, and it can be very painful. If untreated it can lead to damage to the blood vessels in your feet, nerves, skin and muscle."

"Sounds as if it could be nasty! Who has got that?"

"One of your headquarters men, Corporal Corben."

"Corben! He is one of the QM's staff and a trusted and valued man. Is there going to be a problem with him?"

"I don't think so, but I would like to use him as an example to show your S.N.C.O.'s what to look out for in their men should you go permanently into the trenches. I have spoken to Corporal Corben already about my intentions and he is more than happy to participate, hence my talking to you and informing you of his name."

"Does this have to propensity to put him out of action?"

"Not at this stage. We have got it early enough to treat it. He will be excused boots for a couple of days and told to keep his feet dry and warm at all times. He should then be fit enough for duty. He won't be able to do any drill or marching, that's for sure."

"Thank you John. When do you want to do it?"

"After supper tonight, at 7 p.m., in the medical tent?"

"You've got it, and I will be there as well."

"Excellent." He handed the adjutant a piece of paper with an outline of what to look out for. "Can you publish that on orders so that the men will also know the signs as well?

"Of course."

"Thanks. See you later."

After publishing it on the daily routine orders, 2 more men from the Yeomanry reported themselves in sick for they, too, were displaying the first signs of trench foot.

Wednesday, 11th November 1914.

It was a typical training day, commencing with the regiment parading for the usual amount of drill at 8.45 a.m. At 10.50 a.m., and while the regiment was still out in the field, a motor-cycle despatch rider came roaring into the camp. The man ran into the headquarters to urgently seek out the adjutant. One look at the orders was enough to set the adjutant running out of the office and stopping a trooper who happened to be trotting by on his horse.

"You there!" he shouted. "Report to me at once!"

The surprised man immediately rode over to the adjutant. "Do you know where the training ground is?"

"Yes sir. It's over there," he pointed out, thinking he was being helpful.

"I want you to ride at once down there at once and find Colonel Glynn. Tell him we have orders to go immediately to St. Sylvestre. Once you have done that I want you to find the R.S.M. and tell him from me that all drilling is to cease forthwith and he is requested to bring the men back here at best speed – we are to march at once!"

"Very good sir," replied the man and, turning his horse began to walk it away to the training ground.

"Gallop man, gallop" cried out the adjutant in exasperation.

The soldier and horse responded immediately and the they started to hurtle through the camp.

Captain Tyssen happened to arrive on his motor-cycle and, turning off its engine, he removed his leather helmet and goggles. He spoke directly to the adjutant. "Is there a flap on?"

The adjutant grinned. "John! You couldn't have arrived at a much more opportune time, for we have just received emergency orders to march to St. Sylvestre. I want you to take your motor-cycle and go immediately to the G.O.C. 1st Army Corps at Chateau de Trois Tours, at Vlamertinghe, for detailed orders. Do you know where it is?"

"It's about 40 miles away isn't it, just over the border and in Belgium. I think it is somewhere near a town called Ypres, just behind the front line."

Just then the company clerk came racing out of the building, map in hand. "Got it sir," he said breathlessly, pointing out the place.

The adjutant grabbed the map, and together with Captain Tyssen studied the routes. The serjeant who had delivered the message appeared and suddenly intervened. "Excuse me sir, but I am going back there now. If the captain would care to follow me, I'll lead him in."

"Capital, serjeant! Capital! How long will it take?"

"About an hour sir, if we are not diverted."

The adjutant was doing his sums and working out what to do next. He made his decision. "John. This is what I want you to do. Go with the serjeant and get to the G.O.C. headquarters at best speed, find the Brigade Major and get our detailed orders from him. That should take you to roughly a couple of hours from now. When you have got our orders, go straight to St. Sylvestre and find us. Go to the church there, that will be our rendezvous point. If we have not arrived, I just want you stay put. I will request the colonel to gallop ahead of the regiment so that he gets to the church far sooner than any of us. Make sure you deliver our orders personally to him. Got it?"

"Got it." Captain Tyssen kicked started his motor cycle, and setting his flying googles over his leather helmet, followed the despatch rider out of the camp.

The Yeomanry's accredited motor cyclist, Lance Corporal George, was already away delivering a despatch to the Brigade headquarters, so the arrival of the Machine Guns Officer on his personal motor-cycle had been an unexpected bonus.

Four minutes later the colonel arrived. He had taken the trooper's steed and had galloped back to the headquarters. Dismounting, he quickly tied the horse up and ran into the headquarters.

"What's up?" he demanded, a hint of excitement in his voice.

The adjutant handed him the orders, which he had already read. "We are to march immediately to St. Sylvestre, sir. I have directed Captain Tyssen to proceed by motor-cycle to the G.O.C.'s headquarters to collect our written orders. He is then to ride to St. Sylvestre and find you. I have suggested to him that you will be found in the area of the church in the village. May I recommend, sir, that you go on ahead with your batman to that place? That will give you a little time to work out what our next step is going to be."

Colonel Glynn nodded. "Thank you Stanley, that's just what I'll do."

The adjutant added, "I have taken the liberty to have your batman pack your gear and have sent orders for your horses to be saddled and brought around here. With any luck colonel, you will be on your way within 15 minutes."

Glynn grinned. "Dammed good show, Stanley, I will do just that."

"I have also sent for the Squadron Commanders and Major Matthews of the Machine Gun Section to let them know what is happening. They will all be here within the next 10 minutes. The whole regiment should be on the move within the next 2 hours at most."

There was a sharp knock on the office door, and the colonel's batman appeared. "Everything is packed sir. Your kit and equipment are ready for you and our horses are being brought up now."

"Well," thought the colonel, "between them the adjutant and the batman have got everything sorted!" The colonel gave a boyish grin and said, "I'll take 15 minutes before I do anything, Stanley, so I can have a cup of tea before I go."

His batman said, "I have the tea ready sir!"

The colonel nodded. "Have you a map for me Stanley?"

His adjutant grinned and handed it to him, "We are here, sir, and St. Sylvestre is there!"

The colonel took the map from the proffered hand of his adjutant and retired to study it over his cup of tea.

At 1 p.m. the regiment, under the temporary command of Major Lubbock, left their comfortable barracks for the ride to St. Sylvestre. It was not an easy ride, with frequent stops being made for the regiment to move aside, either to let more important and urgent reinforcements pass through them, or to face the grim reality of war. Ambulance after ambulance came streaming by. Along the way the men grimly noted that there were many wooden crosses dotted about, some solitary and others in groups, that marked the last resting place of their fallen comrades. The men were in a sombre mood.

The finally arrived at about 8.45 p.m., and found themselves billeted in 3 farms close to St. Sylvestre. The night was wet and stormy with hardly any respite from it.

Finding the best positions in the open for the horses that they could, they were picketed together in the fields closest to the largest farmhouse. There was a little copse that took the brunt of the driving rain where it was borne coldly by the strong easterly wind. It was not an easy night for the horse pickets either. Besides the noise of the guns, which were much louder now, there was an occasional flash of lightening and roll of thunder, which disturbed the horses even further.

Captain Tyssen had brought orders to the colonel from the Brigade Major. They were to march on even further and proceed to Hooge in Belgium, and without distressing the horses. The colonel surmised to his officers that they were going into battle, and it must be a pretty desperate one if they had to march so far, without rail movement, to get to the Front. Breakfast would be at 8.30 a.m. and the regiment would be in the saddle for 10 a.m. They would eat their rations on the ride, food to be consumed only when they stopped to rest the horses. The men were to tighten their belts. This was the harsh reality of war.

Thursday, 12th November 1914.

The regiment rode to Dranoutre in Belgium at 10 a.m. and proceeded via Bailleul, arriving there at 2.30 p.m. and were billeted in 4 small farms. Once more the steeds were tethered out in the open. The Q.M. reported to the colonel that he had discovered that the water for the horses was extremely poor and on his orders were getting the minimum amount they needed. He did not want the horses to go down with any illnesses. The commanding officer agreed with him.

The colonel made a decision. "Quartermaster," he began, and then changed his mind. "Arthur, I have something to say to you.

"Sir?"

The colonel cleared his throat. He did not have to say what he was going to say to his junior officer, but he was the sort of man who, when he made a mistake, was the first to own up to it. "Before we went to war you may have noticed, Arthur, that sometimes I was a bit short with you."

The Q.M. glanced downwards. "Oh no sir," he responded, but knowing it was exactly true.

He put his hand up. "I want to clearly tell you, Arthur, that I have severely misjudged you in the past. I had not realised how good you and your department were. I was just taking everything for granted."

"Thank you, sir."

"No, I have not finished yet." The colonel cleared his throat. "Since we left Bath I have seen you grow – grow in stature and in confidence. You appear to meet every problem head on and deal with it promptly and efficiently. I am extremely pleased with you. I think that you should know that, although we have not yet been into action, I have had your name forwarded to Sir John French, and today I have been told that your name has been mentioned in his despatches."

The colonel thrust his hand forward and shook that of his surprised Q.M. who seemed to be at a loss for words. "Take comfort, Arthur, in knowing that you are the first man on the North Somerset Yeomanry to receive a recognition for exemplary service in this war."

The startled Q.M. said, "I don't know what to say, sir."

The colonel grinned. "The answer is nothing, old boy. Your Mention in Despatches should appear in the London Gazette next week, and until that happens, only I, the adjutant, and yourself, are aware of the honour. Once the Supplement to the London Gazette has been published, you are free to tell the world.

Lieutenant Holman blushed. "Thank you sir." He thought that how pleased at the news would his dear wife be, for she did fret so about him. Only she knew how he had really felt about the colonel's poor treatment of him in the past. Now all that had changed, and so much for the better. He was really looking forward to writing the news in his next letter home.

Once more Captain Tyssen was despatched to the G.O.C. 1st Army Corp to report their arrival and ask for further orders. These were quickly forthcoming. The colonel could sense that battle was close, so he ordered that all Field Punishment Number 1 offenders were to be set free at this time. He would need every man he had.

There was a fierce battle going on around the Ypres area, and he hoped he would soon be given the opportunity for him and the regiment to take part in it. Everywhere in the unit there was a sense of expectation, for not only could they hear the thundering of the guns, they were close enough to the front line to see the night skies ablaze with light and flares.

It was just his bad luck, Fitch thought, but he really wasn't surprised by it. He had just completed the last session of his penalty that he was to endure when Serjeant Gooding gave them some good news. As he released them from their handcuffs he informed the men that their Field Punishment No. 1 was now suspended, for the likelihood of battle was imminent. Troopers Haskell and Simmons, who still had a long way to go in their sentence, were delighted, for that would now free up more of their time and release them from the daily humiliating ritual.

Friday, 13th November 1914.

The colonel was right in his assumption. Captain Tyssen had returned with orders that the regiment was to immediately proceed to Ypres, just over the border in Belgium and about 20 miles away. They were to proceed by way of Locre and Dickebush to the Ypres railway station, and from there were to follow the main railway line along to Halte, on the Menin Road.

Their orders were to join the 6th Cavalry Brigade as reinforcements. Captain Tyssen was again sent by his motor-cycle to report the regiments arrival to the G.O.C. 3rd Cavalry Division. This influx of the additional 26 officers, 467 men and 498 horses of the North Somerset Yeomanry was most welcome.

The regiment entered the town of Ypres itself and moved along the railway line during the daylight hours. All around them the town lay in smouldering ruins, not a building left standing with a complete roof on. The ancient Cloth Hall was still standing, but it was badly damaged and only its outer walls and tower remained, although two of its pinnacles situated at each end of the hall still remained, scarcely touched. Shells were still falling on the place, but more on the outskirts of Ypres so the Yeomanry got through safely.

They were near to what turned out be a large hospital which had a couple of fields around it with 5 massive shell holes in one of the fields. The craters they had made were large and deep enough to put a horse and wagon into. The occupants of the hospital had been long been safely evacuated. A trench system had already been dug into the field in front of the hospital, ready for any eventuality.

Colonel Glynn halted. He turned to his adjutant and said, "We should be safe enough here. We need to take half an hour to give the horses a rest."

"Very good sir," replied his adjutant, without saluting, for they had been advised that German snipers were still active in the area and were particularly picking out officers and senior non-commissioned officers as their long-range targets. To salute someone was to show to any possible sniper that he was an officer and invite the marksman to take action.

The adjutant called back to "A" Squadron, "30 minutes rest for the horses!" and the call was repeated down the line.

Each squadron knew exactly what to do. The horses were quickly picketed out around the side of the field and without incident. Pipes and cigarettes were lit and the men themselves started to take a well-earned break. Laughs could be heard as the men exchanged jokes and small talk with each other. Suddenly the German gunners, whether by pure luck or prior knowledge, ranged in on the field, and heavy artillery shells coming out of the blue pitched in the field and exploded. The force of the shock wave was enough to bowl several of the men over.

"Leave the horses!" cried the colonel, "and get yourselves into the trenches!" The men needed no second bidding and hastily ran to the relative safety of the nearby refuge. As they ran into them crash after crash of exploding ordnance fell around them, showering them with fragments of stone and earth.

Ernest Summers gave a yelp as something red hot landed on his right shoulder. As quickly as he had cried out in alarm, his chum, Albert Fitch, brushed off a fragment of still smoking shell that had fallen on him. Patting out the smouldering part of the uniform he grinned at Ernie. "Getting a bit hot isn't it!" Both men laughed, Ernie more in relief of the fact that he had not been hurt.

As suddenly as it had begun, the shelling ceased, and the Yeomanry made a dash for their horses. They were up and away without any additional incident.

They arrived at their destination at 2 p.m. without further hinderance and went into billets that had been prepared for them in an old chateau that was located next to L'Ecole de Bienfaisance (The School of Charity) that was beside the main Menin Road, about ½ mile east of Halte. In these billets the horses were tethered in the field, as there was no cover for them.

They were not there for very long before the Yeomanry were ordered forward to Zillebeke to go into the support trenches near that place. They formed up in a large body and they marched promptly at 4 p.m., every man eager to get into the fray. The men were ready. Such was their naivety that they were actually looking forward to serving at the Front for the first time.

As they moved away and had not got very far when several huge explosions erupted in the very spot where the regiment had just formed. Had they still been there, the possibility was that over half the regiment could have been wiped out in one go. The colonel concluded that there must be spies in the area reporting their every move. He turned to his adjutant and instructed, "While we are this close to the enemy we shall not form up again in such a large group. They obviously know we are here and are determined to inflict casualties upon us. In future, no more than 30 men are to be in one place as a formed body."

"I will make it so, sir," replied the adjutant.

They marched on and had halted for an hour but on arrival in the reserve area they found that they were not required for duty. They were immediately ordered to return to their quarters. The North Somerset Yeomanry were somewhat disappointed that they were not actually going into action.

Back at their billets the found that the sector was occasionally shelled, both by day and night. Several shrapnel shells fell amongst the horses, although they escaped without any injury. The men started to ignore the shells, for they had quickly learnt the sounds of those passing over and those that were going to fall short. After a couple of hours, only 1 or 2 men of the Yeomanry would throw themselves flat at the sound of any approaching shell, much to the disdain of their comrades who by now thought of themselves as battle hardened.

One shell dropped close to the officers' quarters. The force of the explosion was so great that every single window in the building was blown out. Luckily no officers or their servants were in them when it happened, but it turned out to be a chilly night for them.

Saturday, 14th November 1914.

Despite the persistent shelling there was only one human casualty, Trooper Yerbury. He and some others were standing near their horses when some shrapnel shells exploded above them. The men turned to run for cover, but Trooper Yerbury was hit and fell. He was rapidly attended to by the Regiment's doctor, and although he was unconscious at the time, all he had to show for it was a badly cut eye. He was quickly removed to the field hospital for treatment.

The horses were not so lucky, and a dozen of them were killed by one of the "Jack Johnson's". 10 of them were slain outright and 2 others had to be put down. The riders of the wounded steeds could only do one thing for them, for both animals had received severe leg wounds. They were ordered by the adjutant to shoot them.

The men soon identified when an incoming "Jack Johnson" was heading towards them by the sound that it made, for it announced its intention very much like an express train passing by. The popular nickname the troops had given to this type of shell fired from the German 15 centimetres gun was the "Ypres Express." It weighed about 93 pounds (42 kilograms) and was named after the American world heavyweight boxing champion of the time. The business end of the ammunition was coloured black and as the outer casing of the shell was blown off to release the shrapnel inside it, it left behind it a tell-tell cloud of black smoke.

The army cooks were soon at the horse carcasses, cutting them up into manageable bits of meat. They would form the basis of a fresh meat stew later that day. For many of the men it would be their first taste of horseflesh, but it would not be the last. They very soon learnt to adapt to the taste of the meat which lay somewhere between beef and venison, but a little gamier.

The North Somerset Yeomanry finally received orders to saddle up at 3.30 a.m. and rode at daylight to the railway that lay just to the north of Halte and on the Menin Road. The horses were tied along the west side of the cutting and the men made small dugouts on the east side. "B" Echelon, which consisted of the headquarters elements, under command of the quartermaster, remained at the billets.

At 1 p.m. the Brigade received orders to march to an area near Vlamertinghe and the regiment found itself accommodated in 2 small farms. These were cramped and the Medical Officer confirmed that the water supply was so bad that it had to be boiled before either men or horses could drink it.

During the day it became very much colder and the snow began to sprinkle down. The horses, not being under shelter, felt it. So did the men.

A motorcyclist appeared at the regiment headquarters carrying their new orders and was received without fuss, for orders were being rapidly changed almost on a 2-hourly basis. The adjutant signed for them and handed them to colonel.

He read through the instructions and explained to the adjutant, "Well, this is it. We have been ordered into action at last. We've to supply 300 rifles for the trenches tomorrow for a period of 48 hours."

"Very good sir. Which squadrons do you wish to provide them?"

The colonel took a moment or two to think about it and then decided. "Instruct "A" and "B" to provide them, and if necessary, take men from "C" Squadron to make up any shortfall in manpower."

"Very good, colonel."

The colonel smiled and rubbed his hands together. "Looks like we will be getting our first taste of real action tomorrow, Stanley."

"The men won't let you down, sir."

Glynn nodded. "I know that," he replied.

Sunday, 15th November 1914.

As it happens in war, the orders were suddenly changed again and without warning. At 2.45 a.m. they were ordered by the Brigade to saddle up. The men were issued with their full ammunition scale and were told to be ready to move. Naught occurred and they were then ordered to stand down and told to parade again at 3.30 a.m. under the cover of darkness, ready for a fast move. Nothing was forthcoming and so they were ordered to stand to at 6.30 a.m., just in case the Germans made a surprise advance. The men waited in an expectant hush in the hastily prepared trenches, their horses picketed behind the trench system. The sound of many a water bottle being uncapped was heard as, for the first time, they experienced that awful dryness of the mouth that men felt just before an anticipated attack.

The breaking of the dawn proved to be an uneventful event, and the regiment was finally ordered to join the Brigade in their concentration area around the Ypres railway station, and they did so. There they were told that the brigadier had no need for horses at the Front, so "B" Echelon were tasked with looking after the animals whilst the cavalry regiment turned itself into an infantry unit.

On foot, Lieutenant Colonel Glynn led the North Somerset Yeomanry the 7 or 8 miles towards the trenches at Zillebeke via the railway line which led to Comines. When they got there at midday the colonel was asked to report to the Brigade Headquarters and "C" Squadron, under Major H.G. Spencer, was ordered to join the 10th Hussars.

The remaining 200 men of the Yeomanry, "A" Squadron, under the command of Major G. Lubbock, "B" Squadron, under the command of Captain F.A.C Liebert, and the Maxims, under Major H.B. Matthews, were placed under the orders of Colonel O. Smith-Bingham D.S.O., 3rd Dragoon Guards, and ordered into the trenches south east of Zillebeke.

Under the cover of darkness, they relieved the 1st Lifeguards at approximately 7.30 p.m. The men were reminded that silence was essential if they did not want the wrath of the German artillery to descend upon them. "A" Squadron went up first, leading the way. They occupied the centre trench in the firing line, and the Yeomanry's 2 Maxim machine guns, together with their officer and 6-man crews, were sited between 2 squadrons of the 3rd Dragoon Guards. "B" Squadron was placed in the reserve trenches. The men of the North Somerset Yeomanry were now well and truly established in the front line, and the night was unusually quiet with only an intermittent amount of shelling.

Trooper George Richardson was stood to in the trench as a sentry. A serjeant was with him, peering out from a small slit between the sandbags. There was a periscope nearby for looking over the trench, but Serjeant Watts had been told by the serjeant that he relieved to use it sparingly.

"Once the Germans see it, they take pot shots at it. If you do use it, pop it up quick like and never from the same place twice. If I were you, whenever it is light, I would look through the sandbags. You can see enough there." Serjeant Watts had taken the advice.

Trooper Richardson suddenly said, "Bah! I can't see anything here," and promptly stuck his head above the parapet to get a better view. There was a strange wizz and splatting sound as an enemy sniper's bullet hit the sandbag just to his right, throwing grit into his eye. He fell back, cursing.

Serjeant Watts shook his head in total disbelief. "You are a silly sod! You've been told there are snipers out there."

"I believe them now," he replied, shaking a little at his close call.

The shelling began to intensify as the men hunkered down into trench life. Those not on duty went down into the below ground bunkers, where they could. If not, they found some sort of safety in the holes scraped into the forward part of the trench, nicknamed by the men as "funk holes". Unless there was a direct hit, they would be far safer there than if out in the open trenches and exposed to the shrapnel shells of the foe.

During the early part of the evening the Squadron had its first real encounter with the enemy. The shelling was happening at the rate of a couple of shells every 5 minutes or so, mostly high explosive but with a sudden switch to shrapnel, hoping to catch out the sentries.

Enemy snipers were out and about in no-man's land, looking out for the unwary. The men soon learnt that if an enemy magnesium flare went up it was usually for the benefit of a German sniper. An occasional near miss took place and then the German's made a mistake.

Up went a magnesium flare, fired by one of the German snipers. All it did was illuminate the stealthy forms of an enemy fighting patrol slowly moving forward from their positions. They were quickly spotted by an alert sentry who raised the alarm. The shelling had ceased all together and the Somerset men were suddenly up to the fire step of the trenches and for the first time, opened fire on an advancing enemy.

Someone shouted out loud in elation as he saw his target fall. The fighting patrol had lost its element of surprise and faded away back into the darkness. The attempt by the Germans to capture a man for interrogation had failed and they returned to their positions.

The North Somerset Yeomanry had experienced their first day under real enemy fire in the trenches. Miraculously there were no casualties.

They also had their first experience of the newly introduced rum ration for those troops serving in the trenches, and they needed it. Men of the headquarters troop came forward, carrying large stone jars of rum that contained 1 gallon, enough for 64 men. The rum was poured into a measured metal cup which held enough for 1 ration and each man and he was given it to drink, but a couple of them were teetotal and therefore declined, much to the delight of the men carrying the ration, for that would be theirs shortly! The idea of supplying it was to warm the men up, for in truth standing in a cold and wet trench gradually sucked the heat out of them. They also had something to look forward to, for the newly introduced rum ration was to be issued twice a day, at dawn and at dusk.

Monday, 16th November 1914.

Heavy shelling had taken place all day and continued into the night. All the men could do was to work carefully in the trenches. The daylight hours were spent by them improving and building up the parapets with sandbags, and everything went well. There were a few casualties received from shrapnel, but nothing major. The dugouts were well constructed and if they were in them, they were safe from the exploding enemy ordnance.

Major Lubbock, the officer commanding "A" Squadron in the trenches, was a worried man. His main cause of anxiety was that at some points the German troops were only about 40 yards away, and although they had wire in front of their trenches, the British did not yet have that luxury. The wire simply had not come up yet from the rear transports.

He turned to his second-in-command, Captain English, and passing him the periscope said, "What do you think we can do about the wiring problem?"

He took the periscope and took a short and hard look towards the enemy trenches. As he pulled the periscope down several bullets cracked the air above them. The men involuntary ducked, although they were safe enough from rifle fire where they were. He turned to his company commander and opined, "I don't think that there is much that we can do, sir. The only consolation is that although the Germans have wire, it means they will have to funnel out along set routes to confront us."

"Yes, I agree," he nodded. "If we can spot the paths that they will have to take I can get the Maxim guns to zero in on their likely points of attack."

"Yes sir."

"Get a S.N.C.O. to use the periscope to see if he can pin-point the exit positions from the wire."

"Of course, sir."

"Remind him to shift his position along the trench line after each use. We only have 2 periscopes and we can't afford to lose one. Have him to draw a sketch map and show it to me before I pass it on to the machine gun section."

There was a whistling sound as a shell landed perilously close and just behind the trench before it exploded with a great roar, pushing the rear of the trench in. It knocked Major Lubbock off his feet but buried his second in command up to his knees in mud and dirt. 2 men from the Yeomanry immediately ran forward with shovels to dig him out.

The major staggered to his feet, covered in mud from the bottom of the trench. "Robert!" he called.

The captain waved the hand. "I'm alright sir, just a bit put off by my indignant position.

"Don't you worry, sir, we'll soon have you out," encouraged the Squadron Serjeant Major, William Reeves, who had rapidly arrived on the scene carrying a shovel. It did not take long to free him.

The first day was spent by "A" Squadron under their baptism of fire in the trenches, and for the men it became a somewhat monotonous experience. This was not quite what they expected. There was no thrilling charge with sabre's drawn and a defeated enemy scattering before them. It was more a cacophony of noise and the different sounds made by each variety of shells. It became a bit of a game for the men, seeing who could correctly identify the type of shell it was before it exploded. Fitch cursed when he incorrectly identified a high explosive shell as a "Jack Johnson" and lost his penny bet with Trooper Albert Summers when it turned out to be a high explosive one.

The lunch meal made for a break in the routine, the only problem being that they had to eat the army rations. In particular, the dreadful Maconochie, named after the company in Aberdeen, Scotland, who manufactured this concoction of barely recognisable chunks of fatty meat and vegetables swimming in a thin and unappetizing gravy. They could not heat it, so it had to be eaten cold, and the taste was one that no-one had a good word for. It made the men crave for the cold bully beef rations instead.

The braver of them munched on the iron hard biscuits that they carried and took a long time to eat. They had to be dipped in cold water to soften them first, for the raw biscuit had the ability to crack or break teeth of the more unwary. They should have been dipped in hot tea, but even this simple luxury was not available to them in the soggy trenches. Men were already up to their ankles in mud and water, and cold feet were a major problem. You could not even stamp them to try and bring warmth back into them, for to do so was invite one to sink deeper into the mud.

At 6.30 p.m., about an hour and a half after sunset, "B" Squadron and one troop of "A" squadron under Lieutenant Bailward were sent forward to relieve "A" Squadron. The remainder of "A" Squadron, who had been in the trenches all day, went back and had a welcome hot meal of bully beef and bread in the reserve trenches which had been brought up by the cooks of "B" Echelon. The Maxim guns remained in the firing line and one cook was sent forward with some hot tea for them. It was "B" Squadrons turn to now learn the harsh realities of trench warfare.

The shelling intensified, and suddenly lessened. The S.Q.M.S. came hurtling out of his dugout and cocked his rifle. "Stand by men!!" he called urgently. He looked towards his company commander and shouted, "When this shelling stops completely, they will be coming at us sir!"

Captain Liebert nodded and looked at his watch. He noted that it was 9 p.m. in the evening, for he would be writing about this later in his diary. He knew about the diagram of the possible enemy routes that had made had been given to Major Matthews. Now he would find out if Major Lubbock's idea had paid off.

2 minutes later the shelling suddenly stopped. "Quickly! Get on the fire-step men!" he urged. His troopers stood on it and for the very first time exposed themselves to the enemy. Sure enough, out of the trenches surged the Germans, screaming for all their worth. Very flares began to be fired overhead and a bright and eerie light illuminated the battlefield.

Captain Liebert yelled "Fire" and the first official shots in anger were fired by "B" Squadron at a bravely advancing enemy, bayonets fixed. The machine guns of the North Somerset Yeomanry chattered into action, firing up to 500 rounds per minute, and the opposing soldiers were being bowled over like nine-pins. Then one of them jammed and a cursing Maxim team busily engaged in attempting to rectify the fault. Major Matthews gave up a silent prayer for the provision of just one Vickers machine gun. "Get that gun back into action," he screamed at the top of his voice, for at a stroke, 50% of his firepower had been lost. Suddenly the stoppage was cleared, and the gun chattered back into service.

No German got any further than a 20 or so yards from their trenches before they were shot down as the attack lost its momentum. Screams of wounded men began to rend the air, and as quickly as the attack had begun, it was over.

The S.Q.M.S. heard the whining of the first German artillery shells coming back over again. "Down boys!" he called, and the men stepped off the firing step and back into the relative safety of their trenches and dugouts.

Captain Liebert made a mental note to send a bottle of port to Major Lubbock, and with his very best compliments.

Someone in the headquarters had decided that enough was enough, and a counter barrage of artillery began descending upon the German trenches. At least the Germans were now getting some of what "B" Squadron had been getting.

Alf Cleall was sat in a funk hole alongside his pal, Charlie Gibbs. They were sharing a pipe full of tobacco between them, grateful for the warmth of the pipe bowl in their cold hands. They both sat with their knees up, keeping them out of the cold water that was slopping about in the bottom of the trench. Lieutenant Bailward had ordered the men to use their mess tins to scoop out of the water and throw it out of the trench, but it was a hopeless task and given up on after ten minutes or so. As soon as they threw it out it would come back in. To top it all, it had started to rain heavily, sometimes turning to cold sleet, and the water was gradually becoming deeper.

"How much has it risen do you reckon?" asked Alf.

Charlie took a puff from the pipe and handed it back to Alf. "About 2 inches in the last hour, I suppose."

Bailward came splashing down along the trench, doing his rounds. The icy cold water was swirling around his knees. He espied the serjeants and headed directly towards them. He nodded a cheerful greeting towards them, a huge grin on his face at the sight of the 2 serjeants huddled together. "What do you think?" he asked. "Do you think the rising water poses any threat to us?"

The S.N.C.O.'s looked at each other and Charlie said, "We might have to think about finding a way to get the water out of the trenches if it keeps up like this, sir."

Bailward nodded. "The furthest trench dips a little for about a foot or so, so the water is deeper down there and some of the men are up to their waists in it."

"Why don't you send a runner back to headquarters and ask for an engineer to come forward with some pumps so we can reduce the water depth sir?"

"Good idea, I'll send someone back straight away."

With a flash of humour Charlie said, "Might it be better to send a swimmer rather than a runner sir?" Bailward laughed at the humour of it all.

There was a flash of lightning followed by a close roll of thunder that even drowned out the sound of the dropping shells. The wind rose and the rain increased in its ferocity. The 2 pals anxiously looked at each other.

Tuesday, 17th November 1914.

At 2.30 a.m. a shrapnel shell burst above the trenches and caught the sentry, Trooper Poole, twice in the side, knocking him bleeding badly down into the trench and leaving him totally incapacitated. Serjeant Major Reeves was quickly on the scene and dragged the wounded man into a dugout and replaced him with another sentry.

At 3 a.m. the heavy shelling dramatically intensified and a continual rain of heavy artillery shells crashed down upon the trenches in their sector. The Germans had found out that the North Somerset Yeomanry, a territorial unit and fresh out from England, had taken over that part of the line. They wanted to teach the English men a lesson they would never forget and were determined to drive them out at any costs. Extra heavy artillery guns had been brought into action by them with the object of either decimating the regiment or driving them away from the battlefield. This was to be an examination of their metal, a test to see if the territorials nerve would break. There was to be no respite.

Every second that passed saw an artillery shell land either in front or behind the trenches. Lieutenant Bailward had his pocket watch out and was coolly counting the number of shells falling. He nodded to Captain Liebert. "About 65 shells a minute, sir," he informed him. It was just a matter of luck that one had not yet exploded in the trenches, but it could not last.

The Somerset men sat in their funk holes, for there was nothing else they could do. Those who did not have these little refuges pressed themselves into the side of the sodden trenches, gritting their teeth and closing their eyes. An occasional prayer could be heard, along with the more often curses as a shell passed close to someone.

Sometimes high explosive shells would crash down nearby, and you knew them by the repugnant fumes they gave off. They usually buried themselves in the ground before exploding, but they were primarily used by the enemy to blow in the sides of trenches and to penetrate dugouts, exploding with such force that they often buried men alive.

Troopers Fitch and Summers were pressed hard against the trench wall, their soft caps giving them no protection at all against the falling stones and earth that continually rained down upon them. All the hats did was to lessen the impact of anything, except shrapnel, that fell down from the heavens above. Albert was not a religious man but he suddenly found himself uttering The Lord's Prayer, with Ernie muttering a fervent "Amen!" on completion.

They were the sentries for their section and it was their job to stay awake and warn of any impending attack, not that anyone was sleeping. This particular trench formed part of a zig-zag which meant that if the trench was hit by a shell any explosive force would be channelled outwards and away from the next.

And then it happened. The first shell struck squarely inside a trench and there was a blinding flash followed by a huge roar and a smell of roasting flesh. Both sentries were thrown off the wall and into the water by the force of the explosion, which suddenly became slightly warm.

Fitch recovered first and pulled Ernie out, for he was lying face down in it and would surely have drowned if not for his actions. "Ernie! Ernie!" he cried. "Are you alright?"

Gasping and spluttering Trooper Ernest Summers sat bolt upright. "Bloody hell" What happened?"

"I think a shell hit in the next part of the trench," he said, pointing towards it. Both men looked around the corner, not knowing what to expect. That part of the trench system had been blown in, and the once perpendicular earth walls were now just a deep hole. In what was a funk hole was now a pair of legs, kicking vainly in a bid to try and extricate themselves from the caved in trench wall.

"Quick, Ern, take a leg. We'll pull him out!" The chums hastily grabbed a leg each and tugged for all their worth. They started to work him out, whoever he was, but then the legs just stopped kicking. Finally the soft earth gave out and they got the man out, his neck extended by his service felt cap and still held in place by his chin strap. The cap had filled up with wet mud when they were pulling him and it had acted like an anchor, stretching his neck out so that instead of saving him they were actually killing him. His neck had been pulled cleanly out and he looked like a chicken whose neck had been wrung. Both men looked on in horror at the sight of the body of Corporal Freddy Hancock.

The shell hole behind them began to rapidly fill with water, and to the top of it the face of a man unexpectedly appeared. By now the water was about three feet in depth and without hesitation Ernie jumped in to rescue him. He grasped his shoulders and gave a huge heave, but that was all there was of him, just the head and shoulders.

Albert Fitch was immediately sick as Ernie just stood there, looking incredulously at the piece of a human being that remained. Curiously the face held a fixed smiled. Ernie let the man go and the remains of him sank below the water.

Lieutenant Bailward arrived. "Bloody hell!" He looked on aghast at the awful scene before ordering, "Nothing we can do here chaps. Back to your posts."

The authorative command snapped the men out of the strange stupor they had lapsed into that had blocked out the sound of the bursting artillery shell behind them. They picked up their rifles and carried on with their duty, the body of Corporal Hancock being left where it was. They looked at each other and neither mentioned how his death had happened. It was the thing of future nightmares, without doubt.

A Chaplain of the Forces came along the trench line, encouraging the men as he did so and singing "Onward Christian Soldiers!" with gusto and feeling. He stopped at the funk hole where Alf and Charlie were sitting. "Any room in there chaps?" he enquired.

The serjeants grinned at each other and moved aside slightly. "Hop in Padre and get yourself some space for a while."

"Thank you my sons." He got in.

Charlie said, "Busy morning for you Reverend?"

He grimaced. "Unfortunately the answer to that is yes. This constant shelling is taking some good men with it."

Alf nodded. "We just lost 2 men a couple of trenches down," and indicated the direction with his hand.

"Oh really?" He rummaged around in his pocket and took out a large bar of chocolate. He broke off 2 squares and gave 1 each to the serjeants. "Here men, something to help sustain you," he offered. Both men gratefully accepted the morsel. There was a huge crash as a shell fell just short of them and the force of the explosion pushed them out of the funk hole and into the foul water. "Damnation!" cursed the Chaplain of the Forces as he staggered to his feet. The serjeants rose from the water and propped him against the trench wall. "You O.K. Padre?"

"Yes, yes, my son," he replied. He shook himself like a dog. "Good luck men," he said, making the sign of The Cross in front of them. Then he was gone, making his way down towards the next trench to administer the needs of the dead and dying. The shelling continued without respite.

At about 7.30 a.m. the dawn began to reluctantly break at last, and the men were getting apprehensive. Very lights started to pop to illuminate the enemy trenches whilst sentries vainly looked to see if there was any movement coming from them. It grew lighter and the sun briefly broke through, but the heavy shelling continued relentlessly. It looked as if the Germans were not yet ready to attack.

The rum ration came up and men greedily gulped it down. This time, there were not teetotal abstentions from the daily issue. It gave the men a seemingly brief respite from the cold.

Trooper Poole and the other wounded men were carried back to the reserve trenches under heavy fire at 8.30 a.m., suffering not only from their wounds but of the effects of having to lie in the cold and sodden wet trenches all night. One of the wounded men was not so lucky, for when they finally lifted him up they discovered that, beneath his tarpaulin, his face had fallen into the water-filled trench, and he had died, not because of his wounds, but from drowning.

It was just before 9 a.m. and the number of casualties was slowly but surely rising, but the men stood grimly at their posts like veterans. One shell had pitched earlier in the trenches plumb centre, and nothing remained of the four men who had received the direct hit. The water in the trench had suddenly turned red with blood, and that was it. They were gone.

Serjeant Reginald Watts was walking along the trench, head down, checking on the men who were supposed to be doing sentry duty. There was a natural tendency to get into the funk holes to take shelter, but if you did that then you weren't being an effective sentry. You had to keep your wits about you, for under the shelter of the bombardment, German snipers would be working themselves forward. A high explosive shell dropped into the trench, burying itself deep before it exploded. That probably saved his life, but fragments of red hot shell casing blew along the trench and he fell to the ground. He tried to get up, but couldn't. Every time he did so, he fell over. The next thing he knew was that Trooper Tom Watts, his brother, was suddenly beside him.

"Lay still Reggie, you've been hit," he said.

"Hello Tom," he replied. "I don't feel anything. Help me stand up and I'll be alright." Reg Watts saw tears in his brothers eyes, for he did not understand that the blast from the shell had removed both of his feet.

One of the regiment's favourite serjeants, Bristow, was also killed on that day. He had been in a dugout together with Trooper Riddle when a high explosive shell had penetrated the top cover of it and had exploded within. Serjeant Bristow had been literally blown to pieces, and the young trooper, who was sitting by his side, had been largely protected from most of the blast by his serjeant, but was badly wounded.

They had succeeded in extricating the trooper from the dugout, and mercifully for him, he was in an unconscious state. He had no right arm. After they had managed to do that another shell burst just short of the front to the collapsed dugout and buried it, along with Serjeant Bristow, completely. 2 stretcher bearers quickly carried the wounded man away and back to the reserve trenches. From there he would be first treated by the doctor in the Regimental Aid Post and then moved back to the Casualty Clearing Station.

Captain Liebert had spotted the remains of a cottage that was occupying a central position in no man's land. If the enemy got to it first it would prove to be a valuable and dangerous asset to them. It had to be secured. He called for volunteers, for the situation was a very dangerous one and the men had little chance, if any, of reaching the building alive. He felt very proud that nine men of his squadron quickly stepped forward to undertake the extremely dangerous task. Corporal Thomas was put in charge of the detail.

Despite the shelling, the men were ordered to man the firing steps and open fire on the German's occupying the opposing trenches so as to give them men some covering fire. As the rapid fire commenced the volunteers dashed out of the safety of their trenches, zig-zagging through the inferno of shot and shell. He grimly watched as the men dropped one by one, their ultimate sacrifice for England made. One man made it, Trooper Tutton, and he dived through what was left of the cottages doorway and immediately started to put down an accurate and telling fire upon the German trenches. Captain Liebert smiled in satisfaction as he saw that men from other regiments were gradually entering the ruins. Quite clearly other officers along the line had also spotted the danger and had quickly sent their soldiers up. He thought to himself, "The cost has been very high!"

As if to prove his point he spotted a German attack immediately going in on the ruined cottage and noted with satisfaction that it was very quickly repulsed. It looked as if one of the other regiments had managed to get a Vickers machine gun in there, for the enemy were dropping like flies and soon retired.

Suddenly the shelling stopped. Captain Liebert was the first to react to the unexpected lull and urged "Stand to! Stand to!" and the men jumped up and on to the fire step, peering across what had been no man's land between the opposing trenches.

"B" Squadron commander quickly noticed that the wire that had been in front of the German trenches had been removed during the shelling and he suddenly knew why. A wave of German soldiers, their spiked helmets called Pickelhaube's clearly visible, came bursting out of their trenches. The Maxim guns immediately opened fire and the German's began to fall, but they came on.

Young Lieutenant Bailward of "A" Squadron gulped and, hardly managing to find his voice, cried "Rapid fire!" The men responded with a volley and then the sound of the rifles began to take on their own individual sounds as each man found his best speed to fire at. The men were coolly picking their targets.

Alf Cleall and Charlie Gibbs had been given a special task by Captain Liebert in the event of any German attack. They were to specifically target the German field police who generally followed in the rear of the attacking men. Their job was shoot down anyone who tried to turn back towards the safety of the trenches.

In front of the field police but behind the men came the German officers, waving their swords above their heads and encouraging their men onwards. In this respect the German army was very different from the British. The British officers tended to lead their men from the front and, consequently, the casualty rates amongst the young second lieutenants in the army was extremely high.

The 2 serjeants had to single out the German officers as well. Captain Liebert held the opinion that without their officers or the field police to stop them, any attacking force would be leaderless and would be much more likely to retreat.

The German troops came on, despite being cut down like corn by a scythe. Alf spotted an enemy officer and nudged Charlie. "I see him, Alf." Both men fired and the enemy soldier fell to the ground. The man standing next to the officer stopped, making himself an easy target as he was only 50 yards away. Charlie fired and the man dropped like a log. Through the rifle smoke they could see the German field police so the 2 chums set about their task of eliminating them, firing continuously until they were disposed of. The Germans came on, yelling and screaming their defiance but the North Somerset Yeomanry never wavered. The weight of fire going down was devastating.

Captain Liebert came running along the watery trench and stopped by the serjeants. "Well done men!" he exclaimed. "I don't think that they can take much more of this." Having said that, the charge wavered and the German's began to take cover. Charlie fired and took out the last field policeman. That seemed to do the trick, and the remaining enemy broke for the safety of their own trenches. A huge cheer went up from the North Somersets.

"Quick," ordered Captain Liebert. "Go out and grab the nearest wounded German and bring him back here, together with his helmet."

Charlie and Alf were out of the trench and dashed forward. Within 20 paces they saw an enemy corporal who had been shot through the legs and was wearing his helmet, so they grabbed him and unceremoniously dragged him back into the trenches, sliding over the top as the artillery barrage started once more.

The officer took the helmet off the injured enemy soldier's head and looked closely at it. It bore the shape of an eagle with outstretched wings and grasping a sword in each talon. In the centre of the eagle was a German cross. "I think that our prisoner is a member of the Prussian Guards, one of their elite regiments." He grinned in satisfaction and said, "We have beaten their best!"

The cry went along the trenches that the North Somersets had thrown back the Prussian Guards and the cheering could be heard above the sound of the explosions. The men were down off the fire trenches and were seeking what shelter they could. The stretcher bearers were going up and down the trenches moving the dead and tending to the wounded.

"Serjeant Gibbs!" ordered Captain Liebert. "Get your prisoner to the support trenches so he can be sent back for interrogation."

2 bearers were immediately summoned and the wounded German was loaded on to a stretcher to be taken to the Number 3 Casualty Clearing Station situated at L'Ecole de Bienfaisance, further behind the lines. Being an N.C.O., he would be a valuable prisoner and if his interrogation was successful, he could probably give the command some interesting facts. Captain Liebert decided to keep the helmet, as it would make a useful souvenir for the mess once the war was over.

As the walls of the trenches were blown in, the men did their best to repair them, but in truth there was not much they could do. Using their picks and shovels they were working under appalling conditions, with shells falling everywhere. The trenches were searched by shrapnel, causing many wounds and deaths amongst them. If the aim of the Germans was to break the will-power of the men, it was not working. In truth it made them more bloody minded and grimly determined to hang on, come what may. There was no engineer support, and no materials for revetting were available. Captain Liebert thought that at this stage the trenches were dangerously vulnerable and sent a runner back to headquarters telling them so.

The shelling slackened a little, and 2 German aircraft suddenly appeared and flew along and above them and at about 300 feet. They were clearly taking photographs of the trenches and Captain Liebert thought that this was probably a precursor to another attack. This was followed shortly by another German aircraft flying along the trenches, but from the other direction. The men fired at it, but with no success. By the time they pulled their rifle triggers the aircraft were well ahead of the space that it had previously been in. The soldiers had no experience of firing in front of the aircraft so that it flew into the bullet. All except Alf. He had been an expert Snipe and Mallard Duck shooter in his day, so he had enough experience to shoot at an aircraft properly.

Alf put 5 shots into the air and the reconnaissance plane suddenly lurched to one side and started side slipping back towards the German lines, belching black smoke behind it. The smoke suddenly turned into flames and the little aircraft nose-dived into the ground and blew up. The North Somerset Yeomanry had shot down its first aircraft.

At noon the shelling abruptly ceased. This time the last artillery shells fired had all been "Jack Johnson's". The men needed no bidding or orders in what to do when this happened. They automatically jumped up to the fire steps, where they remained and hastily got themselves into a firing position that offered them the most safety. Over the enemy trenches they could see a tethered balloon with a couple of men in it. They were using flags to signal to the troops below. Quite clearly they were going to direct an attack. One of the Maxim guns with its crew suddenly appeared close to Alf Cleall and set itself up on its tripod, moving from its original position so that it would take the Germans by surprise. It did not have long to wait.

The Prussian Guards came at them again, bayonets fixed and screaming at the top of their voices, partly hidden behind the clouds of black smoke that the last "Jack Johnson's" had left behind. This time the German Felgendarmerie had learned their lesson from the previous attack, for they had discarded their familiar silver crescent shaped metal badges that were normally suspended from beneath their necks and on a chain and identified them as field police.

Albert Fitch and Ernest Summers were firing, side by side and their rifle barrels were steaming in the icy air as the amount of rounds being fired from them increased.

"Come on Ernie, keep firing!" cried Albert, for his mate had suddenly stopped firing, even though his rifle was pointed towards the enemy. He reached out to give him a shake and to his horror saw a round hole had appeared in the middle of Ernie's forehead. His best mate was dead. A huge feeling of anger overcame him and he fired faster than ever, feeling a coldness about him that he never knew he had. The rifle seemed to have a mind of its own and every time he pointed it at an enemy soldier and squeezed the trigger, that man would drop.

To get to the British, the Germans had to come up a slight hill, and they were bravely doing so. In front of Albert a huge and bearded German officer was urging his men on. He was shouting in English towards them, "Come on out, you Somerset clods. Come on out of your rabbit holes and feel the steel of the Prussian warrior!"

Albert could contain himself no longer. Fixing his bayonet, he stood upright, showing total disregard for the bullets that were whizzing around him, but he seemed to have a charmed life. "I'll bloody well show you what us Somerset boys can do!" he screamed out in pure rage and leapt out of the trench. 5 other men jumped out as well and all 6 of them ran pell-mell down the hill to meet the oncoming enemy head on. Within 30 yards they clashed like knights of old. Serjeant Cleall shouted helplessly after the men, "Get back here now! The remainder of you, hold your positions!" He saw the German officer slash down at Fitch with his sabre, but Fitch parried it with his rifle and buried his bayonet deep into the man's stomach. He was screaming like a madman. There were just too many of the Germans for the six men to stem, and only Fitch got back to the safety of the trench. The rest were killed.

Alf and Charlie kept firing at the advancing Germans, and Charlie's younger brother, Freddie Gibbs and Trooper Gay were passing them up bullets to fire as fast as they possibly could. The Germans were still coming at them and Alf said, "I don't think we are going to make it, chum."

"Then we will bloody well go down fighting and show 'em what the Yeomanry is made of!"

The Germans began coming from their right and Charlie Gibbs hat was peppered by four bullets. He was not quite so lucky with the fifth bullet, for it grazed his skull and knocked him down. His brother jumped up next to Alf and started firing. In the bottom of the trench Charlie held his hand to the top of his head and it came away red with blood. He gingerly felt it and to his relief discovered that it was only his skin that had been broken. He was taken with a surge of adrenalin as his younger brother yelped out and fell backwards, nursing a bullet wound to the upper arm. Forcing himself up he took up his place alongside Alf and began firing.

"Can't be many of the buggers left!" he said casually.

"Not many of us either," he replied.

The Germans courageously still kept coming, but they were slowing down now. Alf pushed Charlie back a bit with his hand and said, "Mind, Charlie, let me have a go at them on your right." He turned to fire and no sooner had he done that when he went down poleaxed, shot through the neck. Trooper Gay jumped up to replace him, and Lieutenant Bailward came running forward and stood up on the parapet.

Alf was alive but bleeding freely. Charlie quickly knelt down beside his comrade and bandaged him up as best as he could before he dragged him to one side and propped him up, sitting in the water filled trench with his back facing towards the enemy. Alf put his thumb up to indicate that he was O.K. and pointed back towards the fire step.

The attack began to falter, for the North Somerset Yeomanry were taking a terrible toll on the Prussian Guards. The enemy soldiers were going down like nine-pin skittles but still they had not managed to get into the trenches. Several of them had fallen, shot dead, on the lips of the trenches, but for the remainder they were kept off to about a distance of 10 yards.

The attack stopped and down came the artillery again, forcing both friend and foe to seek whatever cover they could. Charlie looked on in horror as a German shell exploded on top of a section of Prussian Guards. A white silk handkerchief came fluttering down out of the sky, all that was left of that particular group of soldiers.

After the attack had ended, Lieutenant Davey did a quick check of the men who remained. He grimly reported to Captain Liebert, "A heavy toll, sir. It looks as if we have about fifteen men killed so far, and about twice that many wounded."

"Thank you," he said. He took out his field note book and, using his pencil, hurriedly scribbled a message into it. He nodded and made up his mind. He said, "I am sending for reinforcements." He looked around at those about him before he made up his selection. "Serjeant Gibbs, " he ordered as he proffered the piece of paper in his hand. "Take this message back to the colonel in the reserve trench and wait there for the answer." Gibbs had recently taken the Prussian Guard prisoner back to the headquarter and the Squadron Commander had reasoned that as he knew where it was, he would be the best man to send.

"Yes sir," he said, glancing anxiously towards his stricken comrade.

"Don't worry about Serjeant Cleall, we'll look after him. Quickly now man, go!"

Alf gave a weak grin and once more gave the thumbs up sign, and Charlie ran down the trench with the message in his hand, crying out, "Make way! Make way!" as he did so. The shells were still falling at a massive rate.

Captain Liebert looked over the parapet to get a proper view of the situation, for the periscope that he had been using had been smashed to pieces by a high explosive shell. He could see very little. He turned to face Lieutenant Davey, a look of resolve etched upon his face.

The "Jack Johnson" shell gave its familiar crack as the fuse inside it exploded, blowing the casing off and releasing the lethal balls of lead it carried. This occurred at about thirty feet, and one of the balls hit Captain Liebert square on the back of his head, whilst the others passed through the body of Lieutenant Davey and three other troopers, killing them instantly. Captain Liebert fell down, mortally wounded.

The cry of "Stretcher bearers!" went up from somewhere, and he and the others were transported back to the Casualty Clearing Station, but they were all beyond help. Doctor Edwards was mortified, for he knew Captain Liebert personally, and for the first time as he was tending to the many wounded, he felt a personal pang of regret. He used to ride with Captain Liebert with the Blackmore Vale hunt.

Back in the reserve trenches 2 companies of Grenadier Guards arrived at 3.30 p.m. in order to act as reinforcements. The colonel quickly ordered that Captain English with 30 men of "A" Squadron were to go forward to immediately replace the casualties. Serjeant Gibbs returned with them to the front line.

Much to his surprise he found that Alf Cleall was still there where he had left him. Charlie knelt by his deathly pale chum and produced his water canteen. "How are you, old mate?" he asked in a concerned way.

Alf spluttered a little after drinking the water, and after wheezing a bit suddenly clasped his life-long friends hand with a firm grip. "Tell Winnie," he began, and then his voice and grip just faded away. Charlie bowed his head and wept silently, for Alf had just died in front of him.

There was nothing that he could do for him now, except wrap him in his ground sheet and have him carried back for burial when a quieter moment ensued. But that was not yet to happen yet, as the shells kept raining from the sky.

There was another huge explosion from an high explosive shell and the sides of the trench were blasted over Charlie and 2 other men. His comrades were immediately at the spot, frantically digging the loose earth and pulling them all out, alive. But Charlie had been injured by the force of the explosion, his back and legs hurt terribly and he could not walk. The stretcher bearers took him away.

About an hour later, Major Lubbock and the rest of the Yeomanry, who had been held in the reserve trenches, came up and were placed out along the front line. Including with him came the regiment's popular adjutant, Captain Stanley Bates. He looked in wonder at the damage that the shelling had done to the trenches and wondered how on earth his men had survived. The shells were still falling thick and fast, and being a tall man standing at some 6 feet and 2 inches he was finding it difficult to find somewhere to effectively be safe. He was permanently walking along the trenches with his head bowed, for he did not want to present himself as a target to the ever present threat of snipers.

A "Jack Johnson" exploded and one of the fragments caught him in the chin, bowling him over. He lay stupefied face down in the bottom of the trench, his mind reeling.

"God!" he thought, "I've been hit!"

Another high explosive shell exploded to the rear of the trench sending a wave of earth towards him which rolled him over and left him in a sitting position against the back of the forward part of what remained of the trench. A strong pair of hands reached forward from a dugout in the front of the trench and dragged him in.

The small dugout contained four men and was lit by a spluttering candle. It was shaking every time a shell burst near it and fine earth kept dribbling from the corrugated iron roofing. It was like being in a drum, the sand bagged roof rattling almost continuously as the shrapnel from an airburst rained down upon it. A candle was brought over to the adjutant and he felt a bandage being placed firmly beneath his chin.

"You've been hit in the jaw, Stanley," said Captain Tyssen, stemming the flow of blood. "Nothing major, I don't think, but it is bleeding heavily."

Captain Bates groaned. "Feels like I've punched by Mr. Jack Johnson himself," he said, making reference to the American heavyweight champion of the world.

"I'll get you sent back in a moment or so."

Gingerly putting his hand up to hold the dressing in place he said, "It hurts, but I will survive. I will not be going back yet!" he said in a determined tone.

"As you wish, Stanley." Captain Tyssen tied a knot in the bandage on the top of his head, securing it in place. "There! That'll hold it," he grinned. "You look like someone who has the toothache!" The adjutant tried to laugh but it turned into a grimace of pain.

At 5.30 p.m., just as the dusk was approaching, the shelling suddenly ceased, and the men knew exactly what this meant. They quickly returned to the fire step and waited expectantly. They heard a whistle blow and the Prussian Guards came at them again, screaming madly, although this time their numbers were greatly reduced. Someone said, "For what we are above to receive," and that generated a small trickle of laughter.

The enemy had set off bright magnesium flares in order to help their men to see the way in the gathering gloom and darkness, but instead it made it much easier for the British to see them. The extra rifles of the reinforcements made a huge difference. They had also brought up with them additional ammunition and this was freely shared out amongst the Germans.

Lance Corporal Harold George, the Yeomanry's motor cyclist, had bravely volunteered to come forward with "A" Squadron, and he was stood on the fire trench firing with his newly issued rifle, until it jammed. He tried to free it, but to no avail, so he drew his pistol from his holster. As a despatch rider that was his normal weapon, and began firing at the Germans with that. He emptied his revolver at them and quickly reloaded it. Unfortunately, in order to fire his revolver he had to expose much more of himself to the enemy, and one of their marksman had him in his sights. There was a soft "Thud!" as the bullet took him in the head, killing him instantly.

This attack lasted for about fifteen minutes before it finally petered out, and the heavy shelling commenced once again. Either their ammunition was starting to become low or someone in higher authority had decided that enough was enough, the continuous shelling that the North Somerset Yeomanry had endured for the last 14 hours suddenly ceased. Shells still came over, but at a greatly reduced rate.

Lieutenant Bailward had handled the situation magnificently and had been a steadying influence all through the battle. Another shell exploded, and unfortunately for him he was out in the open of the trench at the time. One of the fragments of the shell caught him in the side of the head, knocking him down and rendering him unconscious. Number 1 Troop of "A" Squadron, North Somerset Yeomanry, would be without one of their most popular officers for about 6 months.

The wounded adjutant came out of the small bunker that had sustained him for a while and took stock of what was left. It was quite dark now but by the lights of the very lights and the magnesium flares he could see that the trenches as a defined defensive obstacle had all but disappeared, they were battered and pitted with shell holes. The dead and the wounded still lay there, so he gave orders to the men to wrap them up in their ground sheets and started to send the wounded back.

At 6.30 p.m. the 2nd Life Guards came forward to relieve them. The officer in commanding of them came towards Major Lubbock with a surprised look on his face. He looked about him, surveying the damage, and said, "Looks like you've had a hot time of it, old boy."

"Oh yes, a hot time indeed." The men shook hands and the relief was made. The men of the North Somerset Yeomanry quickly made their way back along the communication trenches to the reserve trenches, "C" Squadron being the last to do so.

The German's must have detected or guessed that a relief had been effected, and they were determined to have one last go at them. A heavy barrage immediately commenced on to the reserve trenches, either as a begrudging farewell or as a welcome to the men of the Royal Horse Guards who were to occupy them in the reserve positions.

The regiment were tired men. They had not had much sleep in the 2 days period that they had been up in the trenches, and a bedraggled bunch of proud men were walked rather than marched, back to Ypres. Here they picked up the horses which were still tethered out in the open. The animals had suffered badly in the extremely bitter weather and several had gone down with exposure. There were plenty of saddled mounts to choose from and the men rode away from the front line, each leading a string of horses behind them, and returned to their billets near Vlamertinghe.

When they got there the efficiency of the British Army came to the fore, for men of the Army Remounts Company, Army Service Corps, were there waiting to receive the horses. All the men had to do was get to the canteen tent where a hot stew, fresh bread and lashings of tea awaited them. With a hot meal and hot tea inside of them, the men staggered almost drunkenly to where they were sleeping and fell into a deep and comforting sleep.

Wednesday, 18th November 1914.

They were not roused until 10 a.m. that day. The roll call was taken and the slightly wounded adjutant reported to the colonel that the casualties had been exceedingly heavy, and 2 officers (Captain Liebert and Lieutenant Davey), along with 20 N.C.O.'s and men, had been killed. There were another 39 wounded men and he regretted to report that 3 men were still missing. Out of these casualties a total of 59 were sustained by the 200 rifles that were in the trenches at Zillebeke. He also reported that Lieutenant Bailward, of Number 1 Troop of "A" Squadron, North Somerset Yeomanry, had been wounded and would be out of action for some while.

At 1 p.m. the brigadier unexpectedly arrived upon the scene. What was left of the regiment were hastily brought together where he personally congratulated them on the splendid performance that they had put up. He made a great play about the fact that the Prussian Guards were considered to be an elite regiment, and by the actions of the regiment it had ensured that those first 2 days that they had spent in action would forever be remembered by those to come.

After the brigadier had gone a sombre adjutant was talking to the colonel. "I have arranged for the burial of Captain Liebert and Lieutenant Davey tomorrow, sir, if you don't mind. His squadron will be in attendance at the Ypres cemetery."

The colonel nodded. "And what are the arrangements for the men who were killed?"

The adjutant coughed. "They were buried just behind our lines, colonel, but I'm afraid that most of our men who were killed over the last 2 days have not been recovered. Their bodies have just simply disappeared."

"Surely they should be recorded as missing as opposed to killed?"

"No sir, all were seen to be killed. It was either they were blown to pieces, or buried by the shells."

"Do you have the list?"

"Yes sir, I do." He handed the list to the colonel, who read it aloud.

" LIEBERT, Frederick Alexander Charles, Captain. Poor Frederick, he was such a good chap. Of course I shall write to his widow, Frances, at the earliest opportunity. Strange to think that he was born not far away, in Bruges, and in truth his real nationality was that of a Belgian, having spent the early part of his childhood here. But despite that he was a damn fine example of an Englishman! We of The Blackmore Vale Hunt will miss him terribly, for he was one of our most staunchest supporters." The colonel continued reading.

"DAVEY, John Stanley, Lieutenant. Poor John, he had a wonderful future ahead of him and will be sorely missed. I shall write to his mother in Leigh Woods, of course. A charming woman."

He stopped for a moment when he came to the name he recognised so well. "CLEALL, Alfred Ernest, Serjeant." He looked up from reading the list. "I shall write to his wife, Stanley, for I liked and respected Serjeant Cleall very much. He, too, will be badly missed and was a man we could ill afford to lose." He continued reading, nodding his head after he repeated each name.

"GOODING, Harry Charles, Serjeant." The colonel pondered for a moment. "I thought I saw him come back through our reserve trench wounded?"

The adjutant nodded. "He did sir. He had one leg badly broken and the other blown off. They managed to get him back to the Casualty Clearing Station alright but apparently he died through loss of blood."

The colonel looked grim as he continued reading aloud. "BRISTOW, James Douglas, Lance Serjeant.

THOMAS, Thomas Henry, Corporal.

ADAMS, Thomas Francis, Lance Corporal.

GEORGE, Harold John, Lance Corporal.

DICKINSON, Leonard Taylor, Trooper.

CARTER, Ernest Samuel, Trooper.

COMRIE, Alexander Peter, Trooper.

CONGDON, Ernest Frederick, Trooper.

GLASS, Joseph Egbert, Trooper.

HANCOCK, Frederick Charles, Corporal.

HARRIS, Frank, Trooper.

JACKSON, George, Trooper.

WILSON, Wilfred Dick, Trooper.

McILVEEN, Alfred William, Trooper.

RICHARDSON, George Wakefield, Trooper.

POOLE, Edward Henry, Trooper.

POPE, Wilfred James, Trooper.

TUCKER, Francis William, Trooper." The colonel paused and gave a faraway look, for some of the names on the list he had known as personal friends. "I shall, of course, be attending the funerals tomorrow."

"Of course, sir."

"What of the other wounded?"

"They have all been safely evacuated and are being tended to. The doctor tells me that several of the men's wounds don't look too bad, and hopefully they will be returned to us shortly."

"And the others?"

"Some of them have appalling wounds, legs and arms missing, so they will never come back to the regiment, or indeed, to the army. I have asked the doctor to make me a list of the men wounded and to give an indication as to how long he either expects them to return to us and also to mark the names of those who have no chance of returning to us."

"Good man Stanley," he confirmed. "Have you sent the casualty figures to Brigade yet?"

"I am just waiting for the doctor to finalise his list and then they will go by motor cycle despatch rider. We desperately need some reinforcements to bring us back into contention."

The colonel's eyes returned to the list. "I see we lost Lance Corporal George, our despatch rider."

"Yes," replied the adjutant. "I shall have to find a replacement for him. Brigade have loaned us a despatch rider in the meantime."

The colonel agreed. "Well," he said. "Let's see if my decision to let Lieutenant Horner join the 11th Reserve Cavalry as a Training Officer works out. The men he sends to us will have a hard time in living up to the standards of those they will be replacing."

When the men had vacated their billets to go forward into battle, they had left locked boxes with their names on a label that contained all of their worldly possessions. These had been held by the Quartermaster and now the sad task to open those boxes of the men killed fell to that department. They would have to take back any service items and bag up the personal items to be returned to the next of kin of those lost. It was a big task, and a changed Fitch had been detailed off to help Corporal Corben, of the quartermaster's staff, to list the items. Fitch not only could read well but his hand writing was always clear and legible, one of the reasons he had been chosen. He was writing down the items as the corporal called them out.

Fitch felt a bit sad when he was doing this, but he knew it had to be done. They eventually came to the box left by his friend, Ernie. Corporal Corben looked at the numbered keys and matched it to the wooden box and opened it. On top lay his service items, and the corporal carefully went through them, Fitch listing them as he went. Any missing items would have to be paid for, and if the owner of the box had any pay to come, then the cost would be deducted from that.

Curiously, some things that he held he had a duplicate of, and they looked familiar to Fitch. That was his missing bayonet frog! He knew that, because it had his name stencilled on it. Corporal Corben scratched his head and said, "Don't know what he is doing with your kit, Fitch. Perhaps you dropped it?"

Beneath that were Ernest's personal things and a bunch of letters. "Bloody hell!" remarked the corporal. The letters were tied with a piece of red string, one of them not even opened, but what caught the corporal's attention was that they were all addressed to Trooper Albert Fitch. He rifled through them, and then passed them to Albert with a suspicious look on his face.

"I don't know what he was doing with these letters addressed to you Fitch, but I suppose that you had better have them now."

He looked at them, an incredulous look dawning on his bewildered face. He opened the top letter, which was only dated 1st November. It began, "My dearest darling Albert, why aren't you answering my letters, my love? Has something happened between us that you no longer love me?" He stopped reading, for the awful truth about his former friend, Ernest Summers, hit him straight between the eyes, like a piece of shrapnel that had hurtled out from a "Jack Johnson."

INDEX

Printed in Great Britain
by Amazon

59121248R00098